THE WITCHES' PRISON

Maria Melo

Midhallow Books

*To anyone who has ever known the sharp
sting of being an outsider.*

PART ONE

THE WITCHES' PRISON

CHAPTER 1

Petra's aunt loved her, tied as they were by blood, but she'd failed the girl on many counts, and she knew it. On the day her brother, Tom, phoned her from the hospital to say she was an auntie, Alice was full of a kind of joy she hadn't known since her own childhood. They had a special connection, from the instant newly-born Petra gripped Alice's finger with her own tiny one, holding her gaze. As a child, Petra never wanted to be more than an arm's length away from Alice and fixed on her with huge, inquisitive eyes.

When she began to speak, Petra asked endless questions, without pausing for breath. She knew so *much*, and she wanted to share all of her knowledge with Alice. But after Petra started school, Alice grew concerned that she had no friends. There was something in the way she played - on her own, without expectation that anyone would watch or join in – that made Alice picture Petra, isolated and alone, in the unforgiving landscape of her primary school playground.

She asked Tom about it, but he said only that Petra was fine, that she wasn't lonely. Alice didn't believe him and wanted to give her brother and sister-in-law a shake, make them see the need to foster Petra's social conformity, her ability to make friends. There was a difference between natural curiosity and naïve offensiveness – Petra asking Alice if she was trying to grow a moustache, for example – and perceptive boldness – like when Petra asked why Alice's eyes narrowed whenever her mother spoke. Alice realised that she had started to feel on edge whenever her niece was in the room, staring at her, working out what Alice *really* thought.

Petra was twelve years old when she came to live with Alice after her mother died, and she had learned – finally - to keep her observations to herself. She still stared at Alice in that intense, unnerving way, but she no longer verbalised her thoughts. As a child, Petra had spent so much time outdoors that she seemed to Alice to be permanently tanned, but as a newly-bereaved adolescent she was worryingly pale. Shock could do that, Alice knew. Petra had effectively lost both parents; Tom was not coping at all well with his wife's death, and spent every day in a whisky-fuelled stupor of grief. He knew he was failing his daughter, and had been pathetically grateful when Alice stepped in, offering to look after Petra until he got better.

But that was the rub: he never did get better. He'd been a successful cabinet-maker before his wife died, with a reputation for fine craftsmanship. Afterwards, he was unable to focus his energy long enough to complete any work, and eventually lost his business, and then his house. He was forty-five years old, and his life had fallen apart.

As her primary caregiver, Alice knew that she should have been Petra's biggest cheerleader, celebrating her academic achievements and her surprising social success – finding even two friends in the punishing world of secondary school was huge for any young person, and especially for someone as un-used to friendships as Petra. Her niece needed a parent-figure who loved her unconditionally, who was fascinated by her life and her interests, who saw only the good in what she did. But instead, Alice really only took care of Petra's material needs: she cooked, did her laundry, bought her essentials and provided some pocket money, all the while knowing she was failing to give Petra that extra layer of emotional support young people seemed to need. She had difficulty explaining her emotional dis-tance from Petra even to herself. It might have been wariness, or anxiety about her own inability to fix whatever was wrong with her niece's social skills, or fear about Petra inheriting her

3

mother's unusual and unsettling attributes.

Alice never knew for certain that Petra's mother was a witch, but she suspected it was the reason she died suddenly, leaving Petra motherless and Tom broken. She supposed it was natural that Petra wanted to learn about her mother's ways, but Alice didn't approve of the content of many of the books that passed through her niece's hands – witches, witchcraft, the supernatural – and she made her disapproval known to Petra. Years later, Alice would come to see that her condemnation had forced Petra, alone and scared, into dark corners where her anger bubbled over and took on a dangerous, menacing shape.

* * *

After her mother died, Petra was too numb to feel much more than faint relief that her aunt took her in. The first few months were a blur – a new home, new school, a move to the city after growing up in an isolated house in the countryside. She missed her mother and father desperately, and knew how lucky she was to be the centre of their world for so long. When Petra turned thirteen, and started her second year of high school, she admitted to herself that there were good things about living with her aunt. She loved the bright and always impeccably clean flat, and she adored living in Edinburgh – the kind of city you could get lost in. There was always so much to see, so many nooks and crannies for Petra to poke her nose into.

At the end of every school day she walked straight across the Meadows – a vast, open green space that bordered their neighbourhood, Marchmont - to the Old Town, where the ancient cityscape was visible behind the modern shops, cafés and restaurants. Petra read as much as she could find about the history of the Old Town, drinking in the old city's secrets thirstily. She loved discovering a new cobbled lane to wander along, a cluster of brightly-painted tenement buildings hidden there like residential jewels.

Petra adored the buttery hue of the sandstone buildings in

the late afternoon sunshine; equally, she loved how it looked like mist was seeping from the pores of those same buildings when it rained. She was as comfortable sitting on one of the benches in the cemetery at Greyfriars Kirk – said to be the most haunted graveyard in the world – as she was strolling down the gentle curve of Victoria Street, with its candy-coloured shop fronts.

She could not explain what the Old Town *did* to her, but when she was there a buzz started deep in her chest and radiated out through her body. She stopped feeling like Petra – the terrible daughter, the sullen niece – and relished the sensation of stepping out of herself, even if just for an hour a day.

Afterwards, she returned to the quiet of the flat just ahead of Alice. Petra never told her aunt about her walks around the Old Town because she suspected she would disapprove of her interest in its dark history. But she yearned to have someone to talk to about her discoveries. At these times, she missed her parents so much her chest ached. They had always listened to Petra with rapt attention. In Aunt Alice's flat, meals were eaten in silence. Sometimes, her aunt suggested they watch a show on television afterwards, but sitting side by side staring at the TV with nothing to say to each other made Petra unspeakably sad.

She wanted to ask her aunt about her father: what was he like as a boy, what did he like to do, was he kind to you – and funny? Why did you never like my mother? What is it about me that puts you on edge? Petra knew she had done something to upset her aunt, some awful action that propelled them apart. While she waited for her aunt to tell her what she'd done wrong, she thought of her own unspoken words: *I'm sorry, I know I'm an imposition, I'm grateful.*

* * *

Petra was almost fifteen when she found The Third Eye tucked away down a narrow, cobbled lane one Thursday after school. It was December, just the other side of dusk, but already as dark as midnight; winter nights in Edinburgh were for hardy souls. Twinkle-lights framed the shop doorway and the inside of the bay window, which displayed books, tarot cards, crystals, incense, and small glass bottles. Petra was about to walk past when a round, kindly face appeared, then smiled as she added two books to the display. Before she knew it, Petra was stepping through the twinkle-lit doorway, directly into an overpowering waft of incense.

She asked about the books in the window. The owner, who introduced herself as Isobel, pulled the books out of the display with great care and set them on the counter in front of Petra: *Modern Witchcraft for Modern Witches* and *Revenge Spells*. Petra read the blurbs as Isobel watched her, but she was too self-conscious to understand much of what she was reading, and blurted out that she'd take both. As Isobel bagged the books, tallied up the total, took Petra's money and gave her change, she managed to glean – from this sad, lonely girl whose anger bubbled right up from the core of her body – that she was a novice.

"When you start using magic for the first time, it's important to find other people to help you, to be with you. Kind of like magical mentors. And also for protection."

Petra looked like Isobel had just stolen something very important from her. "There's no one I can ask to help me. My friends – they aren't into any of this. My aunt doesn't approve."

Isobel smiled. "Why don't you take these books away and read them and, if you want to try out any of the spells, come back and see me."

Petra thanked her, and rushed out of the shop. Her face burned, and she only just managed to hold back a well of tears. Outside, in the chilled darkness, she took a few steps before the memories of what happened to her mother made her double over in pain that started in her stomach and quickly radiated out to every corner of her body. Then the tears came, and she called out to her mother over and over again in the dark street until her voice broke, and was swallowed completely by the cold night air.

* * *

Isobel's caution regarding the need for others' help and protection worried Petra and she returned a week later, wanting to know more. She'd read the book on revenge spells twice, convinced that she was destined to walk past the shop at the exact moment Isobel was putting the book in the window. She was *meant* to buy it, and to use it.

Isobel greeted her warmly, and suggested they could practise in a room at the back, closed off from the rest of the shop by a thick dark velvet curtain. She had a gentle way with words, and warned Petra against trying any of the spells on her own - before she was ready. She explained about the light and the darkness, about how sending energy out into the world to work on people had implications for the person sending it as well as the recipient. Petra knew this, because of what had happened to her mother. She wondered if Isobel could tell that something terrible had happened in Petra's life, involving the darkness and the light.

When Petra went back to see Isobel the following week, she pulled *Revenge Spells* out of her rucksack, and set it on the counter. "I've decided not to use this one," she said. She did not tell Isobel that she'd dreamed about her mother, who had repeated almost word for word what Isobel had said. Petra awoke from the dream, her mother's soft voice in her ears, the rose scent of her shampoo in the air, and decided to give the book back.

Isobel smiled at her, pulled the book back across the counter and told Petra that she had another one she might prefer. She handed her *Into the Light: Healing Spells.* When Petra reached for her purse Isobel put her hand out to stop her.

"No dear – it's an exchange."

For the next few months, Petra visited Isobel once a week, determined to learn how to use the spells for good. She hoped she could generate enough positive energy to improve her father's life. Isobel taught her how to perform healing incantations, strengthening the spells with crystals, candles and scent.

Isobel lit nag champa incense at the start of every session and, as Petra breathed it in, her lungs and chest grew warm, a physical manifestation of her power. Isobel gave Petra a rose quartz stone, which she held to focus her energy as she stared into the candle flame with half-closed eyes, visualising her father getting stronger.

He was in such a sad place that Petra could not reach him with words. She knew that he still drank too much, from the way he sounded whenever they spoke on the phone. She imagined her real father trapped inside that broken man, trying to get back to her, holding his hand out and offering something he'd made for her: a tiny wooden book, or a candlestick for her doll's house – a token of his love. But the longer he stayed trapped inside the husk of man who was not her father, the more frustrated Petra grew. Her spells were not working. Isobel, patient and kind, told her it would take years to become proficient; she advised Petra to keep practising and it would happen. But when Petra's father was still ill after those few months, she burst into tears in the tiny, dark back room of Isobel's shop.

Isobel put her arms around Petra. She smelled of patchouli and wood smoke, and Petra wanted to stay there, huddled up against the soft wool of Isobel's cloak. Her mother was the last person who'd hugged her. Hot tears flooded her cheeks as she blurted out the story of how she was tormented her in her last school, and about her mother's death and her father's unravelling.

"My dear, you've had far too much sadness in your life. It's a wonder you can bear it," Isobel said kindly. "You've known such unkindness, when all you wanted was friendship. It's hard to know why some people become targets of others' cruelty, for no reason at all."

Petra took a big gulp of air before admitting to Isobel what she never allowed herself to think. "It was me they hated – right from the first day of primary school. My mum tried to help me make friends by asking some of the other mothers around to our house, but they made fun of her, too, and the way we lived."

She took a raspy breath and added, "They started saying that she was a witch."

"Well, that's been an insult for women since time immemorial. And it's nothing to be ashamed of in any case."

"But that's the thing – my mum *wasn't* a witch – she told me that. She believed in living in harmony with the earth, that's all. But even though I knew that, I asked her to do it anyway."

Petra waited for Isobel to ask for more details but she just held her, silently.

"I asked her to make it stop. She'd never have tried it if I hadn't asked. She didn't know how to do the spell properly, and it backfired. It's all my fault. I've never told anyone else, but my mum's dead because of *me*, Isobel."

CHAPTER 2

From the very first day of primary school, Petra was an outsider. She had a knack for saying the wrong thing every time, upsetting someone when she meant to do the opposite. None of the other children wanted to play with her, despite the valiant attempts of Miss Grant, her kindly teacher. On the day that Katie McDougall handed out invitations to her birthday party – to everyone but Petra - Miss Grant suggested that Katie give hers to Petra, since teachers were not really meant to go to the birthday parties of children in their class.

"But I don't *want* her to come," Katie said.

Petra's mother soon realised there was a problem and tried to intervene by inviting other mothers around to their house, so that Petra would have someone to play with. It only worked twice, and the children who came around spent most of their time asking Petra if she had specific toys that they wanted to play with (she did not), and then refusing to play with the toys she *did* have - not even her dollhouse, which her father had made for her. Whenever he had spare time he made another piece of furniture for her, or a special surprise - a teapot, a lamp or a tiny mouse or another cat (there were six already in the dollhouse).

Walking through the school gate after one such visit, Petra overheard one of the women talking about her mother. The tea she made was vile, her home-made biscuits tasted like powder. Claggy powder, at that. The jars of dried flowers on the kitchen shelves – what *were* they? Were they even legal?

Before Petra was out of earshot she heard her say, "I guess the rumours are true - she *is* a witch."

When Petra got home that day she asked her mother why the other mothers called her a witch. Her mother's face froze, her mouth set in a sad 'O' shape, before she fixed a smile and said, "They're just joking sweetheart. I'm not a witch, don't worry."

But the word had stuck, and Petra heard it used to describe her mother many times after that.

She never brought it up again, never told her mother that people were still calling her a witch, years later. Her mother was the one to broach the subject, when Petra was eleven years old. They were in the forest, collecting hawthorn blossoms to hang in the house for May Day, and her mother asked, "Do you remember asking why people called me a witch?"

Still ashamed of the incident, Petra said, "I'm sorry, Mum. I didn't mean to hurt your feelings."

"Sweetheart, you mustn't think that you did anything wrong. I just want to explain why some people might think that."

She told Petra that people still believed in witches, and in fact some people claimed to *be* witches. She explained about black witches and white witches and that, although she did not consider herself to be either, she understood why some people might think she was a white witch.

"I believe in asking nature to help me in my day to day life. I ask for help in growing the fruit and vegetables we eat, in keeping us safe from harm, and in protecting us from illness." She looked at Petra, smiling. "Does that sound strange to you, love?"

She pulled a hawthorn blossom out of the basket. "This will help protect us and encourage good growth in our garden this year. Because I've taken something from the hawthorn tree, I need to give something back to the earth, for balance."

Petra pictured the dark glass jars and bottles that lined the shelves of the pantry off the kitchen – salves and tinctures made of extracts of plants and seeds from their garden – and thought she understood.

***

At primary school, being alone was part of who Petra was. She played her own games in the playground. She never got invited to anyone's house, but Petra stopped caring because she got to spend every out-of-school minute with her mother, her best friend. It hurt when no one wanted to be partnered with her during class activities, but by the final year of primary school it hurt much less. She'd learned to accept that it was just the way it was.

But it hadn't stopped Petra hoping that she would have a fresh start at high school, where there were people from five other primary schools to meet and, hopefully, befriend. She didn't expect that the rumours about her mother would spread to children from other schools, but on the first day of school she overheard two girls she didn't know say that she lived with her mother in the old witches' prison on the coast. On the last day of the first week of school, Petra was in the changing room before gym class, when someone threw a pair of knickers covered in tomato sauce at a huddle of girls. One of them shrieked "Witch knickers!", and batted them away.

The story spread through the school quickly, and by lunch time Petra was subject to an endless stream of taunts: *witch knickers, witch fanny, cold witch tits.*

The verbal abuse continued for a month. Petra sought solace in the library during breaks and lunch time, and hid there after school until the last possible minute, when she'd rush out the side door nearest the library and run to catch her bus home. Petra's ear buds were her only armour, and she played her music as loudly as her ears could take it until the bus stopped outside her house.

She hid the torment from her parents, until the day all of the disappointment and alienation and pain bubbled through her and right up to the surface, the instant she got off the bus. Her parents were pruning the buckthorn hedge that bordered the front garden, and watched in dismay as she stumbled towards the front door, tears streaming down her face.

She wouldn't tell them the whole story, but they heard

enough to understand that Petra had been tormented since the first day of high school, in a cruel, relentless campaign that destroyed any hope she'd had of fitting in.

Her father went to make hot, sweet tea while her mother held Petra close, rocking her. Petra's body shook with deep, wracking, silent sobs. She buried her face in her mother's chest and murmured, "Please make it stop," over and over again.

That desperate plea haunted her later, after what happened to her mother. She hadn't really meant for her mother to intervene. Exhausted, and in despair, she was really asking for the loneliness to end - the years of never finding her place - and for her tormentors to stop.

Her mother, who had never before used her magical knowledge for anything other than good, heard her, and decided to act. She practised all night, while Petra and her father slept. And then, before the moon disappeared from the sky, with her family safe inside the house, Petra's mother carried out a banishing spell, to stop Petra's torment.

But it went wrong, and the spell was reversed. Petra awoke to the sound of her father's low, animal-like moans. When she looked out her bedroom window, she saw him kneeling by the burn at the bottom of their garden, cradling her mother's limp body.

***

Isobel was the only other person who knew the whole story. Petra hadn't told her father, or her aunt, or either of her friends at her new school that she was responsible for her mother's death. She hadn't been able to tell her parents what was happening at school, but she recounted it to Isobel – every bit of it. She told Isobel in an attempt to purge herself of the terrible memories, as well as the dark and dangerous feelings they dredged up. All the while, Isobel repeated the need for Petra to stay away from dark magic, no matter how often or how strongly she thought about revenge.

On the day that Petra was so frustrated by her lack of progress that she broke down and told Isobel everything, she said despairingly, "My father's not getting any better. I practise every day, with intention. All I want is for him to get better. I'm just not good enough."

Isobel did the incantation alone that day. When Petra spoke to her father later in the week, she was surprised at the alertness in his voice as he asked about her life in Edinburgh. When it was Aunt Alice's turn to talk to her father, Petra heard her tell him that he sounded better.

Petra arrived the following week for her session with Isobel, who as usual flipped the sign on the door to "Closed", and led Petra to the room at the back of the shop.

"Isobel, you can't keep closing the shop because you're helping me," Petra told her. "It's bad for business."

Isobel's eyes twinkled. "It's kind of you to worry about me, dear, but I don't think I'll go out of business for closing up the shop for a little bit."

Petra had been mulling it over, and had a proposition for Isobel. "And you're basically providing free mentoring for me, which is also not good business. I have an idea – I'll work for free in the shop until you're ready to close, and we can have our session then."

Isobel was spooning leaves into the teapot as she said, "That's a very decent offer. Thank you, Petra. I'd be happy to accept."

Petra's heart raced – she'd expected Isobel to put up more of a fight. She'd planned what she wanted to say to Isobel the night before, in bed, fully expecting to be told that she was too young to work in the shop. The more she'd anticipated being put off, the more she realised she really *wanted* to work for Isobel. The shop permeated her thoughts during the long days at school, and at night when she was alone in her room. She loved the glass jars filled with dried herbs and plants, labelled in Isobel's elegant script. Although initially she'd found the various smells of incense that mingled in the air cloying, overpowering even, she'd quickly come to love how she was transported to different places when she breathed them in. An entire wall housed Isobel's incredible crystal collection, Petra's favourite part of the shop. It was almost as though she could hear the crystals singing to her, they vibrated with such powerful energies. She loved running her fingers across them – the smooth labradorite and rose quartz, both of which made Petra's fingers tingle when she touched them, the tourmaline, with its jagged edges and mesmerising veins of colour, and the citrine prisms that seemed like they'd dropped into the shop from another planet.

Within a few months, Isobel handed Petra responsibility for selecting and ordering books. She explained that although she'd previously stocked books about dark magic – like the *Revenge Spells* book that Petra'd originally been drawn to – she no longer wanted to cater for customer tastes in that vein. Although Petra suspected it was part of Isobel's plan to educate her about protective magic, and encourage her interest solely in this area, she was happy to scroll through the catalogues of books. The difficulty was in narrowing the selection down to a few new titles at a time.

The arrangement worked well for both Isobel and Petra for almost two years; so well, in fact, that Petra spent most days after school working in the shop with Isobel. Although Isobel tried to pay her in cash, Petra resisted, arguing that her payment was Isobel's teaching and guidance. Isobel was generous as well as kind, urging Petra to take whichever crystals she liked, or books. Through their weekly sessions, Petra felt her strength, knowledge and power increase gradually but steadily, and she was convinced that her father was making small steps forward in his own recovery, largely thanks to Isobel's magic. Petra's goal was for her father to stop drinking, get his business back up and running, and to be well enough that they could live together once again.

***

But despite how hard she worked at staying in the light, at how much care and love Isobel put into Petra's recovery and development as a force for good, the ongoing power struggle between the darkness and the light came to a terrible head after a chance encounter one sunny Saturday afternoon in September. Petra was in the city centre shopping for trainers, waiting at a pedestrian crossing, when a small group of girls her age ran across the street against the lights, shrieking and laughing. When one of them stopped to stare at her, Petra recognised her as Bethany – the co-ringleader of the tormentors from her last school.

The two gawped at each other for a long, silent moment, until one of the girls with Bethany asked, "Who *is* that?"

"Just some fuckface, whose mother is a witch," Bethany said, sneering at Petra as she walked away.

Immediately after the encounter, Petra walked into a large chain bookshop and ordered the book she'd given back to Isobel two years earlier - *Revenge Spells*. She collected it a few days later, but didn't tell Isobel that she had it, that she was returning to the darkness. She practised the spells in her bedroom every night, and plotted her revenge during the long, dull hours at school. Isobel knew that something had changed in Petra, and kept asking in her kind way if Petra wanted to talk about anything. But Petra knew what Isobel thought about her using revenge spells, and knew that she would try to dissuade her.

On the eve of the fifth anniversary of her mother's death, Petra set up a shrine and laid out her tools within a protective circle. She should have had something that belonged to each of her tormentors, but the absence of personal possessions didn't stop her going ahead with the spell as planned. As she chanted, she walked counter-clockwise around the circle. A terrible and wonderful rush of power coursed through her, as she wished for each of the girls to feel the burning humiliation they had inflicted on her.

Afterwards she sat inside the circle for hours, doing incantations to strengthen the magic and its effects, visualising the girls' reactions to whatever humiliation befell them.

Aunt Alice answered the call that came through in the middle of the night: her father had been rushed to the emergency room, after suffering a massive stroke. He'd crawled to the phone to dial emergency services. As soon as her aunt told her what happened, Petra knew that it was all her fault. She had skewed the balance between light and dark, had twisted the energy force out of alignment with her anger, and it had backfired, spectacularly, on someone she loved.

All over again.

***

Petra didn't go back to see Isobel. How could she, when she had defied all that Isobel taught her – everything that Isobel believed about the use of magic? Isobel was kind to her, and loving, and trusted Petra with her teaching and mentorship. And Petra had betrayed her.

After what happened to her father, she packed her books and her tools away in a box and hid it at the end of a shelf in the hall cupboard. Petra was finished with magic. She'd proven that she couldn't be trusted with it, that she would only ever hurt the people she loved.

But she was still fascinated by witchcraft, and she channelled her interest into reading as much as she could about its history in Scotland. The year after she swore off magic, she started studying Scottish history at university. She earned a reputation as an enthusiastic, dedicated and very able student, at least in part due to her almost obsessive need to know as much as possible. In her final year of undergraduate studies, her dissertation supervisor happily approved her request to write an untraditional paper, narrative non-fiction about the lives of the last women to be accused of witchcraft in Edinburgh.

Petra felt destined to write it, and she pored over accounts of witch hunts and trials, spending every spare minute absorbed in reading about the doomed, accused women, then writing from their perspectives. It was gruelling work because of the tragic content, much of which gave her nightmares. She was full of deep sadness for all of the women that had never really stood a chance in the face of such hatred, and a determination to do them justice at last.

Later, Petra blamed what happened next on her impaired state of mind. Exhausted and exhilarated by her work in equal measures, she let herself be distracted by attention. Josh – one of the other final year students – started showing up wherever Petra happened to be, outside of classes. A sudden pervasive presence in her life, Josh endeared himself to her by asking endless questions about her work. Petra thought his rapt fascination was sincere, and she began to look forward to seeing him. She was delighted to have someone she could share her knowledge with at last, and especially someone who seemed just as fascinated by the subject as she was.

She told herself that she wouldn't let his presence in her life interfere with her studies, but she did allow herself the luxury of going to the pub with him from time to time, or to the cinema, or even a few times for a meal. He was always polite, never pushy with his affections. Petra knew it was likely a stretch to call Josh her boyfriend – they hadn't done anything more than hold hands – but she thought that the relationship had the potential to turn serious, once she graduated.

Petra finished a first draft of her dissertation in mid-March, and started editing it in earnest, so busy that Josh's sudden absence from her life barely registered. But then her friend and fellow final-year student, Ana, dropped the bombshell news: Josh had just self-published an eBook about the last women to be tried as witches in Edinburgh, which he was promoting alongside the start-up of his "Witches of Edinburgh" walking tours business.

Although he'd stolen, and published, her dissertation, the university insisted that protecting her work was Petra's responsibility. When she protested that her supervisor had seen her work in progress at regular intervals throughout the year, he rubbed more salt in the wound by suggesting that there was no proof that Petra wasn't the one stealing Josh's work. She was told that her only option was to start from scratch, with a new dissertation topic, and aim to graduate either in November or the following year. But Josh's betrayal destroyed her mental as well as physical stamina. She just didn't have the brain power to continue.

She fought the urge to use a revenge spell on Josh. Even after she dragged the box of her books and tools out of the hall cupboard, she knew she shouldn't do it. She thought of Isobel, and everything she owed her.

CHAPTER 3

Petra honoured Isobel by repressing her strong desire for vengeance after Josh stole her work, but it flattened her. Her brain shut down. She couldn't think of another subject she wanted to write about. She couldn't think about much at all, beyond how badly she wanted to make Josh pay for what he had done. What he had *stolen* from her.

Instead of rallying, like she'd intended, writing a new dissertation and graduating a few months behind schedule, Petra stumbled her way through the first few weeks after learning about Josh's theft. She struggled to get out of bed every day, rarely washed, didn't eat the meals Alice cooked. Intending to tough-love Petra into getting back to her studies, Alice told her she'd need to get a job if she didn't go back to school.

"If you're not a student any more, then you'll need to contribute financially."

Half-blindly, Petra made her way into the job market. Her first job was in the coffee shop at the end of their street, but she was fired after half a day for her listless engagement with customers, and her dangerous use of the very expensive coffee machine, which she managed to break the first time she attempted to use it.

After several other failed attempts at gainful employment, she got a job as a pensions administrator for a large financial company. She answered an endless stream of phone calls and emails all day, every day. She hated the work, but it was mind-numbing enough that she could carry out her role, trancelike, without any real emotional involvement. It saved her thinking too much about the disappointment her life had turned into, and about her role as architect of her own despair. She thought about Isobel every single day, but was too ashamed to visit, after betraying Isobel's teachings.

Nine long months into her job in pensions, Petra finally worked up enough courage to stop by Isobel's shop on her way home from work. At first, she thought she'd taken a wrong turning. Isobel's magic shop was gone, replaced by a shop for traditional Chinese medicine. Petra went into the antique shop next door, because she knew Isobel was friendly with Marian, the owner. Marian's eyes welled up, and she reached for Petra's hand as she told her that Isobel had died six weeks previously, after a short illness.

And Petra, who worried she'd developed a tin heart after everything that had happened in her life, knew that wasn't the case when she broke down, crying wretched, painful tears as Marian tried to console her.

"You are Petra, aren't you?" she asked, when Petra was calmer. Petra nodded. "She left a letter for you, dear." Marian shuffled through to the back of the shop, and came back clutching a brown envelope. "She said I was to give this to you when you came back."

When, not *if* – Isobel had known Petra would come back to see her one day. Petra cried fresh tears, hating herself for leaving it six weeks too late.

She waited until she was in the solace of her bedroom to open Isobel's letter. At the dinner table, her aunt had tried to engage her in a conversation about her fast-approaching birthday, but Petra wasn't remotely interested in celebrating. Eventually, her aunt took the hint and they ate the rest of the meal in silence, but Petra was aware of Alice's frequent sidelong looks in her direction.

Petra held the envelope to her nose, breathing in Isobel's familiar scent of patchouli and nag champa. She took a deep breath, and carefully pulled the letter out of the envelope.

My dear Petra,

I'm going to be a bit maudlin to start, because they tell me I'm living on borrowed time and I want to write this while I'm still able to. I'm sorry we haven't managed to see each other again in person. I should have done more to make that happen. There are things I want to tell you about yourself.

You are stronger than you know. Life dealt you the cruellest hand, and I watched you grow and develop into a strong, intelligent, and kind young woman. Don't let the constant pull between the light and the dark define you – it's a struggle each of us faces, it doesn't mark you out as more prone to the darkness than anyone else. Whatever terrible event happened to your mother that night, you did not incite it to happen. Your mother acted out of love for you, and the darkness reached for her in the most terrifying, extreme way. It's not your fault, my dear one.

The darkness reached for your father, too. The healing magic works, and he will get better if you keep it up. It was an honour and a privilege for me, as your mentor, to watch you grow and develop with the craft. You gave me all of the credit for his improvement, but it wasn't warranted. You have every bit of skill and talent you need, at this very moment in time.

If you step into the darkness, you mustn't hate yourself so much that you give up completely. You must, instead, step back into the light – as quickly as you can. Stay in the light, my dear, and help your father.

When you stay in the light, there is no need to fear your powers, and what they will bring to you, and those you love. Your ability to achieve everything that you want in life – everything that you truly deserve – is boundless.

You mustn't think that I have never strayed into the darkness. I realise now that I should have told you this, so that you did not feel so alone, so full of self-hate. When I was seventeen, I used magic to manipulate my best friend and the boy I loved – who loved her, not me. My magic left her bedridden, and he became my husband. But he could never truly love me, because he was always scared of me. We had a cold, empty marriage. I had all of the power, but that was never what I wanted.

My love was not reciprocated, and we had no children. So, you see, my darling girl, that I didn't just stray into the darkness – I lived with it for nearly forty years, until his cracked heart gave up. What I want most for you is to live a long, happy life in the light. I foresee great things for you, and true happiness.

Your loving friend,
Isobel

***

Petra approached her twenty-fifth birthday without any expectation, fear or even any sense that anything would change in her life. Her aunt asked if she would like to have a party – there in the flat, or she suggested she could hire a venue if Petra wanted to invite her co-workers – but Petra refused. Aunt Alice said she wanted to take her out for a meal but Petra protested – she did not want any kind of celebration. But her aunt had insisted. They agreed to meet after work on Petra's birthday at the Balmoral, one of Edinburgh's finest hotels, for cocktails, and then go for dinner.

Petra felt too conspicuous to relax in the Balmoral's fancy cocktail lounge, and just wanted to leave. The champagne cocktail was fine, probably even delicious, but after seeing the price of it on the menu Petra felt too guilty to enjoy it. She declined a second cocktail, but they were too early for their dinner reservation, so her aunt suggested a slow walk through Princes Street Gardens. At the foot of the Scott Monument, she told Petra a story about how her father, aged seven, had climbed to the top with his sister and mother, and then "screamed the place down, refusing to come back down again."

Petra recognised the story as a gift from her aunt, a little treasure from her father's childhood, and she thanked her.

They huddled together against the icy January drizzle as they walked up the Mound, and along Castlehill to the restaurant - The Witchery. Alice hadn't told Petra ahead of time which restaurant she'd chosen, and Petra felt another rush of guilt because it was posh, and expensive. The gothic opulence of the restaurant's interior was enhanced by the glow of what looked like hundreds of candles, and they were shown to a table next to a huge fireplace, with plush velvet chairs.

Her aunt ordered champagne – silencing Petra's protests – and then, once they had ordered food, she took a deep breath. "You know Petra, you asked me once why I made faces whenever your mother spoke. I was annoyed with you for seeing that, because I believed that I kept my feelings well-hidden. Many, many times over the years I have wondered about that – why was I so cynical about your mother?"

The waiter arrived with the champagne, and Aunt Alice stopped speaking as he popped the cork and poured. She made a simple toast, and then continued. "I don't have any easy answers to that question, but as I have watched you withdraw more and more into yourself over the years, I have realised something. What I resented about your mother was what I was repressing in myself – the desire to be in control of my life – in control of my *time.*"

She paused, and swallowed the rest of her champagne in a single gulp. "For thirty years, I have allowed myself to be governed by the work clock, and by work rules. I work their hours, and I let them tell me what to do. Now Petra, I have had a stream of bosses who I can honestly say have been legitimate idiots, and still I have let them rule me. I have done things I knew weren't right, because they told me to, and I hid behind my subservience to the rules, to absolve myself of guilt. I have allowed myself to be exploited, and verbally abused by every single one of them and even, once, pretended not to notice when my manager leaned against the back of my chair, proofreading my work while he rubbed his groin on my shoulder blade."

With impeccable timing, the waiter arrived with their starters: shellfish bisque for Alice, risotto for Petra. "And, while I secretly criticised your mother for not living in the real world, I have come to realise that that is exactly what she was doing. She lived in the *real* world – the living, breathing, natural world that she spent her days in. While I willingly walked into grey buildings, shut myself away in dim office spaces, put up with horrible people, and told myself I was doing important work. *Serious* work."

The waiter had refilled her champagne glass, which she quickly emptied, again. "I worried about you following your mother's ways, and I worried when I could see that you were taking it much further than she did. I wanted to tell you to stop, but I didn't want to shut off the valve that linked your life to your mother's. So, I stood by, worrying silently. I see the rage in you, and the desire for revenge, and the terrible sadness. I see the guilt you wear, like you're carrying another person around on your back. For too long, I've watched you disappear into an outline of a person – all of your substance has faded away. And I want to tell you, Petra, to fight. Fight back, against whatever has crushed your spirit. Rage and vengeance and sadness and guilt – they can all be harnessed. They don't have to swallow you whole. Fight back, my darling girl, fight."

Petra felt a tingle run through her whole body, from her fingers to the top of her head and down to her toes. Even her *hair* felt like it was tingling. She'd been staring down at her food, looking only occasionally at her aunt as she spoke, going through the motions of celebrating her birthday in such a fancy place. But as Alice spoke directly to her core, the words warmed her veins like whisky. They had never spoken properly before –

not like *this*, and her aunt's words acted like potent magic.

When her niece looked up at her, Alice was startled by what she saw: Petra looked like an entirely different person. Her hair flamed, her green eyes shone so brightly they practically sparked, and in them Alice could see a look of pure, fierce determination.

And when Petra smiled, Alice's body pulsed with a thrill that was equal parts happy relief and terror.

By the end of the night, as the restaurant staff stacked chairs and cleared their throats in an effort to shift the two women, they had a plan. Hunched over their table in animated discussion, Petra told Alice the whole story about Josh's betrayal and theft of her work. After a second bottle of champagne, she told Alice about her lonely years at primary school and the first cruel weeks of high school, how her desperate desire to make it all stop had caused the event that killed her mother. She'd never been able to deny Petra anything, and her fierce maternal love had led to her death.

Alice cried as she listened to the truth. Petra explained that the taunts and jibes of the mothers, passed down to their children, spread first through her primary school and then – to her terrible, dismayed surprise – to high school, when people she didn't even know called her mother a witch. They called Petra a witch, too – said they lived together in the witches' prison on the old Rothmore estate.

She would have continued, would have confessed to visiting Isobel in her shop once a week, but at the mention of the witches' prison Alice took out her phone, apologising.

"I'm not being rude, love, but I remembered something when you talked about the Rothmores. They hold writers' retreats on their estate. I'm checking the dates – there's one coming up in a couple of months. Why don't I see if they have space for you? It'll be a belated birthday gift from me."

Petra stared at her aunt, unblinking, then reached out her

hand for the phone. She scanned the information about the retreat, but spent more time looking at the photographs. She knew something of the history of the estate. Even though the focus of her dissertation was witchcraft in Edinburgh, she absorbed information about its neighbouring area to the east, the place where she had grown up. Although the photographs were brightly lit, showing the estate at its summery best, she could see a layer of darkness below the surface, simmering with the truth of what happened there in centuries past.

She pictured herself there, starting a new story – one about the women taken to the witches' prison on the Rothmore estate to await trial in Edinburgh. Although there were many accounts of the trials, Petra had never been able to find any information about what happened to women in the prisons. Her heart swelled with the possibility of finding out, and writing the women's stories into existence. She would need to use magic again, *and* she would need to keep the promise she'd made to Isobel.

This time, she would stay out of the darkness.

CHAPTER 4

Before they'd left the restaurant, Alice received a reply to her booking request, confirming Petra's place at the retreat. She held her phone out to Petra to show her, and said, "You're in."

Excitement, fear and disbelief welled up in Petra, and she stared at her aunt, unable to speak. She could only guess at the price of the retreat, but was sure it was more than Alice could afford.

"Are you sure?" she asked at last.

Alice reached out and covered Petra's hand with her own. "Of course, I'm sure. You deserve this. I have a good feeling about it."

When they got back home, Petra waited until her aunt was in bed, then crept into the cupboard at the end of the hallway. Gingerly, she lifted up the box full of her magical tools, and carried it back to her bedroom. She lifted the books to her face, breathing in the smell of Isobel's shop, still clinging to the pages after all these years. She rubbed the rose quartz stone, its smoothness soothing at the same time as it sent tiny shocks of energy into her fingers and the palm of her hand. She lifted out the candles – the ones Isobel had made especially for her, infusing them with strength and power. Finally, she took out the shrine of elemental objects – nag champa incense for fire, a smooth beach pebble for water, the feather of a blackbird she'd found in the Meadows for air, a small glass vial of earth taken from the garden behind their tenement building.

Her magical tools were imbued with hope, and promise, from Petra's early days with Isobel. They were suffused with frustration and anger at her lack of progress in helping her father get better, and with terrible sadness about how her desire to exact vengeance had caused her to betray Isobel's teachings.

Petra wondered what kind of a witch she was: a lapsed one, certainly, but now also a hopeful one. She wanted to practise the craft again in order to speak to the women who had been imprisoned at Rothmore, to find the truth in what had happened to them. She would find darkness in their stories, she had no doubt, but as long as her intention was pure and honest, she would remain in the light.

She closed her eyes, pictured Isobel sitting with her, in her room. She asked Isobel to guide her, to help her remain true, to stay out of the darkness. The Rothmore estate was east of Edinburgh, in the area Petra had spent her childhood; it was full of painful memories, which would be amplified when she returned to the place that had caused her so much sorrow.

***

Six weeks later, Petra was cramming her suitcase in the ancient car that once belonged to her father, before he'd lost his driving licence and suggested the car would be better off with her. Neither Petra nor her aunt really ever drove the car, and neither was convinced it would survive the journey to Rothmore and back.

Her aunt hugged her close, then told her to hurry up and get moving before she humiliated herself by crying in the street. Petra gave her a look she hoped was full of gratitude, and love, as she turned the key in the ignition, hoping the car would start. She'd dawdled so much when packing, dithering and debating over just about everything that went in the case, that she was leaving later than she'd planned, and any car trouble would further delay her. Guests were invited to arrive at Rothmore from noon, with an official group-meet scheduled for two o'clock. Petra had hoped to arrive early enough to have some time to acclimatise in her room before meeting the others. Shy, and with a history of making bad first impressions, Petra wanted some time to psych herself up for the social side of the retreat.

But her hopes of a smooth journey were in vain. The twenty-minute journey ended up taking more than two hours, due to a serious accident that had closed the main road just east of Edinburgh and traffic on the coast road – really the only other way to get there – snaked back for miles. Petra drove through a series of not-very picturesque towns, willing her car not to over-heat. The car erupting in flames as she pulled up to the house, leaving a mushroom cloud hanging over the place, was not the kind of first impression she wanted to make.

After miles at a slow-crawl, Petra's reward was stunning, uninterrupted views out over the sea as she drove through the village of Port Seton, and the still-dense traffic provided the chance to enjoy the seascape. As the road wound past the Bents, the long dune beaches that stretched for miles, Rothmore House loomed into view, hanging on the edge of a rocky promontory. Relieved that the car didn't spontaneously combust as she drove along the gravel road towards the huge Art Deco house - its white façade ghostly against the slate sky - Petra pulled up next to a small row of other cars, and saw a man standing at the open front door with a cigarette in hand.

He raised his other hand in greeting and, as she got out of the car, he said, "Petra? Welcome - I'm Fingal. We heard about the accident, and guessed you were stuck in traffic. I'll bet you could use a cup of tea."

Petra recognised Fingal Rothmore, one of Scotland's finest contemporary sculptors, famous for his 'still folk' sculptures of tiny other-worldly creatures. Pixies, fairies, elves, gnomes – the little people that held a special place in Scottish folklore and lit-erature. Once a year the estate held an open-day for visitors to see the still folk in their natural habitat, nestled along a wood-land path. Petra was eager to see them.

He picked up Petra's bag (embarrassingly heavy for one week – she needed someone to show her how to pack) and led the way into the entrance of the grand house. Although it was mid-afternoon, lit storm lanterns lined the entranceway, reflected off the gold-painted walls and created a soft glow. It was beautiful and warm and very welcoming.

Fingal showed Petra to her room on the first floor, and told her to join them in the lounge, on the ground floor, when she was ready. "The others have already arrived and are getting to know each other. Take your time to unpack, though – there's no rush."

Petra's room smelled like freshly washed and pressed linen and of room spray fabricated in a laboratory to smell like sea air. She tried out the bed, which was as soft as a giant feathery pillow, and took a moment to inspect the view of the garden that sloped right down to the sea. Despite her hope to hide away in her room to ground herself before meeting the others, she did not want to keep them waiting any longer. She took a few deep breaths, told herself to stay calm, and try to make a good first impression.

Petra took more deep breaths as she walked, slowly, downstairs to the lounge, which she found without difficulty as she could hear voices – talking, laughing, generally sounding like they were having fun. She stood in the doorway for a moment, looking at the other guests, and taking in the lounge. It was a magnificent room – black wooden floors and ochre walls softened by candlelight, even though it was mid-afternoon. A fire blazed in the open fireplace, testament to the chill in the air on this late April day. Huge floor to ceiling windows covered the far wall, through which Petra could see the distant twinkling lights of Fife across the sea.

Fingal looked up, saw Petra standing in the doorway, and beckoned for her to join them. A woman whose forearms were covered in silver bangles clapped her hands together, bracelets clanging noisily, and called the others to attention.

"Now that everyone is here I'd like to officially welcome you all to our home, and to the retreat. We are very happy to host you and your creativity, here on the Rothmore estate. Please, take it in turns to introduce yourselves, and tell us why you've come here."

A woman with short, spiky blonde hair introduced herself as Gill, and said that she'd recently retired, had always wanted to write a novel, and this was her chance. She described the plot as "lonely commuter picks up hitchhiker on a lesser-travelled stretch of road", adding that she'd had the idea on long commutes from her home in the Scottish Borders to her workplace in Edinburgh. The little-used road to her village was so desolate that she'd often had visions of men standing at the side of the road, shadowy figures whose fingers raked out towards her as she drove past.

"They were just hallucinations, I know that, but they stuck with me. I saw them almost every day, so they were almost like landmarks. Quite terrifying landmarks. It messes with your mind, that road, and I think it would make the perfect setting for a thriller."

A tall man with twinkly eyes and a kind smile introduced himself as Samuel. He said his dream had always been to write "*Treasure Island* for adults. With vampires."

A petite young woman dressed head to toe in black smiled warmly at Petra and introduced herself as Clodagh, who'd come to the retreat to work on a graphic novel. A murmur of enthusiasm passed through the group, and Samuel asked what it was about.

Clodagh bit her lip and said, "Well, I've had a few different ideas, but I'm leaning towards a retelling of a sea witch tale. Instead of being malevolent, my sea witch will be a protector."

Feeling self-conscious, Petra said, "Great minds – I'm writing about witches too. I want to write the stories of some of the women who were brought here, to the witches' prison."

"What an eclectic mix of tales you have to tell!" Jane said, clapping her hands together again. She told the guests that she and Fingal had worked hard to create their "haven for writers and artists to come together, and have the freedom to *become*."

She smiled at them, then nodded at a tall, broad man whose russet hair was sticking out in all directions, his eyes slightly wild. "We're delighted to introduce Erik, our writer-in-residence. Erik has won several writing awards and prizes in Norway, and we're lucky to have him with us in Scotland. He will make every effort to help you discover your inner writer." Erik's face broke into a rictus smile, and he waggled his eyebrows at them, as though to cut through Jane's pretension.

"It's an honour to be here," he said, smiling broadly. "I look forward to getting to know you better, and to hearing more about your stories."

Gill asked for details about the week's social events and Jane said, "We like to maintain an element of surprise, *and* be responsive to your needs. There will be plenty of time for free writing, mentoring sessions with Erik, and some cultural experiences that we'd rather surprise you with than tell you about right now."

"In fact," Fingal added, "this evening, since the weather is fair, I thought we'd take a little trip. Is everyone okay with boat trips?"

Samuel and Gill nodded enthusiastically, whereas Clodagh and Petra gave non-committal shrugs, and shared a nervous look.

Undaunted, Fingal said, "Excellent! How about a trip to Midhallow Island?"

Midhallow was infamous in central Scotland as the island of the disappeared. In the mid-1600s a group of people who had lived in a small fishing village were transported to Midhallow after contracting a plague-type disease. One month after they were banished to Midhallow, the minister of the local parish sailed across with provisions. Every single person had vanished. There were no corpses, nor did any bodies ever wash up along that part of the east coast. Although there were many theories about what might have happened, no one had ever solved the mystery of the twenty-eight who went missing from Midhallow.

Jane and Fingal left the room, returning a few minutes later carrying tiered cake stands peppered with sandwich triangles, small scones, and an assortment of pastries and cakes. Jane handed each guest a hand-written menu with different types of tea listed, and asked for their tea order. The back of Petra's neck prickled with perspiration, as she panicked about her lack of tea knowledge. Fortunately, Jane came to her last, and she repeated Clodagh's order for Darjeeling.

Petra's concerns about small-talk were largely unfounded, thanks mostly to Samuel's spirited conversational skills, and Erik's gregariousness. Clodagh struck Petra as almost as anxious as she was, and hoped she might have met a kindred spirit. But, just as she was starting to relax, Jane disrupted Petra's relative calm by announcing that she had one more ice-breaker activity.

"This will give your creativity a kick-start," she announced proudly. "It works like a charm, every time." She passed each of the guests an envelope. "Don't open this until I give you the go-ahead. When I do, you will have five minutes to write a poem using your given word. Now, start!"

Petra's word was *pleurisy*. She looked nervously at the others, who were already scribbling with the tiny pencil on the tiny pad of paper, both of which were also in the envelope. Clodagh must have felt Petra's eyes on her because she looked up, and gave a subtle shake of her head and a wry smile.

Cringing, Petra wrote the first string of words that came into her head, then covered her slip of paper with her hands, as though trying to keep anyone else from looking at it. Worse still, Jane called time and instructed them to pass their poems to the person on their right. Gill was first to read, sharing Samuel's poem in which he'd used the word *corpse* in every line. Clodagh's word was *didgeridoo*, Gill's was *insatiable* – Petra had the humiliating experience of reading her erotic poem aloud - and finally it was the turn of Petra's poem featuring *pleurisy*. To her surprise, the others seemed to think she'd intended it to be humorous, and she was buoyed up by their laughter.

The experience left her feeling as though every nerve ending was exposed. She took some comfort in another plate of cakes and sandwiches before Fingal announced that it was time for everyone to get their warm clothes, in readiness for the trip to Midhallow.

CHAPTER 5

Fingal gave the guests a safety briefing: stay in the boat, don't lean over the edge, keep the life-preserver on at all times. "It's an old boat, but there's nothing to worry about as long as you stick to the rules. It's taken me to Midhallow so many times in my life, I'm fairly certain it could steer us there without any help from me. Fair warning – the wind off the sea is merciless. Stick close to your seating partner for warmth."

"Do you sail to the other Forth islands as well, or just Midhallow?" Petra heard surprise in Samuel's voice, matching her own. During the summer season, boat tours around the islands in the Firth of Forth were common: to the Bass Rock near North Berwick, which loomed out of the sea like an iceberg and was a sanctuary for sea birds; to Fidra, off of the mainland near Gullane, thought to be Robert Louis Stevenson's inspiration for Treasure Island; and to the Isle of May, home to a colony of puffins. But Midhallow was decidedly off the tourist trail.

Fingal and Erik each grabbed a large basket, and led the group through the French doors from the lounge into a courtyard garden, then down a gravel path towards the shore. On the way, the conversation centred on Midhallow and some of the theories about what had happened to the twenty-eight who had disappeared. The twilight sky was mauve and navy blue as the six passengers climbed into the boat, huddled together in pairs on the narrow wooden seats, and sailed away from Rothmore. Petra sat next to Clodagh, who clutched her hand tightly. Gill and Samuel sat ahead of them, and Erik was up front with Fingal.

Fingal deftly manoeuvred the boat through the shallow

bay near Rothmore out past the cliffs that jutted into the sea to the east, and then they were out in the open and unforgiving Forth wind Fingal warned them about. The cold wind was bracing but Petra felt invigorated, heading towards the site of one of the saddest mysteries that part of Scotland had ever known.

As they approached Midhallow about twenty minutes after setting off, the setting sun had turned the sky blood orange, which was reflected off the dark volcanic rocks and made the island look like it was coated in lava. Despite the loud sound of the wind in her ears, Petra heard Clodagh gasp, and say, "Isn't it absolutely beautiful?". Petra had to agree that it *was* beautiful, in an unsettling way.

As Fingal pulled the boat up to a small jetty there was a little jolt, then Erik jumped out and tied a thick rope to a post. He held out his hand to help everyone off the boat. Samuel led the way, up some roughly-hewn steps. The others followed, until they were on a flat ledge of rock, with a circle of stones and some charcoaled wood, evidence of previous bonfires. Someone had smoothed flat rounds of tree trunks, making little seats, and they each took one. Fingal proceeded to build a fire with some kindling and logs he had brought from the house, while Erik unpacked the picnic supper.

The air smelled of rotting seaweed and something more animal in nature, as though charged with a strong energy, and it prickled the skin on the back of Petra's neck. She was glad when, within minutes, the fire was lit, and was starting to give off a warm glow. Soft filled rolls were passed around and Erik poured warm spiced wine from a large flask.

Samuel asked Fingal if they'd had family picnics on Midhallow, when he was a boy.

"We did, yes. I guess you could say my father had a sense of the macabre, bringing us here. But it always felt natural to us – I don't remember ever feeling frightened. I think my father most likely came here because there was very little chance of seeing other people. He liked his solitude."

"Did you ever camp here overnight?" Clodagh asked.

Fingal laughed. "Many times. My older brother told me if we stayed awake all night, the people who went missing would appear to us, and tell us what happened to them."

"But you never stayed awake all night?" Samuel asked.

"I didn't. My brother claimed he did, although no one came to tell him what happened."

"What a coup – two boys solving the secret of the missing twenty-eight!" Erik laughed.

Fingal took a long slug of wine, then announced that the guests would be the first to see an exhibition of Erik's poetry and Fingal's sculptures, in two days' time. "The idea was based on Erik's interpretation of the legend of the Finfolk, as a way to explain why the twenty-eight disappeared here on Midhallow."

Erik smiled. "When I first came to this island, it had a profound effect on me. I suppose I was like Fingal's brother, hoping if I was quiet enough, I'd be able to hear something to explain what happened here. The answers are *here*, in these rocks that have been here for centuries. Why don't we have the science to tap into the truth – the human truths – in the landscape, in the absence of bones or fossils or any solid evidence?"

"I'm sure there *was* evidence," Gill said, "but whoever was responsible for their deaths got rid of it. They couldn't just disappear without a trace."

Erik smiled at her. "Well, I turned to poetry as a way of writing their stories, drawing on Scots and Norse legends."

He downed the contents of his mug, then said, "The Finfolk of Orcadian legend travelled between their kingdom under the sea and the human world, spending their summers on Hildaland, also called Eynhallow, one of Orkney's magical vanishing islands. You might wonder about the names of these islands: Eynhallow, or the Holy Isle, and this island called Midhallow. Is there a connection?"

He paused, his strong features etched by the light from the fire. "The Finfolk had the habit of choosing a human husband or wife by abducting them, and taking them to their homes on Eynhallow. Our work imagines that the Finfolk took the twenty-eight to live on a vanishing island that no one has yet found. And don't imagine that it isn't possible. After all, the Finfolk could travel between Norway and Orkney with only seven strokes of the oar, so Orkney to Midhallow would take no time at all."

Fingal added, "I started with Erik's poetry and gave the twenty-eight and the Finfolk shape, telling his stories through sculpture."

Samuel asked if they were sitting on the site where the twenty-eight had lived. Fingal explained that no one knew for sure, as every trace of them had disappeared. But, he said, the best guess was that the camp was further up the hill, where there was a larger flat ledge of rock. He said he had brought torches if anyone would like to go exploring, recommending that they go in pairs, for safety. Clodagh said she wanted to go, and Petra offered to accompany her.

They set off, with Clodagh in the lead carrying the torch. Petra stared at the spot of light on the ground in front of her, trying not to trip over anything, or kick Clodagh's heels. They had taken only a few steps before the light and warmth from the fire - and any sound coming from the group - disappeared completely. For an instant, Petra wanted to turn back, but she couldn't leave Clodagh to find the camp on her own. A cold feeling of dread wrapped itself more tightly around her with each step.

After about fifteen minutes, Clodagh came to an abrupt stop, and shone the torch back and forth across what seemed to be a large flat expanse of rock.

"This must be it," she said softly. "Am I imagining it or is it colder here than anywhere else on the island?" Petra agreed with her. "My grandad told me the story of Midhallow when I was a girl. The way he told it, the twenty-eight starved to death after the boatman kept all of the food meant for them for his family. He was supposed to take fresh supplies every week, but he didn't make a single trip to the island. Three months passed, he caught the disease and died, and a new boatman made the crossing with food. He found twenty-eight rotting corpses."

"That makes more sense. Greed won out. And cruelty

I suppose. I wonder, though, what happened to their bones?" Petra shivered as a cold wind blew across the spot. They stood in silence, until Petra heard Clodagh take in a sudden gasp of breath.

She sounded frightened when she said, "I'm glad I've seen it, but I'm ready to go back. How about you?"

"Definitely ready."

When they got back to the fire, Samuel was in the final stages of a ghost story whose ending seemed to be a bit of an anti-climax, if the others' muted reactions were anything to go by. They asked about the camp, and Clodagh looked across the flames at Petra.

"It was horrible," she said. "I saw something I'll never be able to unsee. It scared the life out of me."

***

Sailing back to the mainland from Midhallow, out on the open water with the fiercely cold wind off the sea, Petra worried she might never be warm again. She huddled close to Clodagh, who reached her arm around Petra's shivering body and pulled her close. Her teeth were chattering – she had always thought it was just a turn of phrase, and was surprised by the actual physical phenomenon – as Fingal steered the boat back towards the jetty at Rothmore's pebble beach.

If Petra's legs had not been so cold she would have run back to the warmth of the house, but all she could do was stamp them hard against the ground with each step she took, to get the blood pumping again. Fingal swung open the French doors and led them into the warm glow of the guest lounge. Someone – Jane, Petra guessed, since she had not come to the island – had kept the fire blazing, and she planted herself directly in front of it, holding her hands out over the flames.

"Right, whisky!" Fingal said, and Petra heard the wonderful sound of liquid pouring into a glass. Her fingers still felt like ice blocks as she reached out for the tumbler offered to her, and cupped it greedily. She downed the contents in one huge gulp.

Fortunately, Fingal brought the bottle around again, and she happily accepted another shot. She realised she was hogging the heat at the exact moment Samuel said, "Come on now, shove over – you're stealing all the warmth."

He was smiling and Petra could see that he was just teasing her, but she moved to the side of the fireplace just the same. More whisky was consumed, and the conversation turned from their cold extremities to Midhallow.

"I'm really glad we went – don't get me wrong, Fingal – but it's not an experience I ever want to repeat. I can't quite put my finger on it, but something isn't right about that place. It was almost like it didn't want us there."

"Well put, Gill. I don't believe in ghosts, but I believe in history, and the island has a terrible past. Maybe that's what we were feeling – the fears of those who lived and died there." Samuel raised his whisky glass, presumably to the memory of the twenty-eight who had disappeared.

"Well, I *might* believe in ghosts, and I definitely feel that we're not alone on the island. There's always an overwhelming feeling of sadness hanging in the air," Erik said, staring into his whisky.

Petra was watching Clodagh, who was very pale, and looked like she was on the verge of tears. "It's interesting to me that we – I mean, society generally – are still making up stories to explain what happened there all those years ago. I mean your exhibition," she gestured at Erik and Fingal, "and Clodagh's grandfather's story, which seems like a plausible explanation for what happened."

She looked at Clodagh, expecting her to take this opening into the conversation, but she continued to stare straight ahead of her. When she didn't speak, Petra added, "I hadn't heard that story before, but the boatman kept all of the provisions meant for the twenty-eight for him, and his family. His greed starved them, basically."

Petra saw a flicker of emotion in Clodagh's eyes, but she

stayed silent. Samuel was looking at her, kindly, and said, "So do you think it would be very insensitive of me to set my novel on Midhallow? You know, the vampires are shipwrecked on the island and find twenty-eight weak victims, who can't fight back?"

"That's in very poor taste," Gill said. But it had lightened the mood in the room, and Clodagh even managed a half-smile.

Petra was nicely warm – a bit too warm, actually, which was making her feel sleepy. She would have been happy to stay there in the warm room, with the promise of more whisky, but she had the sudden, sobering thought that this first day of the retreat was drawing to a close. She had seven days to make a good start with her book, and the first day was almost over.

She asked Fingal if she could borrow a torch, and if he could point her in the direction of the witches' prison.

"You want to go and see it right now?" he asked.

"It's as good a time as any. The moon's out."

"You don't want to wait until morning?" Samuel asked.

"I'd like to go and see it in the morning, too. But I'm trying to get a feel for it at all times of the day and night, and in all weathers, so that I can write about it accurately. I've waited a long time to come here and see it."

"Just don't ask me to come with you – I'm not going back outside tonight," Gill said.

"I'll take you there," Erik offered. "I know where it is and, moon or no moon, it's very dark out there." He looked at Clodagh and asked, "Would you like to come with us, Clodagh, since you're writing about witches too?"

Clodagh shook her head, and Petra thought she saw panic in her eyes. "No thank you. I've still not warmed up properly. I'll see it tomorrow."

Petra wondered again just what Clodagh had seen at the camp of the disappeared. She'd been quiet ever since, lost in her thoughts. But she also knew that visiting a place where women had been imprisoned in terrible conditions, most likely after beatings and even torture, was not going to make Clodagh feel any better. Petra questioned her own reasoning for wanting to visit the prison at night; she was linked to the place, and had been since the taunts levelled at her back in high school. The prison was a place for women mocked and marginalised – by other women as well as men – and the very fact that her tormentors had placed her there with her mother made this a pilgrimage of sorts. It was a reckoning with the past, and who they'd made her with their insults, and their ostracism.

CHAPTER 6

Petra was glad Erik had offered to come with her. She wasn't afraid of being in the witches' prison alone, but was happy to have a companion when she visited the place that she had lived with – lived *in* at times, in her mind – for so many years.

"It's a good night to visit the prison," Erik said. "Full moon."

"Waning gibbous actually."

Erik laughed. "I stand corrected. And what does a waning gibbous moon mean?"

"For witches, you mean? The moon is getting darker again. Some believe that this is the time to do spells you want to hide. The darker side of magic I mean. Banishing spells, that kind of thing." Petra could hear her heart thumping, and told herself to take a deep breath, to stop talking so much.

Erik shone the torch over a knee-high curve of stones, then opposite to another similar curve. "These are the remaining walls of the prison - or Marchbane Tower, as it was called."

Petra had seen illustrations of the prison – a tall, narrow tower with only a few small windows for the guards to keep watch, not for the prisoners. The women were imprisoned in groups, except on the rare occasion there was a solitary prisoner, in a tiny, dark room with no windows. They were seldom given food and water, and the guards often prevented them from sleeping. Habitually held in the prison for weeks if not months, the women were subjected to beatings and torture, designed to make them confess ahead of the official trial.

In the many accounts Petra had read of the women accused of witchcraft, the allegations levelled at them, which were ridiculous and obviously false to anyone reading them in modern times, and the terrible punishments meted out were recorded in matter-of-fact ways. She didn't plan to shy away from the horrors of what had happened to the women in her book, but she also wanted to show the fuller picture of their lives - who they were and who they had loved.

A chill wind blew in from the sea, carrying the smell and taste of salt. It was oddly peaceful, as though the women who'd inhabited this space refused to linger, even as spirits. They stood in silence for a few minutes, and then Petra suggested they go back to the pebble beach, so she could get a sense of the distance between the prison and the sea.

"Sure, but there's a better beach I could show you, if you're up for it – it's a bit further away, but I call it the enchanted beach."

An enchanted beach was too tempting an opportunity for Petra to pass up. "Great, let's go."

Getting to the enchanted beach meant walking through the woods, where Fingal's still folk sculptures were. Petra remembered the two ceramic fairies in the garden of her childhood home. Her father had told her to keep an eye out for any movement.

"They have a tendency for mischief," he had said seriously. "If they move to another spot in the garden, just move them right back." She had never known when he truly believed something, or was being mischievous himself.

The woods smelled *alive*, an earthy green smell of things growing, and being born. As they walked through the woods towards the beach, the moonlight illuminated the little statues dotted beside the path. Some were right next to the path, others were perched on rocks or tree stumps. At one point Erik stopped and pointed up at a tree. And then Petra saw it: in a hole in the trunk, a gnome with his head inclined downward stared at them. It was a bit unnerving, and also a little magical.

After about twenty minutes the trees cleared and they

came to an opening in a high stone wall. Petra caught her first glimpse of the water, illuminated by moonlight, and could hear the waves gently washing against the shore. They walked right down to the edge of the sand, then stopped and looked out across the water. Petra could see at least three lighthouses flashing out messages to unseen ships, at different points on the coast.

"It's so still. Is it a cove beach?"

Erik nodded. "It's a private beach, so most of the time you have it all to yourself. Well, shared with the gulls and the cormorants. And it's protected from the wind, so on a sunny day it feels like you could almost be somewhere in the Mediterranean."

They stood together, looking out over the moonlit sea. "Do you ever come here to write?"

"Not very often, but I have a little waterproof notebook I carry around with me, in case the mood strikes. I mostly use it to hold my beach treasures – feathers, petals, little bits that I find on the sand. It's quite handy for that."

They started walking again. At one point, the moonlight on one of the wave-washed rocks looked like a seal's head popping up out of the water, and Petra asked Erik if he knew about the legend of the selkies.

"Scottish folklore – yes, I love it. I'm fascinated by the overlap in our cultural stories, being seafaring, northern nations. All of those silver threads - the links between so many of the stories and the sea. And between witchcraft and the sea, of course."

"Did you know much about the Finfolk before you decided to write about them and Midhallow?"

"A little. When I was a child, my grandmother used to tell my sister and I never to go to the beach alone, because the Finfolk might appear out of the sea and steal us away."

"That's kind of terrifying."

Erik laughed. "It is, but then you could say that it was very effective in keeping us away from the dangers of going into the water without anyone watching. And I suspect she had been told the same thing when she was a child."

They had come to the end of the stretch of walkable beach.

Ahead were towering rocks leading up to a sheer cliff's edge. Erik gently placed his hand on Petra's elbow, and they turned around and began to walk back the way they had come. They walked in silence along the beach, up to the gap in the stone wall that led back to the estate, and then they retraced their steps, silently, through the woodland path, the still folk keeping their watch over them.

***

Back in her room, Petra felt both tired and invigorated by the day's events, and by her extended exposure to the fresh, sea air. She wanted to write a description of the witches' prison before she lost her first impressions to sleep. She'd left the curtains open and a flash of something bright, moving quickly across the lawn, caught her eye. It might have been a rabbit, or a cat or maybe even a fox running across the grass, its shape illuminated by moonlight. But Petra imagined the still folk moving around out there, come to guard the space like tiny sentinels below her window.

She smiled at the thought, and closed her eyes, trying to remember exactly how the prison looked in the moonlight. She remembered hearing Erik's soft breath near her as she stood there, and being grateful for his stillness. In the far curve of the north-eastern section of wall, she saw a faint shimmering and, as she focused her mind's eye, it took human shape. Although Petra had practised the conjuring spell in her bedroom before coming to the retreat, she hadn't used it in the prison – she was waiting for daylight, and to be alone. And yet – had something been conjured, that she hadn't seen for some reason when she was with Erik?

She recognised the shape of the person whose back was to her, because she'd seen it so many times in the past. It was her mother, and she was standing, completely still, inside the prison. She was singing, softly, her daily meditation in and with nature, in which she gave thanks to the life force for their food, shelter, warmth, and their lives together. Petra was enveloped in a deep state of calm, and peacefulness, as she always was when she watched her mother. But then the air around her mother's form turned crimson, moving and shifting like flames. Her mother turned to look at Petra over her shoulder, but it was not her mother's face at all. Petra did not recognise the malevolent face that looked back at her, with hateful eyes.

Petra was startled by a noise somewhere in the house and opened her eyes. She gave a fleeting, longing look at her enticing bed, but she knew she wouldn't sleep. Instead, she grabbed a scarf and her coat, wanting to get out in the fresh night air. Unsure if anyone would still be awake or the doors from the lounge locked, she decided to give it a try. The house was quiet as she crept downstairs and along the narrow corridor. When she reached the lounge, she was surprised – and very happy – to see Clodagh sitting on one of the sofas, her head bent over a large sketch pad.

Petra called out a quiet hello, hoping not to scare her, but Clodagh's body jerked in fright. Petra apologised, and asked if she was interrupting.

"No – not at all. Everyone went to bed but I thought I'd stay up for a bit and do some drawing." She yawned, and patted the seat cushion beside her, inviting Petra to sit. "How was the prison?"

"There's not much left – just the lower parts of walls – but it was surprisingly peaceful. I'm not sure what I was expecting, but if I didn't know it was a prison, I'd never have guessed." She pushed the unwelcome image of the red shape pretending to be her mother out of her mind.

Clodagh nodded, her face sad, and Petra wondered if she, too, was remembering whatever she'd seen earlier in the night, on Midhallow.

"Can I ask what you've been drawing?"

"Sure," Clodagh said, moving the sketch pad closer to Petra so she could see. "I've been toying with the idea of having the sea witch live on Midhallow. Maybe, you know, she made it her home after those people went missing, to make sure it couldn't happen again."

Petra looked closely at the illustration, which seemed to be of the camp nearest the jetty. A fire was lit and a pot sat in the middle of it. A tall, slender woman bent over it, her hair hanging over her face.

"I'm not sure what I want her to look like yet, so I've taken the easy way out for the time being."

"You're very talented."

Clodagh blushed. "Thank you. I love drawing. I haven't done enough of it lately."

"Too busy?"

"Preoccupied is closer to the truth. And not very inspired."

"But Midhallow inspired you?"

Clodagh looked uncomfortable again, and Petra silently cursed herself. "Maybe I'm trying too hard to make something good come from whatever happened to those poor people." She looked thoughtful for a moment, then asked, "And you? What's your interest in writing about the witches' prison?"

Petra considered telling Clodagh about the high school taunts, but didn't trust herself to talk about her mother with someone she didn't know very well. Instead, she said, "Well, actually, I've written about witches before."

Clodagh's eyes lit up. "Tell me more."

Petra took a deep breath, and told Clodagh about her final year dissertation, how researching and writing it had consumed her, and how it had ended with Josh's theft and betrayal. She left out the part about wanting to use revenge magic so much it was all she thought about for months, and how it had left her drained, exhausted, depleted of emotional strength.

Clodagh was shocked, and her indignation on Petra's behalf was like a tonic. Petra smiled as she said, "My aunt took pity on me, and offered to send me here as a birthday gift. I've been really miserable to live with, no doubt, and she encouraged me to try again, not let him win."

Clodagh raised her glass. "Here's to you, Aunt -."

"Alice."

"She sounds pretty great."

Tears welled in Petra's eyes. "She really is," she managed to say, before her voice broke.

Clodagh gave her such a kind, gentle look, that Petra worried she was going to shame herself by breaking down completely. There was so much she could have said to Clodagh, but she guarded the secrets of the past so closely that she'd told no one, apart from Isobel.

Clodagh clasped Petra's hand in her own warm one. "I think we should have another whisky before we turn in. What do you say?"

Petra looked over at the amber liquid, sparking in its crystal decanter in the firelight. Grateful for the chance to blink the tears away without Clodagh seeing, she rushed over to the table and poured two generous measures.

Handing one of the glasses to Clodagh she asked as gently as she could, "I know something at the camp rattled you. Do you want to talk about it?"

Clodagh took a long, slow sip, staring all the while at Petra over the rim of her glass. "Did you see anything strange there?"

Petra shook her head, wondering how Clodagh could have seen anything in that dark place. "Was it a trick of the light? The torch light, I mean?"

Clodagh bit her lip. "I mean, I don't think so, but maybe." She took another slow sip. "I would like to talk to you about it, just not right now, if that's okay. It might be best if I try to put it out of my mind until the light of day."

Petra smiled at her, in an attempt to convey that she understood. And she did, truly, after what she'd seen in her room just minutes before. "Understood. Let's talk about it tomorrow. To tell you the truth, I came downstairs because I closed my eyes for a minute and had a kind of waking-nightmare. I'd rather forget about it, too."

Clodagh clinked her glass against Petra's. "Here's to overactive imaginations. I think we might be two peas in a pod."

The warmth in Petra's chest was partly whisky-fuelled, and partly due to the warmth she felt in Clodagh's company. This was a better start to the retreat than she could ever have imagined, or hoped for.

CHAPTER 7

Gill and Samuel were already in the guest lounge the next morning when Petra arrived for breakfast, sitting at a long rectangular table on the far side of the room, in front of the floor to ceiling windows.

"Good morning Petra," Samuel said cheerfully. "It's a help yourself continental-style breakfast. The machine on the end of the table makes a very good cappuccino."

Gill looked intently at Petra as she chewed her toast. "So, you need to tell us what happened."

"What? When do you mean?"

"Last night, with Erik. We want all of the details." Her beady eyes were gleaming.

"We went to see the witches' prison, and then he showed me another beach."

"Is *that* what they're calling it these days. Come on, spill the beans."

"There are no beans to spill. We went for a walk. End of."

"I don't buy it for a second."

"She said there's nothing to tell, Gill. Let's change the subject and then I'll get you another coffee. So, Petra, tell us about what you saw last night, at the prison."

Petra wanted to tell Gill that she was out of order, but she could see that Samuel was trying to keep the peace, so she grabbed a bowl of cereal and some orange juice from the buffet table, and sat down beside Samuel.

"There isn't much left of the building itself – just some of the lower parts of the walls. In the moonlight, with the sound of the waves in the distance, it seemed peaceful. Not at all what I was expecting it to feel like, actually."

"So, you're writing a book about the prison? Can you tell us more?" Samuel asked.

"I want to set it here, in East Lothian. Maybe right here on the estate, I'm not sure yet. This part of the country – Haddingtonshire as it was called then – had the most persecutions and executions in all of Scotland. I want to get under that, get right down to what it was like to be a woman living here during the peak of the witch hunts."

"Is there much evidence about what happened here on the Rothmore estate?"

"A bit – not much. There was a castle on this site then, but there's nothing left of it now. At least there's still something of the prison left."

"How do you know so much about witches, anyway?" Gill asked.

Petra paused to drink some orange juice, choosing her words carefully. "I've always been interested in stories about witches, since I was a girl. I read as much as I could find – fiction and non-fiction – and I still do. I also studied the history of witchcraft in Scotland at university."

They heard voices in the corridor, and then Clodagh and Erik appeared. Gill's eyes looked like they were about to pop right out of her head.

"Good morning!" Samuel called out. "Help yourselves to breakfast. The machine makes a very decent cappuccino, although I guess you'll know that already, Erik."

"Well, well, well," Gill said. "Do tell – is it a coincidence that you two are showing up for breakfast at the same time?"

Clodagh's cheeks went red, and she said, "Jesus, Gill – have some tact." Petra gave a silent cheer. Gill had nagged Clodagh relentlessly after their return from Midhallow, urging her to tell them what she had seen.

"Yes, Gill. Have some tact. I'm a married man," Erik said, holding up his ring finger and pointing at his wedding band.

Gill had the decency to look slightly ashamed. "Well I for one was inspired by our trip to Midhallow last night, and am in the mood to get my head down and do some writing today. Just don't expect quality on my first day, Erik, but at least the will is there. And you know what they say – writing is ten percent talent, and ninety percent hard work," Gill said.

"You're here for the perspiration, are you?" Samuel teased.

"It's way too early for that kind of joke." Erik grinned, shovelling cereal into his mouth. "While we're all here, I'll just explain how this works. You can ask for a mentoring meeting with me at any point – today, to talk to me about your ideas or share what you've written later in the day, or at any time. Whenever you feel like you want to talk to me, basically. People can feel a bit nervous about sharing right away, but I promise you it's meant to be supportive."

"I'd like to meet with you, as soon as possible please."

"Of course, Gill. After breakfast?" Gill nodded, happily.

"Maybe I could see you after that?" Samuel asked Erik.

"Of course."

Petra gulped the rest of her coffee and said, "I'd like to crack on with some writing today, so maybe we could meet later – but I'm not sure if I'll be ready."

"No pressure – you know where to find me."

Clodagh said, "I need a bit of thinking time but I'll let you know when I'm ready."

Erik pushed his chair back from the table. "Great. Now, can I make anyone a cappuccino?"

After breakfast, Petra went back to her room to collect her rucksack and the picnic blanket she had brought from home. She put on her warm down jacket and a hat, then went downstairs and out the front door, breathing in the crisp morning air. The sun looked impossibly large and orange above the eastern horizon, and the sky was completely empty of clouds. A perfect day to be outside, in the prison. She was excited to be starting to write, at last.

The witches' prison was just as unthreatening in the clear light of day as it had been in the moonlight. Petra hoped to summon some of the women who'd been imprisoned there, so that she could write the truth of what had happened to them, centuries before. She spread the blanket out on the ground, lit a candle and a cone of nag champa incense. Sitting cross-legged, she closed her eyes. Breathing in the salty air, feeling the chill of the morning on her face, she quietly began the incantation. She asked for the women to come to her, to help her understand what had happened to them.

And then she was still.

She heard Isobel's soft voice: *If you are quiet enough, they will come to you.*

Hearing Isobel calmed and reassured her. She kept her eyes closed, and soon she felt a change in the wind. The smell of the incense intensified, and a rush of soft voices filled the air; they came as quickly as a team of horses, passing through the space in front of her and then evaporating just as quickly. When it was quiet again, she felt just the slightest wisp of air right by her face, warm and hesitant, as though someone was asking for permission to speak. Petra silently incanted that she was listening, and she wanted to hear what the voice had to say.

Immediately, images appeared in her mind, staccato at first like a jerky old silent movie and then becoming more fluid. A young girl, in a cotton dress, running through a meadow of bright red poppies. The same girl, slightly older, pressing her forehead against the soft, velvety noses of two horses in a stable. Older still – a teenager now – the girl calmly led one of the horses out into the field, a feeling of total serenity enveloping the scene. Later, as she led the horse back into the stable, she smiled when she saw a tall, thin boy with black hair and a shy smile, waiting for her. Anticipation spiked through the calmness, and she picked up her pace as she walked toward him.

The mood altered completely in the next images. A tired-looking woman yelled at the girl, and lashed out at her with a poker she was using to tend the fire. The girl ran out of the cottage, ran and ran and ran until she was standing on a pebble beach, crying, thinking of the horses, and the boy with black hair.

Later, the tired-looking woman was talking to two tall men, dressed from head to toe in black, who had come to the cottage. The men found the girl, curled up in a ball on the pebble beach, crying, dragged her off the beach and threw her on the back of a horse-drawn cart.

And then they brought her to this place – the prison for witches.

Petra asked her name and, after a pause, she heard it. The young woman accused of being a witch was called Meg.

***

Petra's body jolted and she opened her eyes: the sun was almost directly overhead, tilting westwards. She'd fallen asleep in the prison after the summoning, worn out by it. Gathering up her belongings, she headed back to the house, desperate for something to eat. Clodagh was eating lunch at the large table, alone. Petra grabbed a couple of sandwiches and joined her.

"How was your morning?" she asked.

"Good, I think. I didn't start any writing, but I did a lot of thinking."

"About the sea witch?"

"Yes. I've changed my mind about having her live on Midhallow. Because she's a protective force, I think it would be more interesting to make her a lighthouse keeper. You know, back before they were automated."

"What a great idea! *Were* there any female lighthouse keepers?"

"Some, not many. Usually women took on the role if their husband, or father, died."

"Did they wear trousers? It wouldn't have been easy, doing that kind of work in skirts."

"My research is limited, but in everything I've seen and read they wore skirts. Imagine running up and down those narrow, spiral staircases in skirts – carrying kerosene, oil, or naked flames."

"That's awful - they must have been tempted to ditch the skirts."

"You would think! And lighthouse keepers not only had an active role in preventing maritime accidents and disasters by keeping the lamps lit, they also had to go out into treacherous waters to rescue anyone who might be in difficulty."

"Also in skirts? That's outrageous."

"I agree. How about you? Was it a good morning?"

"Yes. Like you, I didn't start any writing, but I'm ready to, now."

"Can you tell me about it?"

Petra didn't feel ready to talk about Meg's story yet. "Would it be okay to wait until I've written something down?"

"Of course, no problem. We'll have lots of sharing, when the time comes." Clodagh pushed her chair away from the table. "I should get my head down and do some work. Talk later?"

Petra smiled, and nodded, and inwardly hoped that she hadn't offended Clodagh, or put her off. She tried to silence the voice in her head that was saying *You have quite a way with people, Petra.*

Back in her room, Petra sat down at the Spartan – but perfectly functional – desk. It was placed directly in front of the window and she sat for a long moment, staring out across the garden, thinking, then told herself to get her head down, and start writing. If she worked hard enough and made a good start with the beginning of Meg's story, she would reward herself with a walk along the cove beach before dinner.

She tried her best to remain true to Meg's story as she had seen it, adding some details about her life in the cottage.

Petra doubted that her poker-wielding mother was usually non-violent, so she wrote about Meg's difficulties living in that place. Petra wondered at Meg's mother's motivation for calling in the witch-hunters: had there been a reward? Was it because she hated her daughter? Had she actually thought she was a witch, or had been bewitched by the young man she had loved?

Petra made a reasonable start, but there were still some gaps that required more research and thinking about, before she could continue. She'd worked hard, and it was time for her reward: the beach.

***

The afternoon was gloriously warm when Petra stepped through the front door, and out into the sunshine. The air was full of the smell of things coming to life – the earthy, warm, heady scents of spring. Petra walked through the woods, nodding at the still folk, and then out into the sunshine again and through the wall to the cove beach.

Erik was right: it was so sheltered, so warm and still, that it could have been a beach somewhere on the Mediterranean.

Petra had planned a quick walk along to the cliffs and back, but it was the perfect day for ambling. Looking for tiny treasures washed onto the shore was one of her favourite activities, one she hadn't had the chance to do in years. Almost immediately, she found a pair of legs from an action figure, separated from the rest of the body. They were intact - a pair of plastic sea legs.

Several metres along the beach, she found what beachcombers might call the holy grail of sea glass finds: a bottle stopper, beautifully frosted and seafoam green. Petra picked it up and put it in her pocket, wanting to keep it close to her body, like a good luck talisman. This was a rare find, from a time long past when glass bottles were in common use, and Petra thought it was a good omen.

At the edge of the beach, below the cliffs, she spotted some driftwood and almost walked past it until she realised what it was - a paintbrush, minus the bristles, smoothed by the sea and bleached by the sun. She turned around and headed back in the direction of Rothmore and found, just a few steps apart, right arms from two different dolls: one large white arm and a much smaller black arm. All of the sea treasures had tales to tell about how they'd been lost or discarded, and now found again.

She reached the hole in the wall, but didn't feel ready to go back to the house just yet. It was perfect weather, for this last day in April, and she wanted to enjoy it a little longer. She sat down in the sand, warmed by the sunshine, and stared out over the calm, still sea.

Petra heard a crunching sound behind her, turned around to look for the source and saw Erik emerging through the gap in the wall, with hair that looked newly-combed, and a huge smile.

"Ah, here you are – back on the beach!"

"I came out for a walk and couldn't bring myself to go back indoors. I *love* this beach."

Erik sat down in the sand beside her. He laughed when he saw her collection of sea treasures, laid out in a row in the sand. "What's this?"

"All things I found on the beach today."

As Erik picked each sea treasure up, he scrutinised it and made up a back story. He seemed to be delighting in them as much as Petra.

"Do you know, I was down here one day and I stepped over a brick that had been worn down by the waves. Not ten steps along I found another one, so I picked it up, went back for the other one, and now I use them as book ends in my room. Sea brick book ends!"

"Kindred spirits," Petra said, smiling. They sat in companionable silence, watching the birds and one sailboat, most likely out from the harbour at North Berwick.

Erik looked at Petra, mischief in his eyes, and asked, "Have you ever gone swimming in the sea?"

"Never! Not even during heatwaves. Are you kidding? Do

you know what the water temperature is this time of year?"

"Yes, I do. I swim in it most days."

"In this water?" He nodded. "Right here?" He nodded again. "No, Erik. I am not going to go swimming with you."

He stood up, took off his jumper and the long-sleeve shirt he wore underneath and then unbuckled his belt. Petra averted her eyes. 'What could be better in the afternoon than an invigorating swim?'

"It sounds like torture - no thank you!"

Erik walked towards the water, in his swimming trunks. He called over his shoulder, "Why don't you roll up your jeans and just put your feet in? You'll feel amazing, I guarantee it!"

"I'll feel hideous, and then my heart will stop and I'll go into cardiac arrest. I hope you know CPR."

He just laughed. Petra hadn't gone swimming in the sea off the east coast since she was a child – before she knew better - but something made her decide to risk it. She took off her shoes and socks, and tried to roll up the bottoms of her jeans. They were too snug to budge more than a centimetre, so she unzipped them and took them off. Erik stood by the water's edge, staring out over the sea.

Petra started running toward the water then, and Erik looked back over his shoulder and whooped. He ran into the water until it was up to his thighs, then did a graceful dip-dive right in. Petra hopped from one foot to the other, yelling out a medley of swear words, aware that she must look completely ridiculous. Erik was graceful in the water, doing the breast-stroke until he was so far out Petra nearly lost sight of him completely, and then he turned back and started swimming towards her. He swam right up to where she was still doing the ridiculous water dance, grabbed her hand, and they ran back onto the sand.

"You did it! Congratulations! Life will never be the same!" He shook himself like a dog, jumped up and down a few times, and began to put his clothes back on his wet body. "I never remember to bring a towel, for some reason."

"It's your mind blocking out the agony it knows you're

going to inflict on yourself," Petra said, shivering. She looked down at her jeans, lying on top of her bag. "Those aren't going back on anytime soon."

Erik handed her his trousers. "Here, put these on. It'll be better if I go back to the house in my swimming trunks than you in your underwear. Just think of what Gill would say."

CHAPTER 8

There was an air of expectant excitement in the lounge when Petra arrived for dinner, and she had the strange feeling that everyone else was in on a secret. Fingal was circulating amongst the guests, a bottle of white wine and a bottle of red in each hand, topping up glasses. Petra happily took a glass of red wine, and joined the others. Jane nodded to acknowledge Petra's arrival, and then announced that she would like to say a few words before dinner.

"First of all, we would like to thank you all for being here. Fingal and I have worked hard to build this creative space, and we hope that you are off to an enjoyable and productive start. Hopefully you have already started to make the best use of Erik's experience and talent as a writer and mentor. He's truly talented. So please join me in a toast: Here's to us, who's like us?"

Glasses raised, everyone chimed, "Damn few, and they're all deid!" Petra noticed that Erik joined in the traditional Scottish toast, too, as though he was already accustomed to their cultural rituals.

Jane and Fingal excused themselves, and when they came back a short time later, they were preceded by the mouth-watering aromas of comfort food. No one wasted any time in sitting down at the long table, where they tucked into garlic-buttered rolls, two types of lasagne, and a warm lentil salad. It was just the kind of food that Petra adored, and she tucked in with gusto.

During dinner, Petra learned more about her fellow guests, and what had brought them to the retreat. Samuel talked about why he had not started writing until his retirement. He took it on the chin when they pantomime-booed him when he said that he had been a bank manager, and again when he told them he had retired at fifty-five. He said that this was his chance – at last – to do what he had always wanted to do.

"It was my father who knocked my plan to become a writer on its head. He said it was nothing more than a pipe dream, there was no way I could make a living at it, so that was that."

"Was it your father who made you become a bank manager?" Clodagh asked.

"He got me my first job, in a bank. It kind of snowballed from there. By twenty-two I was married, with our first child on the way." He took a sip of wine, then sighed. "I think I knew before we ever got married it wasn't going to work. I don't know if she ever even *liked* me. I always seemed to be in her way. You know, I'd come home from work and try to talk to her about my day, while she walked around saying 'Excuse me!' and huffing while she was putting tea towels in drawers or whatever."

"Maybe she was fed up putting tea towels in drawers," Gill said.

"I mean, no doubt she was, but she was making it clear that she didn't *want* to talk to me, or be around me. She started sleeping in the spare room shortly after we were married. She just didn't want to touch me, or have me touch her."

"Do you have any children?" Petra asked.

Samuel beamed. "Donna – my pride and joy. She's the spitting image of her mother, but we're alike in every other way. That was another reason for my wife to hate me, of course."

Gill talked about how her husband's disdain for any attempt at a writing career had put her off completely. "The divorce freed me, I suppose you could say. He used to laugh at me, saying that commuter fatigue was giving me an overactive imagination. But it was pure fear I felt on those long journeys home, and if I can translate that into tension and suspense I'll be happy."

"Just like in those terrifying films where someone gets in

their car and a killer pops up from their hiding place in the back seat," Clodagh said.

"Exactly. Driving on the dark, cold days of winter, I was convinced that someone was going to get in my car, somehow, even though I always kept the doors locked."

Clodagh said she'd been hoping to avoid distraction at the retreat, so that she could knuckle down. "The thing is - I wasn't taking into account how many *more* distractions there are here. What I really need is to stop daydreaming and staring at the view, and get down to work."

Petra didn't want to answer any more questions – no matter how innocent - about her motivation, or what she was doing in the witches' prison; instead, she followed Clodagh's lead and said she was hoping the serenity and space at Rothmore would allow her to focus on what she wanted to do more than anything else – write her story.

"Skål to that!" Erik said heartily, raising his glass, and the others followed and drank a toast to each other, and to the week ahead.

Jane and Fingal cleared the dinner plates, then served warm pear crumble with custard, and some very strong coffee. "I'll not be getting up from this chair for some time," Samuel said, puffing out his cheeks and rubbing his stomach. "I've definitely overdone it."

Jane rubbed her hands together and looked at Fingal, who asked the guests to move to the garden, because there was a surprise in store: they'd arranged a special performance in honour of Beltane, the Gaelic May Day festival.

***

Traditionally, the Celtic people of Europe marked the changing seasons, upon which their very survival depended, with the ritual of the fire. To mark the passing of winter into spring, and of the cold days with little light into the longer days that enabled and sustained growth of nourishing crops, they celebrated Beltane, meaning bright fire. Symbolism through action was very important to the Celtic people, and thus the extinguishing of old fires and the lighting of new ones to mark the end of the dark days of winter was central to Beltane. Although by the start of the 1900s Beltane celebrations had all-but-disappeared across Scotland, the later part of the century had brought a renewed interest, and the re-emergence of Beltane festivals across the country.

The modern-day Beltane festival in Edinburgh took place on the last day of April on the city's Calton Hill, a perform-ance involving the key symbolic figures and, as the climax, the huge bonfire. To experience it as a live event was to feel the primal thumping of the processional drums as they announced the arrival of the May Queen, marked the death and rebirth of the Green Man, and provided the atmospheric accompaniment to the lighting of the bonfire. Petra had always thought that the relentless pounding of the drums seemed, eventually, to merge with her own breath, and that it was possible to feel connected through time and space to those people for whom the length-ening days meant the difference between death and survival. Legend held that Beltane Eve was the time when the filmy layer that separates the spirit world from the earthly realm was thin-nest, the time when human beings were most likely to see one of the creatures from the otherworld – a fairy, or a sprite, one of Fingal's still folk come to life.

Washing one's face in the dewy grass at dawn on the first of May was meant to bring good fortune for the rest of the year. Almost every year of her adult life, Petra had attended the festival, and engaged in the face-washing ritual with her fellow revellers, as they made their way home at dawn.

The guests filed out onto the back lawn that led down to the sea, and Fingal gave each of them an unlit torch. It was a beautiful evening, clear and mild, and they huddled together in anticipation of what was to come. Everyone but Erik had been part of a Beltane festival before, but never one as small and in-timate as this. Clodagh stood next to Petra and she leaned close and said, "I can't believe they've organised this for us. I *love* Beltane!"

"Me too. The raw power of it. Celebrating our interconnectedness to the earth."

Clodagh's eyes were shining and she was about to say something, but just then they heard loud drumming. A minute later the drummers appeared in the garden with their blue-painted faces, and Petra's neck prickled. The male drummers had bare torsos, and the combined visual and aural effect was of something very primal. The eight drummers stared ahead sombrely as they passed through the group and formed a circle around them. One of the performers following behind the drummers stopped to light Gill's torch, who lit Samuel's, and the group followed suit until every torch was lit.

The May Queen appeared, walking slowly with all of the grace and dignity of a ballet dancer. She wore a white sleeveless dress clipped with a thick red sash. Her exposed skin was painted white, with red lines drawn around her eyes. On her head sat an enormous floral crown. She was a captivating figure and the group watched her in nervous expectation, as it was one of the crucial moments of Beltane: the May Queen could choose to turn back the way she had come, symbolising a return to the darkness of winter - or to what *was* - or she could keep moving forward, towards spring and new life.

Next came the Whites – six women dressed all in white, who symbolised the preservation and reawakening of the life force, of spring. As they moved past the group, Petra heard them chanting, "Earth, air, fire, water". Clodagh started to chant, and then Petra joined in, too.

The Green Man appeared next, with his green-painted face and body, his body covered in foliage and evergreen branches. Petra always thought the person playing the Green Man had to work very hard to look dignified, when wearing only a skimpy pair of green briefs.

Then came the elements – Air and Earth – before chaos awakened, represented in human form by the Reds wearing only underwear, their entire bodies painted red. Their shrieks and wails were ear-piercing as they raced past the group, baring their teeth. Fire and Water were next, dressed entirely in orange and blue respectively, arms outstretched, hands touching, dancing delicately together.

Fingal broke away from the group and followed behind the Beltane players, gesturing that the others should, too. They followed the players down the sloping lawn and gathered together at the bottom, overlooking the sea, watching transfixed as the May Queen chose her consort. This May Queen broke with tradition; instead of choosing one of the players, she held out her hand and summoned Erik, who looked delighted if somewhat bemused by what was happening. The May Queen kissed Erik, then took his torch and threw it down onto the grass. Fingal threw his next, and indicated then everyone else should, too.

Everyone cheered the May Queen, and the coming of spring, and the players who had put on such a spectacular show. They stood around the bonfire, with the drummers once again standing in a circle behind them, continuing their frenzied drumming. Most of the players were dancing around the bonfire, spinning and twirling, the light from the fire catching their painted faces in ways that made them look sometimes frightening and gruesome, and other times enchanted, as though possessed by otherworldly spirits.

Petra was mesmerised by the dancers, as the heat from the fire and their dancing held her in something of a trance. She loved dancing, and she decided to join them. Erik cheered, and then joined in the dancing, too. Some of the braver players jumped and leapt over the fire, as the others cheered them on. Fingal and Jane passed around spiced wine, the drumming and dancing continued incessantly, and Petra thought of nothing other than what was happening in the moment: she did not want to control how her body moved, just wanted to be swept up in the music and the fire and the primal abandonment all around her.

Much later, her body completely wrung out of energy, she

moved away from the crowd and stretched out on the damp grass. She felt the drums pounding through the earth and up into her body, and she reached her arms out to the side, letting the ground cool her down. A tingle of air brushed across her face, and she could sense her mother's presence there, with her. Her mother had loved Beltane, and Samhain, the winter festival, and there were always small celebrations – with Petra and her parents – to mark these important events.

They would light a fire, and her mother would cook something on it: sausages and beans, baked potatoes, a hearty stew. While their dinner cooked, each of them would say what they were most grateful for, and what they hoped the next year would bring. Petra's wish was the same every year, but it was not one she could say out loud for her parents to hear: she wanted her days at school to be less hostile and isolating, and she wanted a good friend. The wish that she *did* share was the same every year: she wanted the three of them to stay healthy, and to stay together. She was so grateful for her parents, and their boundless love.

On the last Beltane they ever spent together, Petra spoke aloud her wish that she wanted the three of them to always be together and, when she had finished, she looked up from the fire to see her mother wiping away tears. Had she known, Petra wondered, that it would be their last-ever Beltane? Or perhaps she had been saddened by the passing of time, and the fact that it was Petra's last year at primary school.

Petra's Beltane wish had not come true: the three of them had not stayed together. Her mother was not alive for the Samhain festival, at the start of the winter.

Petra missed those Beltane celebrations, and all of the rituals that had been so treasured in their family. As much as she loved the wild Beltane festival in Edinburgh with its huge crowd, the anonymity of celebrating the coming of spring with strangers engaging in primal behaviour, it would never match the small, very special times her parents had created.

CHAPTER 9

Her skin chilled by the damp grass, Petra stood up and went in search of a warm drink. She found an urn of spiced wine in the guest lounge, and was about to pour a cup when she heard someone sniffling. She turned around and saw Clodagh, huddled up on one of the sofas.

"Clodagh, what's wrong?"

Clodagh wiped her cheeks with her sleeve and said, "Don't mind me - something about Beltane triggered this. Sorry – I'm not trying to be a downer. I'm so embarrassed."

"You don't have to be embarrassed." Petra sat down beside Clodagh, wondering if it was inappropriate to put her arm around her shoulders. "It's a powerfully symbolic event, isn't it? All of that rebirth, death, out with the old in with the new kind of thing."

Clodagh started crying again, and apologised through her tears.

"You don't need to apologise. *I'm* sorry, for setting you off again."

Clodagh laughed. "What you said is spot on. That's exactly it. It's just kind of – brought things to a head, I suppose."

"Do you want to talk about it?"

"No. Thank you, but no. It's just some stuff I need to work through on my own."

"Would some spiced wine help?"

Clodagh laughed. "Yes, I think it would."

Before Petra had the chance to get some, Gill and Samuel walked into the lounge, in animated conversation. When they saw Clodagh and Petra, they stopped talking and hurried over.

"What's happened?" Gill asked.

"I'm embarrassing myself. Please just ignore me."

Gill gave Petra a stern look. "Has Petra done something to upset you?"

"No! No, it's nothing like that. I've got some unresolved issues, as they say. Something has made them bubble up to the surface tonight."

Gill continued to give Petra the stink eye. "Anything you want to tell us about?"

"I was just about to get us some spiced wine. If you could bring over a couple of glasses that would be great," Petra said.

Samuel went to get the wine, as Gill sat down on the sofa opposite. "So - you were like a whirling dervish, dancing out there," she said to Petra.

"I do love to dance, and I don't really get the chance these days."

Samuel handed Clodagh and Petra their wine. "I thought you looked terrific – completely unreserved. I only wish I had the guts to do it myself."

They talked about the performance, and how it compared to other Beltane festivals they had been to. Clodagh told them that she had been a drummer one year, in Edinburgh.

"Well aren't you a dark horse!" Gill said.

"It was really amazing," Clodagh said, looking cheerier. "To think our ancestors created a festival to celebrate fire, and the May Queen's procession – it's all so beautiful."

Petra had a sudden memory of her father at Beltane one year, asking her if she could imagine what it was like for people before fire was discovered, and she said no. He took her hand, and they moved away from the bonfire, around the side of the house where it was cold and no light from the fire reached. Petra had a brief flash of primal fear and panic, a split second of knowing how it might feel to live in a time of complete darkness, and cold.

Petra snapped back to the conversation when she heard

Gill say her name. "I'm sorry, what did you say?"

"I said isn't it true that farmers and landlords used to pay witches to stay up all night at Beltane to make sure that no one stole their cattle," Gill said.

"Yes, that's true." Petra was still in the past, outside with her father in their garden, and didn't want to be dragged back into a conversation with Gill.

"They used to make sacrifices – human and animal – a long time ago," Gill said.

Samuel shuddered. "I'm staying in here, then. Although, as the oldest, I'm probably safe. It's the young ones who have to look out."

Gill slapped his arm. "We're supposed to be cheering Clodagh up – not making her feel worse!"

Petra snapped out of her reverie, alarmed by how pale Clodagh suddenly was. She looked terrified, and ready to burst into tears again. Petra searched for a story, an anecdote – something she could pull from her memory to change the subject.

"My father once told me that I was conceived on Beltane," she said, which she knew was over-sharing, but it worked: her frank admission cued some lewd conversation about naked people and fire, and Clodagh, finally, appeared slightly more relaxed.

***

With three cups of spiced wine coursing through her, Petra went back outside, where the festivities were still in full swing. Erik was still dancing. One of the Reds was eating fire, which was both compelling and horrifying to watch, like a form of self-torture. It was spectacular, though, Petra had to admit. Seeing her, Erik motioned for Petra to join him. At one point, Petra realised he was no longer dancing in the space near her, and was surprised to see him running towards the fire: with a huge leap, he cleared it, and everyone cheered loudly.

The drumming and the dancing continued until the sky

in the east began its fade from black, and those who were still standing washed not just their faces in the dew, but their whole bodies. Petra knew she should drag her tired body to bed, but she could still feel the pulse of the drums coursing through her, and didn't feel ready for sleep yet. Her face still moist with dew, she sat on the eastern-facing wall of the old prison. She closed her eyes, and willed all of the gaps in what she'd seen of Meg's life to come to her.

Without any summoning, they did.

Meg was blindfolded, but she knew she was still by the coast because of the fresh salty air on her face. She heard the heavy, creaking sound of a door opening, and then someone shoved her. Her knees grazed several steps as she fell, and she landed on her side, tasting dirt. The heavy sound came again, and she realised they had locked her in.

If she'd known what was coming next, she would have slept. Instead, she tried to work the shackles off her hands, but they were too tight. She couldn't get her hands around the front of her face to even try to shift the blindfold. She stood up, and took tiny, tentative steps, trying to figure out where she was. Three small steps forward, and her toes touched something solid. She took three sideways steps, and again felt something solid. She shifted so she was turning slightly in the other direction, counted three steps and again came up against a wall. She thought of the horses, of how small the stalls must feel to them. She lifted her face up, but there wasn't any light coming through the blindfold, nor could she smell the sea air, so she knew there was a ceiling. She was trapped in this place.

In an act of comfort, and of despair, she started to sing – first the lullaby she had used to tame the wild horse, then other songs from her childhood. At first her voice was quiet, but it became louder with each song. The sound of the door opening stopped her mid-song, and a rush of cold, foul-smelling water coated her.

"Shut up, witch!" a man shouted. The door shut again.

From then on, she sang silently. She was cold, and she

stank, and almost every inch of her body hurt. She wondered what they were planning on doing to her. She sat on the cold, damp earth, rocking back and forth for comfort and for warmth. She didn't know how many hours passed, but she was on the verge of sleep, when the door opened and she heard squealing noises. Almost immediately she felt sharp scratches on her skin. Rats. They'd thrown rats in with her.

The rats didn't keep their distance, but kept scrabbling over her, or coming up to sniff her. Trying to keep them away kept her on high alert, but also tired her out, and soon she was on the verge of sleep again. Her chin fell onto her chest, waking her up, and she heard the door open again. This time there was frantic flapping, and squawking. They'd thrown birds in, this time. This seemed to unnerve the rats, who scrabbled over her and up her legs and arms, looking for hiding places.

Every time she fell asleep, or was about to, her captors seemed to somehow know it, and they'd wake her up in one unpleasant way or another. They threw live creatures in with her, banged wooden spoons on copper pans, yelled "Wake up, witch!"

She had no idea how long this went on for. Time became one long frustrating red ribbon of fear that stretched out ahead of her into what she knew was a grim future, as the past twisted away. The more they interrupted her solitude, and her attempts to sleep, the less she could remember those crisp mornings riding her horse on the beach, the quiet nights putting the horses to bed in their stables.

When she lost the ability to remember the beach, and the horses, they came for her. She cringed when she heard the door open, but for the first time it was followed by the sound of boots on the steps. Rough hands grabbed her under her arms, yanked her to her feet, and dragged her up the stairs. There was the smell of salty air, and the grunts of the man dragging her. She tried to tell him to stop, but didn't recognise the words that came out of her mouth.

Someone yanked the blindfold off, and through eyes unused to the light, Meg could see that she was in a room with several men. One of them repeated the accusations that had led her to that forsaken place: fornicating with the devil on the village green in moonlight; having the power to make animals and men do her bidding; having the devil's mark. At this last accusation, a man she couldn't see lifted her dress above her waist, and another man pricked her stomach with needles.

"Witness the devil's mark!" the first man shouted. "When we prick her, she feels no pain. Smell her – the devil's smell! Listen to her – speaking the devil's tongue!"

The pain of the needles, the humiliation of being partly naked in front of these men, the lack of sleep, the fear – all of it roiled together and caused words she'd never heard before come out of her mouth, in a long stream, as though she had no control over her own tongue.

She heard them say she was guilty, and deserved death. With that, she was dragged out of that room and out onto the green, where a crowd had gathered – women and children as well as men - chanting "Witch! Witch! Witch!" They hadn't put the blindfold back on her. They wanted her to see what was about to happen to her.

Petra opened her eyes, felt trickles of tears running down both cheeks. For a brief moment, she could see Meg sitting on the ground next to her, a pale outline of the young woman who'd been brought to this place to await her execution. She told Meg she would honour her memory by sharing her story, so that she was not forgotten. Petra vowed to return with flowers to commemorate how Meg had lived, and given colour to her world – every living creature she'd come into contact with in her too-short life.

She performed an incantation of gratitude, and of sorrow, and of peace.

As she walked back to the house, none of the exhilaration she'd felt during the Beltane celebration lingered; instead, she carried only deep sadness and pain. It absorbed her, and she had no awareness of the pair of suspicious eyes that watched her from an upper-floor window as she trudged through the dawn light, her body heavy and calling for sleep.

CHAPTER 10

Petra slept through breakfast and almost through lunch. No one was in the lounge, and fortunately they'd left one sandwich, which she ate greedily while making an espresso, and then another. She set off for the woods, hoping to find bluebells and perhaps even wood anemone to take to the prison, in honour of Meg.

She was a short way along the path when she heard loud swearing coming from deep in the woods.

"Clodagh? Is everything okay?"

"I went over on my ankle. Ow! Shit."

Petra clawed her way through the undergrowth, following the sound of Clodagh's voice. When she finally reached her, Petra was so overwhelmed by what she saw that she couldn't speak. They were in a clearing in the wood, large enough that the sunlight reached the space. Clodagh was sitting down, inspecting her ankle. As she drew closer, Petra could see that she was sitting on a seat carved from wood, next to which stood its twin.

"I know – can you believe this place?" Clodagh patted the seat beside her. "Come and sit with me."

Petra sat down, and they both laughed. "How did you find it?"

"Fingal told me about it. I told him I was coming to look at the still folk, and he said I would find a secret, if I went off the beaten path. He wouldn't tell me what it was."

"Did he carve these?"

"He didn't say, but he must have done."

"This feels like a dream."

Clodagh laughed again. "It's like a little enchanted part of the forest."

She rubbed her ankle, and Petra asked if she was okay. "Oh – fine, I'm sure. I was looking up and tripped over a tree root."

"Well, this is a good place to sit and rest awhile. I can help you walk back to the house when you're ready."

"What were you doing in the woods? Or were you going down to the beach?"

"I came to gather some flowers to take to the prison. In honour of the women."

"That's a lovely idea. I'd go with you, if I wasn't hobbling."

Petra smiled. "How are you feeling, after last night?"

Clodagh took a deep breath, puffed her cheeks out, and said, "Okay, I guess. A bit embarrassed."

"There's no need to be."

"Well, I'm not much of a crier. It just all bubbled over last night, I guess."

"Maybe you just need a quiet night in your room."

Clodagh laughed. "Tonight's the exhibition. Maybe after that I'll go to my room, try to get some work done."

They sat in silence for a few minutes, listening to the cheerful sounds of the blackbirds, robins and tits, only occasionally interrupted by the piercing squawk of a gull. Petra was about to comment on how peaceful it was, when Clodagh said, "Listen – about Midhallow -."

"You don't have to talk about it if you're not ready."

"I think I am ready – I mean, I do want to talk to you about it. It'll sound a bit crazy though." Petra nodded her encouragement. "And can we keep it just between us?"

"Of course."

"You remember how dark it was? The torch was lighting up the camp – I mean, just the flat rocks. That's what you saw?" Petra nodded again. "That's all I saw, until a figure appeared suddenly. It looked like a young girl, lying there. She started to rise up in the air – still lying on her back – and then she turned to look at me."

Clodagh paused, and Petra said, "No wonder you were terrified."

"I was. But then it got worse. I could see her face, and she looked exactly like me."

"My God, Clodagh, that's horrifying."

"It all happened so fast – I blinked and she was gone."

"I can't believe you didn't scream."

"I think I was in shock. But that's why I wanted to get back in such a hurry."

"I can understand why."

"You'll think I'm out of my mind."

Petra shook her head. "Not at all."

"But if you didn't see anything, it must mean there's something wrong with me."

Petra wasn't planning to tell anyone at the retreat about the summoning spells, and her visions. And Clodagh hadn't voluntarily seen her ghostly doppelgänger, so it wasn't really the same thing.

"You said you've been dealing with some issues lately. Stress can do that – cause visual hallucinations. And auditory ones too."

Clodagh turned to look straight into Petra's eyes. "Really? It can?"

"It could be your brain's way of dealing with what you're going through. Making sense of it all."

Clodagh's look was so intense Petra could hardly stand it. "That makes perfect sense." She reached over and covered Petra's hand with her own. "Thank you, Petra. I thought I was going crazy."

Petra gave her a sad smile, wondering what Clodagh would think if she told her the truth about her own life, and what she was doing at Rothmore.

"Do you want to go back now?"

"Oh sure, okay – let's see how this ankle is." Petra stood up, and offered her elbow to Clodagh. As soon as she stepped down, putting her weight on the sore ankle, Clodagh winced and said,

"No, no, no – I'm not ready to walk back yet. Are you happy to sit awhile longer? Or, if you want to go back no problem – I'm sure I'll be fine in a bit."

"I'm not going to leave you alone in the woods with a gammy ankle. Haven't you seen the carrion crows circling?"

Clodagh's eyes flashed upwards, but only for an instant, and then she smiled at Petra. "It's not nice to pick on the infirm."

They sat in pleasant, companionable silence for a few moments, and then Clodagh asked, "So, is the retreat everything you hoped it would be?"

Petra took a deep breath, considered how much to tell Clodagh. "I think – because this was my aunt's idea – I hadn't built up much in the way of expectation. Actually, that's not really true because I'm expecting myself to work hard and make good progress with the book." She glanced at Clodagh, then added, "I guess I'm really hoping that this will be the start of something new in my life. My aunt will be hoping that too, I think, because she was worried about me. I mean, I guess she could see that I was depressed."

Clodagh reached across the narrow gap between the chairs, and put her hand on Petra's forearm. "I know all about depression, if it's any consolation."

Petra gave Clodagh a sad smile. "The thing was, I didn't even think I was depressed, at the time. Now that I've started to come out the other side, it seems so obvious."

Clodagh nodded. "My brother saw it – I didn't. When you're right in the middle of it, it's hard to remember what you felt like *before*."

"Exactly right. My aunt told me I had to fight back – and I saw myself through her eyes. It's a cliché, but it's true."

"Fight back against the complete arsehole who stole your story – I agree with your aunt."

They laughed, and Petra realised how good it felt to share a laugh at Josh's expense. "But really, it will be the perfect revenge when your new story is a best seller. And how can it not be? The true stories of the women imprisoned here."

Petra smiled at her. "I don't know about a best seller, but even just thinking of it being out there in the world is very exciting."

"I know you've been spending time in the prison, but I don't know anything about your process. What are you actually doing in there, if you don't mind me asking?"

Thinking about it later, Petra realised her guard was down when Clodagh asked the question – a combination of feeling relaxed and happy, sitting on a chair carved out of wood, with her new friend. "Have you ever heard of summoning?"

Clodagh frowned, and shook her head. "A summoning spell is designed to call on a non-living spirit. I summon the women who were imprisoned here, and someone comes forward to communicate with me."

Clodagh laughed, but stopped abruptly when she saw the serious look on Petra's face. "Oh – I thought you were joking."

"I've used magic since I was fifteen. But this was my first attempt at summoning. It went very well, though."

She told Clodagh about the rush of voices, and Meg coming forward with her story. She described how she saw Meg's past, like a silent film.

Clodagh looked confused. "But – forgive me if this is a rude question – how do you know these are *real* women, and not products of your very rich imagination?"

"I've done enough magic to know the difference. With my dissertation, I just used research records to write about the last women to be tried as witches in Edinburgh. I didn't write anything down if it wasn't part of documented record. My imagination was out of bounds. But with these women – the ones brought to the prison – there are no records of their experiences here, just factual information about names, ages, what they were accused of. This is the only way I know to find out what really happened to them."

Petra was relieved to see that although Clodagh still looked confused, she wasn't looking at her like she was crazy. "The summoning spells – aren't they dangerous?"

"They can be. There's always a risk that a spirit energy will come forward under false pretences, with ill intent. There are ways you can protect yourself – to a certain extent. But it's a risk I think is worth taking, because I want this book to be brilliant."

Clodagh's eyes widened. "And I suppose you must be quite good at it, if you've been doing this since you were fifteen."

A crevice opened up between them, in which the darkness of Petra's past sat hidden, waiting to be exposed. She couldn't, though – she couldn't tell Clodagh about her mother, or Isobel, or her father. Not yet, anyway.

"Can I ask – what I saw on Midhallow – is there any chance *that* was summoned?"

Petra shook her head. "I don't think so. Someone on the island would have had to do it, and I can't see that happening. It's more likely it was a manifestation of extreme stress, a strong emotional response made visible. That's why it looked like you – it was your brain telling you to be careful, or identifying imminent danger, or a risk to your wellbeing."

Clodagh smiled wryly at Petra. "I can't believe it – I come here to get my head down and do some work, to this place with a definite otherworldly vibe. I make a new friend who's so adept at magic that she can summon up women from the past."

Petra knew Clodagh was trying to give her a compliment, but she pictured the crevice between them, opening up ever so slightly, threatening to reveal her secrets.

She changed the subject, asked Clodagh if she was content to sit for a little while, while she gathered some flowers to take to the prison. She was glad to be on her own for a few minutes as she carefully picked a few wood anemones, and some bluebells.

She helped Clodagh up out of the wooden seat, and supported her as they made their way out of the woods and back to the house. Clodagh's ankle was tender but not swollen, but Petra helped her into her room and made a pillow-stack on Clodagh's bed so she could prop it up. She promised to come back and collect Clodagh in time for dinner, and carried the flowers to the prison.

Petra gently leaned the flowers up against the north-facing curve of the wall, then carried out an incantation of gratitude to Meg for sharing her story, which was also intended to bring peace. She sat in stillness, waiting in case Meg wanted to come back to communicate anything else to her, but the air all around her remained quiet, unmoving. She closed her eyes, and saw again the image of her mother standing in their garden, as the burn turned crimson and swallowed her up. Haunted by the same living nightmare since her mother died, Petra thought of Clodagh's question: *How do you know that the stories are real, and not a product of your imagination?*

She'd asked herself that question, many times, since she'd first had the vision. Neither she nor her father could ever be sure of what happened to her mother, before her father awoke just before dawn to an empty bed, went to search for his wife, and found her lifeless body outside by the water. Petra had only one source of evidence as to her mother's actions the night she died: the small notebook in which she wrote details of her "mixings", as she called them – the brews, tinctures and balms she mixed up for various ailments.

Petra had always loved looking through the book, which chronicled her minor illnesses and her mother's treatments since she was an infant. The very first entry was for a honey balm her mother had mixed when Petra developed a full-body rash, at just a few weeks old: *For Petra – honey, one spoon rolled oats, one spoon milk.* When Petra experienced a prolonged period of anxious, sleepless nights the summer before starting high school, her mother had prepared a brew every night before bed: *For Petra – valerian root and chamomile; lavender pockets.* Petra closed her eyes and could smell the lavender sachets her mother hand-sewed and hung above her bed – pockets from old clothes, filled with crushed lavender flowers and sewn across the top edge. She'd always thought of them as scented bunting. The most common entries in the book involved onions: *For Petra –*

onion poultice (chest); For Petra – sliced onion, socks; For Petra – onion poultice (ears). The frequent chesty coughs and ear aches of her childhood were cured quickly by her mother's onion poultices and onion socks, but Petra hadn't dared to suggest her aunt make one for her in all the years they'd lived together.

The very last entry was the night of her mother's death: *For Petra – black salt, belladonna, wormwood, rue.*

Petra pictured her mother grinding plants into the salt in their kitchen, carrying them carefully to the place at the bottom of the garden where she did her daily incantations, but she couldn't bear to think about what happened next.

Her tears flowed freely as she repeated her incantation for peace and gratitude, for Meg and for her dear, beloved mother.

CHAPTER 11

Petra was more than a few minutes late picking Clodagh up for dinner, and their awkward shuffling steps down the stairs and along the corridor to the lounge meant that they were unfashionably late. Gill gave Petra an impatient hurry-up-and-sit-down-so-that-we-can-eat look, but the others reacted with concern and kindness when they saw Clodagh's injury.

Once they were both seated Jane said, "We hope you have all had a productive day. I'm sure you will agree that there is plenty of inspiration here at Rothmore. And this evening we hope to inspire you further with Fingal and Erik's work. You have the great honour of being the first to see their exhibition, which explores their imagining of the fates of those who disappeared from Midhallow."

As everyone cheered, Erik said, "Don't cheer yet – you haven't even seen it. It might be terrible!"

"I can assure you it is *not* terrible," Jane said. "But first, let's eat."

She tinkled a little brass bell, and two men in kilts appeared – catering staff, hired for the evening - carrying platters. There was whole roasted salmon with new potatoes, braised red cabbage, roasted root vegetables and, afterwards, the most impressive cheese board Petra had ever seen - she *adored* cheese. The food was delicious, and everyone was more animated than Petra had yet seen them, in anticipation of being the first to view Erik and Fingal's work.

After the plates were cleared Jane, Fingal and Erik excused themselves. Jane appeared a quarter of an hour later and invited the guests to follow her. As they neared the exhibition room, which was beside Fingal's studio, they saw and smelled that the corridor was filling up with the acrid sweetness of dry ice. It caught in Petra's throat and she had a brief coughing fit before Erik appeared in the doorway, looking very dramatic in a long black cloak.

"Welcome to Hildaland," his voice boomed out. "Here you'll discover answers to a centuries-old mystery: what happened to the twenty-eight women, men and children who were quarantined on Midhallow in 1642? How could twenty-eight people disappear without any trace? It was once thought that pirates might have taken them, or giant birds of prey, capable of lifting human bodies into the air. But the answer is even stranger, even more other-worldly. Finwives stole the men, for as we all know, without a human husband they lost their beauty forever. Finmen stole the women, taking them as brides to their kingdom under the sea. The children were taken to live in this magical land. Come inside, and meet them, and hear their tales."

Petra thought that the whole effect might have been silly, but instead she found it completely enthralling. Everyone was silent, their body language revealing how eager they were to get inside, to see what awaited them. Erik held out his arm, and they entered the dark room.

Inside, it was as though the air was infused with magic. The room was low-lit at floor level so that people could find their way around the space, and as the dry ice cleared away they got their first glimpse of the work. Little lights, like candles, illuminated Fingal's small sculptures, arranged on their own pedestal stands, with Erik's poems – one version in Norwegian, the other in English - encased in glass and affixed to two sides. There were sculptures of each one of the disappeared, with their own story told in verse. Petra thought that Erik's poems were little masterpieces, managing to capture the essence of each person's history up to the point of abduction, and their new life in the magical kingdom. Fingal's copper-glazed clay sculptures captured one of the significant moments in each person's life so that through facial expression, body language or gesture, that moment came to life.

And then there were the sculptures of the Finfolk whose fins, as legend had it, could be easily disguised as human clothing. The Finmen had handsome, serious faces, and the Finwives' beauty – preserved through the act of taking a human husband, according to legend - was striking. Often portrayed as troll-like, Fingal's Finfolk were beautiful and beguiling, hiding their malicious natures. Petra was amazed by how much detail he had managed to get into such small sculptures.

But the most remarkable sculptures, in Petra's view, were those of the children. Six children went missing from Midhallow and, in Erik and Fingal's representation of the legend, the children were full of joy and delight at being taken away to live in a magical land. Instead of suffering with the disease, they had been taken away to live long, healthy lives. As Petra read one of the poems about the children, Clodagh appeared beside her.

"This is very special, isn't it?" she whispered, her voice heavy with emotion.

"Absolutely beautiful," Petra agreed.

They moved around the room, in reverent silence, until Jane reappeared and announced that there was champagne in the guest lounge, to celebrate Fingal and Erik's remarkable achievement. Perhaps sensing their reluctance to leave the exhibition, she added that it would be open for the remainder of their stay, and that they could come back as often as they liked.

No one rushed away, almost as though they could not bring themselves to leave that beautiful, magical world. Eventually, once they had all found their way back to the lounge, the waiters from dinner handed them a glass of champagne. Jane gave a toast to the artists, and Samuel led the cheering. Fingal gave a short speech, in which he praised Erik's work, and thanked him for providing the inspiration for the sculptures with the poems.

When it was Erik's turn to give a speech, Petra was surprised that he had lost the casual, jokey way she had come to associate with him; instead, he looked decidedly emotional.

"I would like to thank Jane and Fingal for inviting me here. I was at a low point in my writing career – to say the least – when the letter arrived inviting me here for a residency. It was such an honour that they even knew of my work, never mind wanted me to come here. Scotland – particularly this strange corner of it – has worked its way under my skin. I am so lucky to be here, and to have the chance to meet exciting writers like yourselves." He raised his glass and said, "Skål!"

Everyone echoed Erik's toast, and then gave Erik and Fingal a warm, extended round of applause. They both looked pleased, and modest, and more than a little uncomfortable.

When the applause died down, Jane announced that the following evening after dinner, it would be the guests' turn as the centre of attention; they would each have a few minutes in which to speak about their work in progress, or give a reading from their new work. Gill and Samuel looked ecstatic, while Clodagh and Petra shot each other nervous looks.

Observing the differences in their reactions, Erik said, "Please don't be nervous about it. It's a chance for you to talk about your work, to share it if you are ready. If you've never done that before, I know that it can be very daunting. But it will be a friendly crowd, rest assured!"

Fingal nodded, adding that he was excited to hear what they had been working on. "There are no limits to the talents of human beings, I've learned over the years. I'm constantly amazed."

"No pressure, then!" Samuel laughed. He shifted his body so that he was standing between Clodagh and Petra and the rest of the group. "Are you not looking forward to sharing, then?"

"I don't even have anything to share yet," Clodagh said sadly.

"But they said you could talk about your ideas. Come on, this is your chance to practise. Tell me."

Clodagh told him about her plan for the sea witch to live in a lighthouse, recasting her as a protector of those at sea.

"Moody, atmospheric, I like it!" Samuel enthused.

"I'm ashamed to admit this, living on the coast, but I don't really know much about lighthouses. I've done a bit of reading about them – about women lighthouse keepers, mainly – but I don't even know what one looks like inside."

"Hold that thought," Samuel said, turning around and calling to Fingal. When Fingal had joined them, he said, "Can you help us? Are there any lighthouses nearby that are open to the public?"

Fingal nodded. "There's Sealcraigs lighthouse, just past Dunbar. It's not open to the public as such but we've held events there before. I could contact the owners and see if they'd be able to open it up. When were you thinking of?"

"Tomorrow, if possible. Clodagh needs some context for her story."

"I'll see what I can do."

"That would be wonderful. Thank you so much Fingal," Clodagh said.

Ten minutes later, it was all set up: the owners would open the lighthouse for them the next day. Clodagh did not have a car, so Samuel offered to drive. Gill wanted to go, too, but Petra said she would stay back and concentrate on her writing, as she was worried about her lack of progress.

When Jane heard about Clodagh's idea for her story, she said, "There was a very tragic case at Sealcraigs, involving the young bride of one of the keepers. The very first lighthouse keeper was Robert Chalmers, who married a local girl. They raised a family of four children in the lighthouse."

"Imagine that," Samuel said. "Four children, growing up in such a small space."

"And isolated. It gives me the shivers," Gill said.

"Tradition had it that the eldest son - also Robert – would take over as keeper when his father died, or became too ill to carry out his duties. For Robert, that happened when he was only seventeen. His father was lost at sea, and he became principal keeper. Over the next few years his siblings all left the lighthouse to live and work elsewhere, and Robert's mother died of consumption."

"How awful for him," Clodagh sad sadly. "To be such a young man, all alone in that place."

"Although I can think of a few men who would love to be left all alone," Gill said.

"Not me – I need human companionship," Samuel said.

"I have no idea how or where he met the woman who would become his wife, but a few years later he married Eleanor Skittles, and she moved into the lighthouse."

"Skittles!" Samuel said, gleefully. "Best surname ever."

"You should definitely name one of your vampires Skittles," Petra said.

"Well, poor Eleanor Chalmers née Skittles did not have an easy time as the lighthouse keeper's wife. The first winter of their marriage was one of the most brutal ever known in this part of Scotland. Winter storms raged solidly for five months, and Robert was regularly called out to save boats in distress. It's very likely that Eleanor went with him on those rescue missions, even though it's doubtful that she had any experience of the sea."

"It's bad enough going outside in a storm, never mind going out in a boat on treacherous waters," Samuel said.

"Exactly. What's more, the track of road to the lighthouse was completely washed away in a storm in early December, stranding the couple. The storms raged on and it took months to repair the road. No one could get any supplies to them until early March."

"What did they eat?" Gill asked. "And what did they use for fuel? It would have been perishing in a lighthouse in the winter."

"When the road was passable again, a team of two men went to check on them, and they found Robert dead. He was sitting in his finest clothes, propped up in his chair, his corpse tied with ropes to keep it upright. Eleanor was in the chair next to him, holding his hand and singing him lullabies."

"Eleanor was alive? But how?" Gill asked.

"No one ever found out how she'd managed to survive. She'd stopped talking, and had kept no record or diary of her time there."

"But she was singing when they found her?" Clodagh asked.

"That's right. She continued to sing lullabies until she died, but she never spoke another word. Although the men reported that she'd screamed bloody murder when they tried to move her away from Robert. She didn't want to let go of his hand."

"What happened to her?" Petra asked.

"Well, of course there were locals who said that she must have murdered Robert, and deserved to be punished. Some, at least, could see that she had lived through a traumatic time. Both she and Robert were so thin, the men who found them reported, that they suspected neither had eaten in some time. They concluded that Robert had starved to death, and Eleanor was on the verge of starvation when they found her."

"Tragic – just tragic," Gill said.

"Well, the faction that felt she was a murderess who deserved to be punished persisted with their accusations, until it was decided that she should stand trial for Robert's murder."

"Oh God, I don't think I want to hear the rest," Gill said. "I'm pretty sure I know how this story ends."

"It didn't end well for Eleanor," Jane confirmed.

"Poor Eleanor Skittles," Samuel said, sadly.

***

Later in the evening, as the celebrations were drawing to a close and people started to head to their beds, Petra overheard Clodagh asking about a cairn at the eastern edge of the garden. Fingal told her that, when he was a boy, a white cross stood on the spot. After the cross was blow into the sea during a severe winter storm, he built the cairn. His father told him that two of the women awaiting trial died in the prison, and the cross had stood for centuries, marking the spot where they were buried.

Petra interrupted their conversation, asking, "What about the accounts of three women who were burned here instead of Edinburgh? I read that the clergymen decided to make an example of them and burned them right here, so that all of the locals would see, as a way of preventing them from consorting with the devil."

Fingal frowned. "My father's father told him that was a vicious lie, spread against our ancestor Lord Rothmore, by a rival landlord who hoped to drive him off the land. Because he held sway with the church, the accounts became part of the public record but, apparently, there's no truth in them."

Clodagh yawned, and Petra said she'd help her back to her room. As they said goodnight at the door, Clodagh said, "You're going to look for the cairn, aren't you?"

Petra nodded. "I'm intrigued. If I went to bed now I'd just lie there thinking about it anyway."

Clodagh gave her a look that was one part disbelief, another part admiration. "Be careful."

Petra smiled, and wished her good night, and set off in search of the witches' cairn.

CHAPTER 12

The moon was hidden behind thick cloud, and the only light visible was across the sea in Fife, distant on the horizon. Even with the torch, Petra stumbled often, almost falling over when she tripped over a rise in the earth that she had not seen. *Don't walk into the cairn*, she told herself. *It would be way worse than sacrilege to topple it.*

She felt the place before the torch illuminated it. It was almost right at the edge of the land, as close to the sea as it was possible to get – whoever had buried the women had no doubt wanted to keep them as far from the house as possible. During the witch hunts, it was common for the burial sites of women found guilty of witchcraft to be covered with a large stone, to keep the devil from rising up out of the ground. The wind off the sea was bitterly cold, but it seemed to Petra that something else was chilling the air hovering over the spot.

This was a bad place, a place where the anger and paranoia of the accusers had condemned innocent women to death, a place where the women's bodies – violated and tortured – had been discarded, abandoned to the earth. The earth and the air had not forgotten them, Petra knew; she could feel it.

Isobel's voice came to her: *Not now, love, it's not safe here. You need protection.*

Petra would not defy Isobel again. She walked away from the cairn, vowing to come back when she had the tools to make a protective circle. But she wasn't ready to go back to her room, and recognised her thirst to communicate with more of the women. Even in the dark, she found her way back to the witches' prison easily, as though it had hold of her and was drawing her in. She closed her eyes, sent thanks to Meg and the other women who were yet to tell their stories, and walked back to the house.

She opened the door to the lounge, not expecting anyone to still be there, but was pleasantly surprised to see Erik, who was staring into the fire. Until he was aware of her presence, he looked decidedly sad – forlorn, even – but once he saw Petra he unleashed a huge grin.

"Hello! Have you come to join me for a night cap?" he asked, jiggling the tumbler in his hand, which was almost empty.

"Don't mind if I do." Petra poured herself a small shot, and a generous one for Erik. "It's cold out there tonight – almost like winter's trying to return."

"No thank you – it's May now. I think we deserve spring."

They clinked glasses, and Petra congratulated Erik again on the exhibition of his work.

"Why, thank you. I was just sitting here, thinking it all seems like a bit of a dream."

"What happens next?"

"Jane's organised another private exhibition, for some people she knows. They're considering opening it to the general public."

"Wow – just think of how many people would see your work. But what I meant was – what happens next for you? How long will you be in Scotland?"

"Until July."

"And will your wife and family be coming over to visit you at some point before then?"

"No, my wife isn't able to travel."

"It must be difficult, being apart for so long."

Erik sighed. "It is. For me. She's not really aware that I'm not there."

"I apologise – that was intrusive. I have a knack for asking the wrong questions."

"It's just – a very difficult situation. Very sad. And I feel guilty, every day, because I am so far away. It was my mother-in-law, actually, who told me I should come."

"If you don't want to talk about it, I understand."

"I don't talk about it, ever, really, apart from with my mother-in-law. You see, my wife was in an accident – hit by a car cycling home from work. She was in a coma for weeks and when she woke up, she was a changed person. She couldn't walk, or speak, or do anything independently. The worst part – the very worst – is that any time I go to visit her, she screams. I seem to scare her, or make her angry. If I try to go anywhere near her she just screams."

Petra could see that Erik was only just managing to hold back tears. At that moment she realised that, underneath his gregariousness, there was unbelievable sadness. "I'm so sorry for you, Erik."

"In this place – this strange and magical place - every day, for at least a few minutes I forget completely about what happened. And that is both wonderful and terrible." He took a deep, shaky breath. "I shouldn't forget, even for a second, that she's living in a home while I am here." He looked sideways at Petra, frowning. "You must think I'm a terrible person."

"Not at all. I think you are a very good person in a terrible situation."

Petra couldn't shake the thought that Erik might be wrong about the reason why his wife reacted the way she did whenever she saw him. Perhaps she was screaming out of frustration because she couldn't communicate with him, couldn't tell him that she wanted him to take her home, so that her life could go back to the way it was. And here he was on an extended residency in Scotland, while she waited in vain every day for a visit from him.

For a brief moment, Petra thought about telling Erik about her father – if anyone could understand how she felt to see her wise, strong father locked away in himself, it was Erik. But then, just as Petra was about to open up to Erik, the last log on the fire tipped into the ash, and the flames died out.

"That might be a sign that it's time for bed. Thank you for

listening to me." Erik smiled sadly at Petra, and stood up, holding out his hand to help her up.

She took his hand, and the moment was lost.

***

Petra was up early the next morning, determined to devote the day to writing. But she was the last one at the breakfast table – the others were there, finishing their coffees and talking animatedly about their trip to Sealcraigs Lighthouse.

"You're sure we can't tempt you to come?" Clodagh asked, her eyes shining.

"Thank you but no – I've got to knuckle down and get to work today." Petra noticed Gill raise her eyebrows, but she said nothing. She watched as Samuel helped Clodagh - still hobbling, but moving more quickly than the day before - manoeuver her way through the lounge, and out into the corridor. She would have been interested to see the lighthouse, but with all of the other planned events she hadn't made the progress with her writing that she'd expected to.

She grabbed her rucksack, and set out for the witches' prison, deciding that she would summon the women buried at the cairn another time. She was worried about her capacity to protect herself adequately, based on past experiences, and she could only guess that she'd need more recovery time after communicating with the women buried there. All of the women who'd been hunted, beaten, tortured and imprisoned had terrible stories to tell – stories that taxed the recipient mentally, and physically. Petra knew that summoning the women who'd been executed there would take strength, and time.

Petra stepped into the protective circle, and fortified it for the day's work. She incanted words of protection, and then called on the women, telling them it was safe to come forward, peacefully.

The air was still only for a fraction of a second before a ripple of air tickled Petra's cheek. She heard a soft voice identifying herself as Betsy Hendricks.

Betsy's story flashed across Petra's closed eyelids. She'd had a baby of her own. Her husband had not allowed him to be named, not until he reached three months of age, but Betsy had named him Alistair, after her father. Alistair had been healthy when he was born, such a good size, the woman who had helped deliver him said so. He was always hungry, and she had plenty of milk for him. He hooked his little finger onto hers when he suckled, as though he was thanking her, she always thought.

His death at ten weeks old, in his sleep, was so unexpected that she refused to accept it. She had tried to revive his little blue body, with its blue lips and cold, cold skin, until her husband had to wrestle Alistair away from her. She had screamed, then. Screamed and screamed and screamed until her husband slapped her cheek repeatedly to stop her.

He forbade more screaming and he forbade any crying.

She felt she was walking around in someone else's life, after that. She didn't recognise her thoughts and her body felt strange – limp and rubbery – like it belonged to someone else. She thought she must be someone else. This must be happening to a stranger, and she was imagining it. She would wake up in the morning and Alistair would be there waiting for her, rosy-cheeked and ready for his breakfast.

But when the morning came it was worse, because she was still the stranger and her husband was shouting at her to make his breakfast.

The kindly lady who had helped bring Alistair into this world came to see her, when her husband was out in the field. She had said how sorry she was, how she had an idea of how much she was hurting, and was her milk still coming.

She had nodded, crying, because the milk was still coming and she could not pick Alistair up and give it to him.

I know another woman, the kindly lady said, *who has two babies, but no milk for them.*

She lifted her eyes up, her own eyes, not the stranger's eyes, looked at the kindly lady and said *I can help.*

They went to the other mother's cottage right away, and with each step she felt less and less like the stranger who could not move, could not think.

The babies were beautiful – so much smaller than Alistair. They were hungry and they were angry, but they calmed as she fed them, and then they slept.

The other mother wept.

She could not go back home to where her angry husband would be waiting, so she stayed. She slept in the chair she nursed the babies in, or sometimes on the floor. She stayed until the men showed up. Two men, dressed entirely in black, calling out her name. The babies started to cry, the other mother cried, as they put an iron bridle over her head. The witch's bridle, designed to stop women from biting. They led her out of the cottage, towards their horse and cart.

A banshee-scream pierced the air, and the two men fell to the ground. When she saw that they were unconscious, she started to run. The scream had unlocked the bridle and, when she could feel it loosen around her head, she pulled it off and threw it as far away from her as she could.

She ran, and stumbled over her skirts and her feet, and ran, and stumbled.

Exhausted and on the verge of passing out, she came upon a small byre. She banged on the door, but no one answered. She pushed the door, and walked into the dark, damp space.

No one had lived there for some time, she knew. The fire had not been lit in a long time.

There was a single wooden chair in front of the open fire and she fell onto it.

She dreamed about the babies, crying, and Alistair, silent. She dreamed that her husband was one of the men who had come for her, the one who had shoved the iron bridle onto her head with such force.

When morning came, weak light shone through the tiny window, and she looked for anything she could eat. Any food there might have been had been long since eaten by mice or rats, or maybe by other women in hiding. She opened the door slowly, looking for any sign of another human being and then, as quickly as she could, picked whatever she could find to eat: sorrel leaves, chickweed, ground elder, young plantain leaves, a few pheasant-back mushrooms.

As darkness descended on the cottage she wanted nothing more than to set the wood she had found alight, but she was frightened that it would signal to the people looking for her that she was there. She pulled her clothes around her as tightly as she could, imagining that she was sitting in front of a fire, with Alistair huddled to her breast.

The next day, and the next, after the sun rose she went outside looking for anything she might eat. On the third day, a sudden storm blew in and brought with it torrential rain, soaking her. She went back to the cottage, still with nothing to eat, and huddled in front of the cold, dark fire.

Her body shook with the shivers, and after a while she was drenched with sweat, too. Alistair was there with her in the cottage, older than when she had last seen him, and able to talk. He was telling her to get up, and light the fire. She told him the men would come if she did. *They're coming anyway*, he said.

I'd rather die here than go with them. Maybe the cold will kill me, she told him.

Her husband was next to visit her, shouting that she had killed their baby, and she had left two more to die. He moved to strike her, but his hand stopped before it made contact with her skin. He tried again, and the same thing happened. *They're coming for you*, he told her, teeth bared. *I've told them about you and they're coming for you.*

The kindly woman came, and told her to come with her, she'd get her to a safe place. The men were searching all of the buildings in the area, they would find her soon. Betsy tried to get up and go with her, but she could not move.

Her mother and father, dead since she was a child, stood in the open door, light streaming in behind them, beckoning to her. They told her to come with them, they would lead her to a better place. *Carry me*, she tried to call out, but her voice wasn't working. *Help me.*

The men came for her, after that. They put the iron bridle on her, again. They dragged her outside, where she was accused of killing a child, calling on the devil to use sorcery against her captors, and speaking the devil's tongue. She was found guilty, and blindfolded, then taken to the prison at Rothmore, where she was held for only one night.

The next morning Betsy was taken to Edinburgh, where she was burned on Castle Hill, without strangling beforehand. The men told her that this brutal punishment was suitable for her terrible crime of killing her own child.

Petra opened her eyes, and spoke to Betsy Hendricks. She told her that she had heard her story, and she would make sure that others heard it, too.

She could not bear to hear any more voices, not then. She buried her head in her hands, and she wept. She wept for Betsy, and for Meg, and for all of the women who had been accused and killed by fear and lies. She wept for her mother, and for herself.

The tears wore her out. She closed her eyes and silently carried out an incantation of sorrow and of gratitude, for the women who'd shared their stories. Although she wanted to lie back in the grass and sleep, Petra packed up her rucksack and heaved her heavy body up off the grass, determined to write Betsy's story while it was still sharply framed in her mind's eye.

CHAPTER 13

Petra sat at her little desk and wrote Betsy's story, even though remembering what Betsy had lived through pained her. In her grief, Betsy had found a way to help another mother and her babies, and yet the men had come for her. Accused of killing her own child, they had burned her to death. How many other women were there like Betsy, Petra wondered, sick with grief and despair, then blamed for it, and found guilty in the eyes of the law? She remembered reading one tragic account of a woman accused of cavorting with the devil who asked her accusers – naïvely, innocently – if it was possible to do so and have no memory of it? Through pure blind fear and terror, confusion, and the effects of torture, how many women had become convinced that they really *were* witches?

Petra knew something about what it was like to turn in on yourself because of the way others treated you, to come to accept that you were as small and insignificant to the world as they led you to believe. She had felt it all through primary school, hoped for more at secondary school – and was sorely disappointed at first, then surprised by unexpected friendships at high school in Edinburgh, and at university, because she'd never really quite believed that people really cared about her, and wanted to spend time with her.

And then Josh had come along. After he stole her work, Petra was angry with him but she was even more angry at herself for being fooled by him. She'd let her guard down, allowed herself to believe that he was attracted to her. Instead, he was only attracted to her work, and in using it for his own gain. Here, at Rothmore, Petra could feel that she was letting her guard down again. She wanted to believe in these burgeoning friendships with Clodagh and Erik. They were both bursting with talent – they didn't *need* anything from her, so there was every reason to trust that they wanted nothing more than friendship, and she had to believe that.

Petra's reverie was disturbed by the sound of voices outside - the others had arrived back from their trip to the lighthouse. She thanked Betsy again for sharing her story, then left the stillness of her room, eager for company.

She walked into the lounge and saw Gill grabbing a handful of sandwiches. Petra did the same, then sat down at the table and listened as Clodagh told her all about the lighthouse, which she said was spooky and terrifying and wonderful, the perfect place to set her story. Samuel said that the visit had inspired him, too, and he was now planning to include a lighthouse in his book.

Gill said that the damp, musty odour was unbearable, and disagreed vehemently with Clodagh, who said that after a bit she'd stopped noticing it.

Samuel asked how Petra's morning was. "Good, thanks. I got my head down and wrote."

Gill's eyes narrowed as she looked at Petra, and she didn't break eye contact. After spending the morning writing Betsy's story, Petra's tolerance level was low. After a brief stare-off, Petra said, "You have a bit of chocolate in the corner of your mouth, Gill. No – on the other side."

"That's what you get for pinching the last dark chocolate ginger biscuit!" Samuel teased, explaining that the tour guide had served them tea and biscuits in the tiny room where lighthouse keepers and their families had once communed.

"Claustrophobic is the only way to describe it," Samuel explained. "It's hard to imagine a couple living together in harmony, never mind an entire family."

"Rank is the way I'd describe it," Gill said. "I'm sure the smell has intensified over the years, but I have no idea how anyone could live with that degree of damp."

"No choice," Samuel said, shrugging his shoulders.

During lunch, they discussed the progress they were making with their writing, ahead of the celebration event planned for that evening. Afterwards, Petra returned to her room and busied herself by editing what she'd written about Meg and Betsy. She felt so close to both women – like she knew them personally – that she was having trouble choosing which of the stories to read at the sharing event. In the end, she decided she would share Meg's story, since Meg was the first woman to come forward.

***

Petra didn't realise that people would be getting dressed up for the sharing event, and arrived for dinner distinctly underdressed, in jeans and a jumper. Only Erik was as casually dressed as she was. The sea fog – or haar, as it was called in Scotland - had rolled in, and was curling up against the window like a thick white blanket, but the numerous candles dotted around the lounge made a cosy counterbalance. The night was Spanish-themed; Jane brought several tapas dishes, as well as large jugs of tinto de verano wine cocktail, to the table, a stark contrast to the weather outside.

About an hour after they sat down for dinner, Jane asked who was brave enough to share their work first. Samuel stood up, and enthusiastically read the first chapter in his Treasure Island-vampires novel. The foggy real-life backdrop was the perfect setting for his reading, which Petra thought was silly and funny and very well-written.

"Bravo, Samuel! I think you might have a best-seller on your hands!" Erik cheered. "It would make a great film."

Samuel grinned as they all applauded, then took a gracious little bow. "I have to say, I don't think I would have known how to start this without your help, Erik. Many thanks from me to you for your guidance."

Jane excused herself and came back a few minutes later with a few fresh, hot tapas dishes. But before anyone had the chance to tuck in, Gill stood up.

"Ah-hem. I hope you'll indulge me next. I want to share my first chapter with you." She looked around the table at everyone. "Is everyone ready?"

"I don't think any of us are ready for this!" Samuel teased.

Gill's first chapter was a bit of a slow-burn, describing the home stretch of the main character's commute back to her home in a small Scottish Borders village and how she pulled the car over and got out to investigate, after hearing a sound like she had driven over something big. There was nothing obviously wrong with any of the tyres or the underside of the car, so she got back in and started the car. At that moment, the passenger side door opened and a man – more of a shadow figure really – snaked it open with his long, ghoulish fingers, and climbed in.

"Oooooooh, spooky!" Samuel said. "Way to crank the suspense, Gill!"

They all applauded, and Petra had to admit that Gill had the makings of a terrific story.

Nerves took hold of Petra and Clodagh, such that neither volunteered to go next. As Jane gathered up the tapas dishes and announced that she'd come back soon with more, Clodagh gave Petra a stoic look then stood up, and began fiddling with cables and her laptop.

"This looks intriguing," Samuel said, rubbing his hands together.

"Well I hope it lives up to your expectations. First of all, I'll start by telling you *about* my story, because I haven't started to do any actual writing yet and don't have anything to read aloud. As I think you all know, I want to retell the sea witch story. Witches were often blamed for causing storms and tragedies at sea, but in my story the sea witch calms the sea, and protects sailors."

She paused, and took a large swig of her drink. "My sea witch lives in a lighthouse, not under the sea as is common in most legends. Visiting Sealcraigs today made me even more convinced that a lighthouse is the perfect setting for this tale. I'd been thinking about having the lighthouse on Midhallow, but after a lot of thought I've decided that might be disrespectful to the memory of those who disappeared."

Clodagh paused again, to take another sip of her drink. "The lighthouse will be somewhere along the coast here in East Lothian. But the important part is that she will be the protector of the sea, keeping all who sail in it safe. Except the vampires, of course," she smiled at Samuel.

"Ooh – a mash-up story. I like it!" he laughed.

"We'll look forward to reading it," Erik told her.

Clodagh smiled at him, and then told the group that she had sketched some of Fingal's still folk, which was what she had brought to share with them. Fingal switched off the lights, and Clodagh showed them her first illustration, of the mischievous greeting gnome at the entrance of the woods. She read out a short passage about his behaviour at night, after the humans fall asleep. After enthusiastic applause, she shared more illustrations and stories about a fairy, a pixie and a sprite. Because Petra knew that Clodagh's planned expedition to draw the still folk was scuppered by twisting her ankle the day before, she was amazed that all of these illustrations had been accomplished in a single afternoon.

"It's a celebration of your amazing sculptures," she told Fingal. "And it was inspired by the exhibition."

"We should definitely discuss a collaboration," Fingal told her, clearly impressed.

"Result, Clodagh!" Samuel cheered.

Clodagh gave a shy smile. "I have to ask – I found twenty still folk today, Fingal. Is that all of them?"

He looked wistful as he said, "Well, all but one. But the one you didn't find is buried so deep in the woods that no one but me knows where it is. It's been there for over fifty years."

He paused, and Petra realised that Fingal would have been a child when it was made. "Fifty-five years, to be exact. My father made it for me when I was five years old, and too terrified to go into the woods. I'd seen something with red eyes in there, staring out at me one day while I was playing, and I was too scared to go near the woods, let alone into them."

They all waited for Fingal to explain what had been in the woods with red eyes. He continued, "My father tried a number of different tricks to loosen my fear, but nothing worked. I screamed if he tried to make me go with him towards the woods. And then he presented me with a protective spirit, carved from a large tree limb that had fallen in the winter storms. This was important, he told me, because he would never harm a tree to use it for carving. The protective spirit had the kindly face of a wise old man, and my father told me if we placed it where I had seen the red eyes it would keep me safe forever. Because I had seen the red eyes peering out at me from part-way up one of the old oak trees, that's where the protective spirit went. It's still there, but is completely covered now by the canopy of the old trees."

"What a wonderful story, Fingal," Gill said.

"And did it work?" Samuel asked. "Did it make you feel safe enough to go into the woods?"

"It did," Fingal said, smiling. "My father carried it in the crook of his arm, and we walked along the path right through the woods and out the other side towards the beach. I was trembling the whole way, but we made it."

"And is that where your love of still folk began?" Clodagh asked.

"I don't remember my father ever talking about protective spirits before that, but it seemed to open the dam of folklore and mythology that he then shared with me whenever we were outside together. I learned so much from him. Even as a boy I knew that they were stories, but I also knew that they held a certain truth for my father. And now for me. I want to believe in their power, and so I do."

Jane replaced the votive candles, which had all burned out as the fog pressed ever-more insistently up against the windows, and they talked about the little creatures that were part of their cultural heritage, both in Scotland and in Norway. Inside the warm, candlelit room, with the golden glow of the fire, Petra found it entirely possible to believe that they might catch a glimpse of the uncanny world, just for an instant.

Erik interrupted her thoughts. "Now then, there is one person still to tell us about her work. Are you ready, Petra?"

The fog had given Petra an idea, although she wondered if the others would think it was a step too far. "Yes, I'm ready. My story is set in the witches' prison. I'd like to do the reading there, if everyone is up for it?"

"Spooky!" Samuel said. "Yes, I'm up for it!"

"Absolutely – great plan!" Erik beamed.

Jane said that no one had ever done a reading in the prison before, and Fingal added that they had plenty of torches. Gill said she would rather stay in the warm house but, seeing as everyone else wanted to go, she didn't want to be the party pooper.

As Petra rode the wave of the others' enthusiasm, she didn't notice Clodagh's look of desperation. Although she was trying not to draw attention to herself, she willed Petra to remember that she'd seen the apparition on Midhallow, and change her plan. But, when Fingal passed around torches and everyone stood up to go, she followed them, even though she was terrified.

They walked slowly, in a procession through the fog to the old prison, Samuel and Erik keeping up the banter the entire time. Clodagh tried to make a plan, to avoid any unwelcome visions. If what Petra had said was true, the terrible history of the place could trigger another visual hallucination.

She hoped that squeezing her eyes shut once they got there would work. As they stepped into the confines of the three walls, the fog seemed to blanket any sound, and she was grateful that she heard nothing, unlike the night on Midhallow. She closed her eyes as tightly as she could, as Petra started to read the story of Meg's imprisonment in the space in which they all stood.

The events in the story were terrible, and Clodagh felt a

rising anxiety to get away from the words, to get away from the prison. She silently begged Petra to end it, to finish the story and let them all get back to the safety and warmth of the house. But at that moment something poked into her arm, and she opened her eyes to see what it was. The murky outline of a girl, lying on her back, appeared in front of her. The girl's body was even with Clodagh's waist, as though she were levitating. In an echo of what had happened on Midhallow, the girl's head tilted to look at Clodagh. Again, her own face stared back at her.

Clodagh couldn't stop herself from screaming.

Petra's blood ran cold, and she stopped reading. "Clodagh – was that you? Is everything okay?"

Clodagh didn't reply, just started running back to the house as quickly as she could. She stumbled once and almost fell flat on her face. She heard the others call to her, shouting her name. But she continued to run, virtually blinded in the fog, until she was back to the safety of the house.

CHAPTER 14

As soon as Petra realised Clodagh was running away, she started after her. But she couldn't catch her. Just a few steps away from the prison, she dropped her torch. As she bent to pick it up, the others ran past, calling out to Clodagh. By the time she arrived back in the lounge, everyone but Clodagh and Erik were standing near the fire. Gill glared at her, eyes blazing.

"What did you do to her?"

Petra couldn't find the right words. She couldn't say that Clodagh had seen a ghostly vision on Midhallow, which had just reappeared in the prison. She was angry at herself for not suspecting it could happen again, in the prison, because she thought of it as a place of safety. She could see now that it was insensitive of her to suggest a reading there. But she hadn't even considered that Clodagh might have *another* vision.

Erik appeared in the lounge, looking concerned, and reported that he'd knocked on Clodagh's door, but she'd asked to be left alone.

Petra apologised to everyone. Gill said it was Clodagh she should be apologising to.

"I will. I'll go and see her right now."

"I'm not sure that's a good idea," Samuel said gently. "She said she wanted to be left alone, that she didn't want to see anyone. I think we should respect that."

Petra nodded.

"What happened in there? Why did she scream?" Gill asked, shaking with anger.

Petra took a deep breath. "Something happened on Midhallow, something I can't tell you about. I think the same thing might have happened tonight."

"What do you mean by the same thing?" Jane looked rattled, and more than a little angry.

"I can't tell you. It would be breaking Clodagh's confidence. All I can say is that something really scared her on the island, and it might have happened again tonight."

"Well thank you very much for clearing that up for us. It's as clear as mud," Gill spat.

"Whatever happened, I'm sure you didn't mean to upset her," Samuel said, kindly.

"I wouldn't – I didn't – I'm so sorry."

Fingal said he'd make pots of tea, and hot chocolate, to warm everyone up. The fog had seeped into their bones, and they huddled close to the fire – variously cold, angry, sad and morose.

"It's a shame that it ended the way it did, but I wanted to say how much I enjoyed your work," Erik said, giving Petra a sad smile.

Samuel said, "Me too. You have quite a powerful story."

Petra thanked them, angry with herself for not just reading out Meg's story in the lounge. The truth was that she had *wanted* everyone to be in the old prison as she read it, didn't want to let them away with sitting in a warm room as they listened. She'd wanted them to feel uncomfortable, and cold, and scared – even if just for a few minutes.

But she had not wanted Clodagh to be terrified. And here she was, at the centre of yet another disaster of her own making, all over again.

Before she went to bed, Petra wrote a note to Clodagh, and slipped it under her door.

I'm so sorry, Clodagh. It was a stupid thing to do, and it's all my fault. Please forgive me.

Petra

Petra knew sleep wouldn't come, not when she was plagued by memories of the other times she'd hurt someone with magic. After the revenge spell she'd used had backfired on her father, Petra deliberately avoided finding out if it had worked on Bethany and the other girls. She'd long suspected, though, that nothing had happened to them - that her lack of skill, errors she'd made without the skilled guidance of a mentor like Isobel, had undone her intention to cause harm to her tormentors.

***

It all started with the poppet. The day that Petra saw Bethany, and the memories of those terrible first weeks of high school came flooding back, it was as though forces she could not control guided her actions, leading her to the book shop, to buy *Revenge Spells.* Isobel's voice came to her often in the days that followed, urging her to turn away from the darkness, to stay in the light. But the forces steered her towards what she saw as inevitable; the *need* to cause pain to Bethany, and to the others who'd treated her so cruelly, which was greater than her loyalty to Isobel.

The book contained detailed instructions about making a poppet to intensify the spell. Although it suggested that the greatest effect would be realised by using something belonging to the person at the heart of the spell – strands of hair, a bit of clothing – Petra had nothing of Bethany's, and she knew she'd attract too much attention by showing up at her old school out of the blue to collect something (plus, she had vowed to never – ever – set foot inside the place again). No, the poppet itself would have to stand in as the physical manifestation of Bethany.

At first, Petra considered making the poppet out of paper, because it was the quickest way to exact her revenge. Perhaps something of Isobel's teaching was with her after all, as she decided she should take some time to practise the revenge spells, which would also give her more time to make a more sophisticated poppet. Using felt, yarn, herbs and small quartz stones, she constructed the tiny representation of Bethany.

The night that Petra performed the awakening spell, her body shook with nervous excitement. When she told the little doll that it would thereafter be her servitor, a searing flash of heat passed down Petra's spine. The feeling *electrified* her; she could feel the power emanating between the poppet and her own body.

Every night, for two weeks, Petra carried out an act of revenge on the poppet. Each one was meant to bring physical pain to Bethany in short but intense episodes. Petra's plan was to build up to an ultimate act of revenge, to coincide with the fifth anniversary of her mother's death, an act which Petra hoped would leave Bethany as harrowed and hollow as she herself was.

The poppet started as a source of fascination, and quickly became an obsession. Through some invisible connection between them, Petra's body tingled whenever the poppet was used. She devoured information about poppets, and learned about their use in protective spells and white magic. She made a second poppet, to represent her father. Her nightly ritual expanded, starting with healing spells for her father, followed by revenge directed at Bethany's poppet. As Petra's confidence grew, so did her anger and her desire to help her father become the man he once was. As much as she needed to hurt Bethany, she needed to help her father.

Petra would later realise that, on the night of her planned act of ultimate revenge, she erred in two significant ways: she failed to seal the protective magic she'd used on her father's poppet, and she invoked dark magic - out of ignorance rather than intention – as she walked around the circle, chanting the revenge spell.

As a novice witch, Petra didn't yet know about widdershins – or walking counter-clockwise, the opposite direction to the movement of the sun. In doing so, she walked away from the light and into the darkness. Her symbolic action matched her strong intent, and the magic worked.

She would never know what happened to Bethany as a result of her magic, because the night's events had led to her father's hospitalisation and all of her focus shifted to him. She was no longer interested in the consequences for Bethany. Her only concern was reversing whatever she'd done to harm her father.

With absolute certainty, Petra knew she was to blame – her lack of skill, her inexperience, her mistakes. The very knowledge that she was complicit in her father's incapacitation became almost unbearable. She was frightened about trying to reverse the damage, in case she caused even more.

Every time she saw her father she told him she was sorry. He looked at her with glassy, unfocused eyes, and spoke only in mumbles and grunts, but she thought he knew what she was saying. She believed that her father knew she was the reason he was stuck inside an even less cooperative, less functional body. They had never – not once – talked about what Petra had asked of her mother that led to her death. Petra wondered if some dark, opaque light shone out of her, a clear sign that she was impure, something only her father could see. Maybe her aunt could see it, too.

Petra didn't make the connection between the poppet, the widdershins and the misfiring magic until years later. She suspected her father's poppet was involved in the revenge spell, and her suspicions increased when she replayed every second of that night, over and over in her mind, as she waited to fall asleep each night. Had she only made a poppet for Bethany, she believed her father would have been spared his sudden, crippling stroke. Walking widdershins was an error that took years to discover and, when she finally read about the role of counter-clockwise movements in black magic, she wept.

She'd released the energy from both poppets the evening following her father's stroke, sobbing as she spoke the words to unawaken them. Her aunt was in the next room watching a soap opera, the characters screaming at each other loudly enough to mask the sound of her sorrowful weeping. But, even though her father's poppet was released from its role as magic enhancer, she spoke to it every day, asking it to help her father be well again. In that way, the benign, innocent-looking poppet became the only aspect of Petra's world that knew of her pain, her self-directed anger and hatred, and her deep sense of regret at betraying everything Isobel had taught her, as well as her mother's memory.

But the itch of magic – of its incredible power, of its potential to help Petra right the many wrongs she'd brought about in her short life – prickled away just under the surface of her skin, ever since that terrible night. She'd fought the itch to honour – if it wasn't too late – Isobel, and her parents. She fought the itch because she knew her aunt was afraid of the unseen world that magic inhabited. She fought the itch because she was afraid of her dark urges, and her ineptness. In the dark corners of those long, sleepless nights, she beckoned silently to a magical shadow-mentor, who worked in opposition to Isobel; her heart's desire was to find a mentor who showed her how to walk in the darkness without hurting those she loved.

The darkness was a part of her, and she'd known this even when she was a child, even when she had no words to describe what she knew about herself. She'd known it because of the way others chose not to be near her, were frightened or disgusted by her. After Josh stole her work, she'd wanted nothing more than to embrace the darkness, to cause him pain for what he'd done. For Isobel and for her mother, for everything they stood for and believed most deeply, she'd stayed in the light.

She'd meant for no harm to come to Clodagh, and yet twice in Petra's presence – on Midhallow and in the witches' prison – she'd been terrified by a ghostly vision. Petra, summoning women with true and pure intention to gather their stories for her book, saw with sudden clarity the overlap: something in her magic must have gone wrong, again, and brought pain and suffering to someone close to her.

This time, Clodagh – someone Petra thought of as an ally

and a kindred spirit, who she had come to care about deeply in such a short space of time – was the victim.

She couldn't let the situation get out of hand, again. She had to make it right.

CHAPTER 15

The ancient oaks on the Rothmore estate had witnessed so much cruelty, violence and death over the centuries. The dead stayed silent, they had learned, unless the living asked them to speak.

They knew of the three women who were buried in the ground near to where the grass ended and the tall cliffs plunged to the sea below. The women lay, mostly forgotten, for more than four centuries. The oaks had stood while the women were brought to the prison – two of them together, hands, eyes, mouths bound, their bodies already bent and twisted from beatings. Held in the prison they received further beatings, and worse. They gave up the name of a third woman, one the oaks saw every day staring out at sea from an upper-floor window. She was taken from the castle to the tower, where she was held in a dark, windowless place.

The oaks had seen many other women taken from the tower, loaded onto a cart, and driven away. They had not seen what befell them in Edinburgh, at the trials, or afterwards.

But they saw what had happened to these three women. Before they were loaded onto the cart, the people came for them. There were not enough guards to hold the people back, and they got to the women, who were still bound at the eyes, hands and mouth. The women could do nothing to defend themselves, did nothing to draw on the powers they were accused of having.

Most of the people left, quickly, when it was over and done, but some stayed to watch as the guards hastily dug a hole for their bodies.

No one came to visit them. No record was kept of the

women's burial. The people forgot about them, quickly, and about their own part in the women's death.

The oaks remembered.

***

Petra braced herself for an onslaught of abuse from Gill as she prepared for the walk of shame into the lounge for breakfast the next morning, but was surprised – and relieved - to see that Erik was the only other person there. Gill and Samuel had been and gone, he said, and he had not seen Clodagh yet. Petra was about to apologise, again, when Erik spoke.

He gestured at the fog, still thick outside the glass. "Have you heard of Niflheim?"

"Pardon me?"

"In Norse legend, Niflheim is one of the nine worlds, the world of fog and mist. It's the coldest and darkest region." He nodded his head toward the window. "Yesterday and today, I feel like we're stuck in Niflheim."

"Here on the east coast, we get fog all year long."

"I've noticed."

"Some people say that the dead can speak to the living through the fog, as though it's a curtain between the worlds of the living and the dead."

"That's handy."

Petra laughed – she couldn't stop herself. She didn't want to spoil this light mood by asking Erik if Gill and Samuel had been talking about what had happened the night before. Instead, she asked if he ever went swimming in the fog.

"It would be too easy to be lost at sea, I think. I'll dunk myself in the water, but I don't swim out."

"Like a baptism, in the fog."

Erik stared at her for a moment, then said, "It *is* a bit like a baptism. Not that I can remember mine, but you know – the sense of giving yourself over to another force. That's what it feels like when you go under the surface of the icy water. You can't see anything when you go under, and you can't see anything when you come back up."

Petra's brain was too fuzzy with shame about the night before, about how she had made Clodagh feel, to pinpoint what it was about Erik's analogy that prodded her consciousness. Was it a dream she'd had, about being drowned in icy water, or a flash of a memory from one of the women in the prison?

As she fought to focus her thoughts, Fingal appeared in the lounge and asked to speak to Erik. Petra excused herself, giving them space to talk privately. She had decided to practise the protection spell, alone in her room, then go back to the burial site. She knew that she could be in danger even in broad daylight, but she felt a pull to the place and had to go back. She would channel all of her shame and self-loathing into self-protection.

***

Petra found her way back to the burial site with ease, even in the fog. The stone cairn looked like a small, misshapen person, looming up through the mist. She lit a candle, and stood for a moment in silence. Then she delivered an incantation of sorrow and understanding, asking for the truth to be told.

You will not be forgotten, she told the women. *You will be heard.*

She lit the incense and sat down with her eyes closed, signalling that she was ready to listen.

The voices came to her not as a rush of whispers, but as a steamroller of wails and shrieks. She tried to separate them out, to listen to one at a time, but a wave of pain and sadness, built up over centuries, rushed towards her. The candle went out – she could smell the tang of smoke as it did so - and she felt a brief flush of fear. She commanded the voices to speak to her in turn.

But when they did - two women sharing their tragic intertwined tale, before the third joined in - Petra could hardly bear it. They had held onto their stories for centuries. No one had come to claim their bodies, or to listen to what had happened to them.

These were the women accused of being the Midhallow witches. When no one had been able to explain how the plague victims went missing without a trace from Midhallow, word quickly spread that witches were to blame. The hunt then began for the witches responsible. Lilias Rankin and Margaret Thomson were sisters by marriage, healers in their village of Saltpans. Margaret told Petra that Lilias was the kind one, who visited anyone ailing with no thought of her own safety. She did what she could for anyone, with plant potions, and with prayers. Yes, they were prayers, Margaret said, not spells that came from the devil's mouth. They accused her of talking to the devil, when in truth she was talking to God. As kind and gentle a woman as you would never again meet, Margaret said of Lilias.

Margaret said that she was Lilias's opposite, impatient and quick to anger. She had neighbours that were always griping about something – she and her husband and weans were too loud, they must have been thieving from them, because they had less each week than the week before. They complained about the loathsome smells that emanated from the Thomson house, which Margaret said was her bad cooking and her husband's ale. It did have a terrible smell when it was fomenting, she explained. But she used the ale to heal, infused it with her own potions and poured it into the mouths of the unwell.

She was a different kind of healer than Lilias, but they were both good at it, and the villagers had come to know that they should visit one or the other if they were ailed. Margaret was revered, for a time, but she was also feared. Her arguments and physical fights with the neighbours were witnessed by many. Similarly, people who were healed and those who had witnessed her healing others began to spread fear about her, because no one could explain how it was that she was making people better.

Lilias suffered the backlash by proxy. No one had ever witnessed Lilias saying a harsh word to anyone, but paranoia spread about what dark force was helping the sisters to make other people better.

Three men came for them on the same dark day in November. It was just past three o'clock in the afternoon, and the sky was already black like the middle of the night. The women were alone with their children in their cottages, but the men showed no mercy. They demanded they confess to making an unholy pact with the devil and, when they refused, they beat them. They beat them to the sound of their children screaming and pleading with them to stop.

Two of the men pulled on Lilias's arms, until they popped out of their sockets. Next, they pulled on her legs, dislocating both of her hips. They ripped her dress down the middle, took a copper kettle off of the fire, and held it to her breast.

She confessed then, of everything they were accusing her of, to stop the physical pain and that of knowing that her children were watching what the men were doing to her.

They threw Lilias into an open cart, and went for Margaret next. When the men kicked down the door, Margaret could see Lilias lying like the poorest creature she had ever seen in the back of the cart. She told them that whatever Lilias had said she had done, Margaret had also done. One of the men drew back his arm, and punched her with full force in the stomach. The children wailed and screamed, but Margaret could not look back at them, did not want to have the last images of their faces, terrified for her.

The cart bumped along the road, to the tower at Rothmore. The men pulled them roughly out of the cart. Lilias could not stand, so they kicked her where she lay, every part of her body. She could not raise her arms to protect her face and head. Margaret tried to protect Lilias, but they turned on her, hitting her with their arms and with thick pieces of wood. They stamped on her feet, spat in her face repeatedly, pulled on her hair so that large chunks came out at the roots. When they smashed a piece of wood into her pelvis, she went down, landing hard on the ground.

With both women on the ground, the men demanded to

know who was the third. Who was the third witch who had lived with them on Midhallow, who had worked with them to kill every last person sent to live there to keep the plague away from others. Who was the third witch who consorted with the devil.

As the men screamed down at them, Margaret stared up at the sky, begging God to make this come to a quick end, for Lilias and for herself. As she lowered her eyes, she found herself looking right into one of the windows of the castle. At a window on one of the high floors, a pale face stared out at what was happening to them. God forgive her, she felt such hatred in her heart for that woman, safe and warm up there.

"Lady Rothmore," she said through broken teeth.

The men looked up to the castle window. And then they went for Lady Rothmore.

Lady Rothmore had always known they would come for her. She had watched them bring all of the women – and two men – to the tower. She knew only one of the women imprisoned there: the minister's wife from the church at Haddington, because they'd had afternoon tea together once in the reception room of the castle. She had hardly believed it could be possible, the wife of a man of the kirk, but then Lady Rothmore wondered if perhaps that might have made her *more* susceptible. She would have been under more scrutiny than most.

She should have guessed that standing at the window might make her an obvious choice for women tortured into naming their accomplices. But she had felt it was an act of honour to watch as every single woman was brought to the tower. Someone – another woman – needed to bear witness to everyone who was brought there, and how they were treated. How they *had been* treated already by the men who came for them, for every single woman arrived with the physical markers of a beating.

When the men came for her, they seemed to delight in her humiliation. They tore her clothes off her body, then pricked her skin all over for evidence of the witch's mark. She felt the pain of it – the shame – everywhere, but they announced that they had pricked the small of her back and she had felt no pain.

They told her to confess, that she should admit to being one of the witches who was said to live on Midhallow at night, and come back to the mainland by daylight, as though to trick their husbands into thinking they were good women.

She refused. She knew what had most likely happened to those people: instead of transporting them safely to Midhallow, where they would either recover or die of the plague, the boatman had tipped them – one by one – into the sea. A stone or two in their pockets and they would sink, so far below the surface that they would never rise again.

It had not been witchcraft. It had been cruelty towards the most vulnerable, not three old crones exacting revenge on the twenty-eight for bringing their pox to the island.

So, she did not confess. She would not confess. Even as they inflicted more pain on her body than she ever thought possible – worse, even, than the intolerable pain of childbirth – she would not say what they were waiting to hear. If she had been a witch she would have caused the men's limbs to rip from their body as they beat her, for all of the blood vessels to burst in their heads as they bent over her. She would have summoned the very devil himself into the room, to exact on the men a death as cruel as the ones that women, every day, suffered.

But none of those things happened, and she was dragged to the tower, with the two other women. The woman who had accused her repeated, "It wasn't me," until the doors were locked behind them, and Lady Rothmore thought she knew what she had meant: it was not her, not her true self who had accused her – those men had turned them into something that they were not, had never wanted to be.

She did not remember much of what happened when they were in the tower. Each day stretched into the next. Cold, dark, wet, hungry, unable to sleep due to the torments that were inflicted on them. When the door to her cell was opened again, she thought she had been saved: her husband, or her son, had brought forth the truth, and she was free.

But that was not the case; no one came to save her. The three Midhallow witches were being taken to Edinburgh, where they would be tried. And executed. They had all known that would be their fate, from the moment the men arrived for them.

Word had spread through the local villages, and the crowd reared up when the women were brought out of the tower, yelling profanities and wild accusations at them. And then they surged forward – the guards were too few in number to hold them back – and they attacked the women with anything they had: fingernails, stones, fists, teeth, feet, sticks.

Each of the women, through the agony of the terrible beatings, had the same thought: *Soon, it will be finished.*

CHAPTER 16

After leaving the burial site, Petra went straight to her room, and crawled into bed. She curled up in a ball and pulled the duvet over her head. She hoped to fall into a deep sleep, to put the images of the women's torment out of her mind, even for a short time. But the images ravaged her mind. One of the most disturbing scenes was of a young child – maybe seven, or eight – running straight up to Lilias and throwing a stone, hitting her right between the eyes.

She wondered if Fingal knew anything of what had happened to his ancestor. There was, increasingly, recognition of the hate crimes perpetrated against innocent women during the witch hunts, so any family secrets that the Rothmores had tried to keep might be received with compassion. If he didn't know, Petra was unsure how to tell him what she'd seen, because she was afraid to reveal how she'd come to know the women's stories.

When she did, finally, sleep she dreamed of Clodagh, sitting in the chair at the desk in her room, looking out the window. Although her back was to Petra, she knew it was Clodagh because she was wearing the pink jumper that Petra loved, and coveted. When she called to her, Clodagh disappeared through the window, like a wisp of air.

Petra awoke with a start. It was almost half past one, and she was famished. There was a good chance that all of the sandwiches were gone, but the silver lining was that she might not have to see the others. See *Gill* was what she meant – Samuel and Erik did not seem to blame her for Clodagh running off, but Gill had made it very clear that she believed Petra was responsible.

There was some lunch left when she got downstairs, but Gill was also in the lounge, agitated. Erik and Fingal were also there, and Fingal asked Petra if she'd seen anything of Clodagh since the night before.

When she said that she hadn't, Fingal said, "Gill has knocked on Clodagh's door a few times this morning, to check on her after last night. There's been no answer."

"I've knocked on her door every half hour, and I'm getting very worried."

Fingal bit the side of his lip. "I know this is a sensitive topic but Petra, do you know what upset Clodagh so badly last night?"

Petra did not want to say anything to betray Clodagh's confidence, but she knew how distressed she'd been after seeing her ghost doppelgänger. "I do know, but she asked me not to tell anyone."

"For heaven's sake, this isn't a game – she was terrified Petra! You have to tell us what is going on!" Gill's eyes bulged and her face flamed, she was so angry.

Petra looked at Fingal, and took a deep breath. "She was convinced that she saw something on Midhallow – a hallucination. She thought she was losing her mind. I told her I'd heard that it's not uncommon to see visions, in places where terrible things happened."

"And knowing that, still you insisted on doing your reading in the prison?" Gill demanded.

"I had no idea that it would happen again. Yes, terrible things happened there, but to me it's not a frightening place. Not like Midhallow."

Gill started to say more, but Fingal interrupted. "We need to decide what to do next. I could go into her room, but if she's there and doesn't want to be disturbed that's an invasion of her privacy. And if she isn't there I still won't know what to do about it."

"If she's not in her room, why don't we go out looking for her?" Gill asked. "If she's somewhere here on the estate, we can at least offer to talk to her about what she saw. If she doesn't want to talk, at least we've tried. I'm very worried about her, Fingal."

Petra, Erik and Gill followed Fingal up to Clodagh's room on the first floor. He knocked and called out to her and, when there was no answer, used his key. The door swung open and they all looked inside. Clodagh was nowhere to be seen, but her bed was made, her laptop was on the desk, and some clothes were draped over a chair.

"Okay, let's go and look for her," Fingal said, looking worried.

They called on Samuel, who was at work in his room, and Fingal went to get Jane. After they'd all assembled in the lounge, Fingal organised everyone into search teams: he and Jane would search the pebble beach and the land adjoining the house; Gill and Samuel would search the cove beach; and Erik and Petra would search the woods.

The fog seemed thicker than ever as they began their search, their voices ringing out from different directions calling to Clodagh. Petra and Erik followed Gill and Samuel as far as the woods, but then diverted from the path into the trees, calling out to her. Gnarled tree roots protruded from the ground, causing them to stumble. At one point Erik hit the ground with a thud, and Petra heard the sickening snap of what sounded like bone.

"Erik! Are you okay?"

"I'm fine, I just snapped a branch."

They had strayed so far from the path that, in the fog, Petra couldn't tell if they were making progress, or circling back on themselves. They both took it in turns to call out to Clodagh, then wait and listen for any reply. But they only ever heard the other's voice. Petra knew, from seeing the woods in daylight, that they were not very dense, but still she worried about finding their way back to the house in the fog. She felt the tight claustrophobic grip of fear as she imagined them lost forever in the trees. She told herself not to be ridiculous – *someone* would surely come and find them.

After what felt to Petra like hours of searching, Erik finally called it off.

"I don't think she's here. And if she is, I don't think she wants to be found."

***

Erik and Petra were the first ones back to the house. They sat quietly, silently hoping the others were having more luck with their searches. But then Fingal and Jane came back, both ashen-faced.

"The boat's gone," Fingal said solemnly. "We're worried that Clodagh might have taken it out."

After some discussion, they all agreed that it was doubtful Clodagh would have set out on the boat in the fog, but Fingal called the lifeboat station at North Berwick anyway. The captain said he had a crew ready, who would leave right away and search along the coast to the Rothmore estate. Jane and Fingal said they would go and wait on the pebble beach.

Gill and Samuel arrived back minutes later, and Erik updated them.

"But she's a smart person," Samuel said. "It just doesn't make any sense that she'd take the boat out in this fog."

Everyone agreed; it made no sense at all.

Gill said that there was no way Clodagh would have risked her life in that way, unless she was suicidal. She shot an angry look at Petra, and asked if anyone had noticed anything telling in Clodagh's behaviour to suggest she was depressed? Did anyone know anything about her, really?

She said, "I know it's a terrible thing to say about someone, but what if it's true? We don't really know anything about her state of mind. It has been a pretty intense few days. And, if some-one was depressed -."

No one really knew anything about Clodagh, apart from the little she'd told them over the previous days. Everyone went quiet again, imagining how desperate Clodagh would have to be to harm herself in that way.

Gill broke the silence, again, with another theory: What if someone had sneaked onto the estate, and abducted Clodagh? "It wouldn't be that difficult, let's face it. They don't even have any security at the entrance to this place. It would be very easy for someone to just come up to the house, and then who knows what they might have done."

She looked at the others with frantic eyes. "Think about it – someone who knows that people come and go here, that the doors aren't locked all day. I'm not saying anyone planned to take *Clodagh* - she was likely the nearest warm body they were able to reach."

Samuel pointed out that Jane (and most likely Fingal, too, Petra thought) would not want this theory to be made public. "Imagine what that would do to business, if the rumour spread that someone had snatched her from here."

"It's hard to believe that we wouldn't have heard *something* – some kind of noise that would alert us to Clodagh being in trouble," Petra said.

There was a pause and then Gill said, "No one has mentioned this, but it needs to be discussed as a possibility. For the last few days we've been more or less immersed in stories about what might have happened to people who disappeared without a trace. It's possible that's what's happened to Clodagh."

Samuel said, dismissively, "That's just fiction, Gill. Or fantasy, whatever you like."

"I know, I know. I'm not saying that the Finfolk took Clodagh. I'm just saying there are mysteries that have never been solved, things we cannot know. We might never find out. Sometimes people's bodies are washed out to sea and never found."

"We're just making ourselves worry more sitting around in here. Why don't we go and wait on the beach with Fingal and Jane?" They all agreed that Samuel was right, and walked through the fog down to the shore.

***

Fingal was standing alone on the beach when they got there. He'd lit the storm lanterns, which were providing only partial illumination in the dense fog. He said that Jane had gone to get some foil blankets that they kept inside for emergencies. Petra thought it seemed likely that the lifeboat crew would have had these, but figured perhaps Jane just wanted to keep busy, like the rest of them.

Standing with Fingal on the beach, the discussion about Clodagh's disappearance ceased, and they huddled together silently in the fog, waiting and hoping. After a few minutes, they heard the crunching sound of footsteps on the pebbles and Jane appeared, holding blankets.

"She'll be so cold when she gets back," she said sadly.

They waited in silence for what felt like hours until they heard the sound of a motor, then something heavy slapping against the waves, and the lifeboat's lights surged into view. There were three crew members, in bright yellow gear. The boat banked sharply and then pulled up beside the dock. All three crew members jumped out of the boat deftly into the shallow water, and Fingal stepped forward to greet them. Petra saw that two of the crew were wrestling with something behind the lifeboat, then tied it to the dock.

"Hello Fingal," the captain said, shaking his hand.

"Hello Derek."

"No sign of her, I'm afraid. We found your boat drifting just a few miles to the east. There was no one in it, no signs that anyone had been in it. We've called the helicopter out to do a search of the water just in case."

"I don't understand – how would the boat get out into the sea if no one was in it?"

Derek shook his head. "No idea. The rope was inside the boat, like someone had untied it and thrown it in."

"It makes no sense," Fingal said. Jane stood behind him

like a shadow, wringing her hands. "I know we tied it up when we sailed back from Midhallow the other night."

"We'll do a slow crawl along the inlet beaches on our way back to North Berwick, to look for any signs of life. I'll ring you once we're back at the station. By then I should have news about the air search."

Fingal shook his hand again. "Thanks Derek. And thanks for bringing the boat back." He thanked the rest of the crew, too, gripping Jane's hand as he waved them off into the fog.

"They'll keep searching for her. I'm going to phone the police. Please come back inside where it's warm. Jane's got some blankets if anyone needs one."

Jane looked startled, as though hearing her name had brought her back to reality. Petra felt reluctant to leave the shore, imagining there was an answer hovering there, waiting to be plucked out of the fog.

CHAPTER 17

While they waited in the warm, cosy lounge for the police to arrive, Erik suggested that he would go out and search the land to the east of the estate, on the coastal path that ran along the top of the cliffs.

"The area to the south of the path is dense with trees and shrubs – it would be almost impossible to search, especially in this fog," Fingal said.

"What if I search the coastal path, just in case she went that way? Maybe she got turned around trying to get back to the house, or was so upset that she went that way deliberately, but got lost?"

Fingal said he would go with Erik because it was dangerous, walking the path in the fog.

"I should go," Petra said. "I'm the one who upset her, after all." Fingal, Erik and Samuel protested, but Gill said it was the sensible option; after all, Fingal needed to wait at the house in case the police arrived.

Kitted out with head and hand torches and high visibility jackets, Petra and Erik set off on their search of the land to the east of the estate, along the coastal path. Just as they had done in the woods, they took it in turns calling out to Clodagh, and waiting for any response. Sound got sucked up into the fog, Petra knew, and she worried that they would be unable to hear Clodagh calling out to them. Despite the fact that there was zero visibility, Petra had a clear vision of Clodagh standing at the end of a tunnel of fog, waiting for them to reach her, trusting them to find her.

They searched the land roughly a mile and a half to the east before Erik suggested they turn back, since they couldn't hear or see anything. Petra didn't tell him about her vision, but it filled her with hope that Clodagh was safe, somewhere. She hoped so, because she was so cold - even through her many layers – that she didn't know how Clodagh could survive if she was lost and alone, out in the elements.

***

Fifteen minutes after they got back to Rothmore house, still shivering and clutching mugs of hot tea, the police arrived. They announced, sombrely, that they would need to speak to everyone, to build up a picture of what had happened in the run-up to Clodagh's disappearance. They asked Fingal and Jane if there was a private room they could use, which made Petra's heart thud so ferociously she was sure everyone could hear it.

Fingal was the first person to speak to the police. While he was out of the room, Petra's eyes were drawn to Jane, who didn't join in the group conversation. Her bottom lip quivered, and she stared down at the carpet. Samuel and Erik kept the conversation flowing, but Jane just stared into the fire, not even attempting to engage.

When Fingal came back, he said the police wanted to speak to Jane next. She rushed out of the room, looking like she might burst into tears. Fingal looked weary, and worried, but he at least did join in the conversation. He apologised to everyone, for the distress this was causing.

Gill shot Petra another dirty look. "There's no need for *you* to apologise to us, Fingal. I'm worried sick about what has happened to the poor girl. You were with the police for a long time – do they have any leads or theories?"

Fingal frowned, looking pensive. "They wanted me to show them the boat, and the beach. I suppose they'll tell everyone anyway, but they found a jumper on the beach that I'm fairly certain is Clodagh's. The strange thing is - I didn't see it down there earlier."

"It just doesn't make any sense that she would have taken the boat out," Samuel said. "Why would she do that? And why wouldn't she have taken her jumper with her?"

"This just doesn't make any sense. I don't see Clodagh getting into a boat, in the fog, no matter how upset she was." On this occasion, Petra fully agreed with Gill.

"Maybe I wasn't supposed to tell you about the jumper," Fingal said, looking apprehensive.

"Fingal, you have to know that none of us would harm Clodagh. We're all very fond of her." Samuel looked very sad, and Petra knew that he was trying his best to reassure Fingal, and her.

"I do know that," Fingal said, looking down at the ground, sadly.

***

Petra was the last to speak to the police. Samuel and Erik sat in the lounge with her until it was her turn, doing their best to keep her calm and relaxed. Gill had come back after her conversation with the police, carrying with her the self-importance of someone who had just told them everything they needed to know. She had not come back for moral support, Petra knew, but to hear what the others had to say about their own conversations, to glean every bit of information she could.

The interview was held in a formal room at the front of the house on the ground floor. Petra loved the casual sophistication of the guest lounge, and had imagined every room in Rothmore house was decorated in a similar elegant style. But this formal room spoke of another, less tasteful time in the Rothmore family's history. Or maybe it was just that – this room had been decorated by another, older generation of Rothmores, not by Jane and Fingal. The carpet was ruby red-coloured, likely expensive, certainly ostentatious. The furniture was elaborately ornate. Portraits lined every wall; people from the past stared down at her from all around.

She tried not to look nervously at the two male police officers, in their imposing black uniforms, sitting together on one of the overstuffed settees. She did not want to think about the last time two police officers had sat across from her. Then, their looks were compassionate; today, she saw something else in their eyes.

They started with the basics: her name, age, where she lived, why she had come to Rothmore house. They asked about her relationship with Clodagh, and she heard herself give too much detail. It just poured out of her, in a nervous torrent. They interrupted her, frequently, asking for more details or clarification. When she reached the point of telling them about the reading in the witches' prison, she stopped, and thought carefully about what she was going to say.

"I mean, I guess the others have told you what happened. I suggested that I could read my work in the prison, for extra impact, even though it was foggy. It was insensitive of me, I can see that now, but I had no idea Clodagh would be upset. I really didn't. I was shocked when she ran off."

"Why do you think she ran off?"

"She told me that she'd seen something – a vision – the night we went to Midhallow. I didn't even think about the possibility that she'd see it again in the prison, but after she ran away, I thought that must be what happened."

"And you were with her at the time, on Midhallow?" Petra nodded. "But you didn't see anything?"

"No."

"What did you do when she ran out of the prison?"

"I ran after her to apologise but I dropped my torch and couldn't catch up with her and then later, back here, I wanted to go and say sorry, but the others said to give her some space."

"Did she say anything to you about wanting to go out in the boat?"

"No."

The younger officer reached down to the floor, and lifted

up a pink jumper. "Do you recognise this jumper?"

"Yes, it's Clodagh's." Petra was confused. She had loved that jumper the moment she saw it, the soft pink boiled wool, and ivory piping along the seams. "But -."

"Yes?"

"Is that the jumper you found on the beach? Fingal told us that you'd found one." The officers nodded. "It's just – when we went into her room to see if she was in there, I saw it hanging on the back of her chair."

"And you're sure it was this jumper?"

"Yes, unless she has two of them."

The younger officer took notes, while the older one kept up his intense eye contact with Petra. At last he asked, "Did you have other arguments – any disagreements - with Miss Sullivan, before she went missing?"

"No, none. I thought we were getting on very well, until the incident. Which I regret deeply, by the way. I feel terrible about it."

"And you've had no contact with her since she ran off during the reading?"

"None. I wrote her a note to say I was sorry and slipped it under her door, but I'm not sure if she saw it."

The younger officer lifted up a second item of clothing. "Have you seen this before?"

"Yes, that's my scarf. Where did you find that?"

"When did you last wear this?"

"I wore it the night we went to Midhallow, because Fingal said we needed warm clothes. Did you find that on the beach?" The officer nodded. "I had it with me the next day, because I was outside for a long time. I don't remember if I wore it, but I'm sure I put it in my bag. You know, just in case. It doesn't make any sense that you found it on the beach today."

Neither officer said anything immediately, but both continued to stare at Petra. Finally, the older officer asked, "You're sure you weren't with Miss Sullivan on the beach at any time last night or today?"

"I'm sure."

"And you're sure you saw the pink jumper in Miss Sullivan's room?"

"I'm sure."

"And you have no idea how your scarf ended up on the beach, with Miss Sullivan's jumper?"

"No idea."

The officers were absorbed in their notes, and did not say anything for a few minutes. Anxious, wanting nothing more than to be told she could leave the room, Petra looked at the portraits of Rothmores past. The portrait on the wall directly above where the officers sat stared down at her. She realised with a start that she had seen the subject of the painting before: it was Lady Rothmore, who had been accused as one of the Midhallow witches.

When the officers said at last that she could leave, she bolted out of the room, pulling the door so hard behind her that it made a loud cracking noise as it closed.

***

With all of the interviews finished, the officers compared notes, and thoughts. Four people had looked inside the missing person's room, and two of them mentioned that they had seen the same jumper that was found on the beach draped across a chair in her room. How had the jumper got from her room to the beach? If Clodagh was coming and going without the others seeing her somehow, *why* had she taken the jumper to the beach?

Two people identified a third person who they thought might have something to do with Clodagh's disappearance. More than just by giving a reading in the old prison and frightening her, they suggested this person's involvement might have been more serious. One was fairly robust in her accusations; the other was more tentative, but still clearly pointing a finger.

That person's scarf had been found on the beach, along with the jumper, yet she had told them that the last place she had worn it was not the beach.

Three people – all male – asserted that this person had done nothing more sinister than hold back information about what Clodagh had seen that night on Midhallow. They also pointed out that she had been asked to keep it a secret. With hindsight, they believed that they should have refused to go to the old prison for the reading. But, at the time, they had thought it was a good idea - were excited about it, even.

The person herself took responsibility for upsetting Clodagh, although she said she had no idea that the setting would trigger another vision.

The facts were not at all clear. The jumper and the boat were confusing. Opinions were split about Petra. She *had* looked rattled towards the end of their interview, but why?

CHAPTER 18

Back in the guest lounge, Petra braced herself for an onslaught of questions from Gill, but she merely looked up in disgust when Petra walked in the room, and then looked away again. Of course, Petra realised, the police had shown everyone her scarf, just as they'd shown them Clodagh's jumper. Did everyone know that it was hers? It was dark when they had gone to Midhallow, so perhaps not.

And yet the fact was that *someone* had taken her scarf and left it on the beach, to make it look like she had been there with Clodagh. She'd been shocked, when the police had lifted up her scarf. Why hadn't Fingal mentioned that a jumper *and* a scarf were found on the beach? How had someone got hold of her scarf, anyway, in order to plant it on the beach? She remembered the day she had come back from the prison, so hungry that she had left her bag and the blanket outside the guest lounge. If her scarf was in her bag, had someone taken it out? But that made no sense – no one knew that Clodagh would go missing, so no one would have taken her scarf to plant as evidence.

Unless – she had dropped her scarf, or it had fallen out of her bag, and someone had picked it up, intending to give it back to her. The scarf might then have become an opportunistic way to put her in the frame.

But who would do that? She looked around at the others. She could not believe that Erik or Samuel would do it. Gill was making it very clear that she blamed Petra for Clodagh's disappearance. But would she go so far as to stage the scene on the beach? Petra didn't think so; Gill had a problem with *her*, not with Clodagh.

Petra did not want to sit there a minute longer. But, just when she had decided to go back to her room, Jane appeared with plates and cutlery, followed a minute later by Fingal, carrying a large dish of curry, and another of fragrant rice.

No one said very much during dinner. No one said *anything* about Clodagh. They talked about the fog, and said they hoped it would lift soon. They all praised Jane's curry, which they agreed was completely delicious and just the kind of comfort food they needed. Petra ate a small amount of dinner, thanked Jane, and excused herself. She was back in her room before nine o'clock.

***

Petra channelled her worries about Clodagh into searching for any information she could find about her online. Oddly for a woman in her early twenties, Clodagh had no social media presence Petra could find. There were no hits for her name whatsoever.

Was Clodagh Sullivan not her real name? If that was the case, how could Petra find out who she really was?

She remembered a photograph that she had taken of the two of them, sitting in the sand at the cove beach. She did a reverse image search, and found two photographs that were most certainly of Clodagh. In both of them, she was smiling and standing next to a handsome man, who looked so much like Clodagh they could have been twins. In one of the photos, standing on the other side of her, was a woman who might be described as Clodagh's opposite: tall, willowy, with long blond hair, her serious face in contrast to that of Clodagh and her maybe-twin. She did searches of both of the people in the photos. Petra found no matches for the woman, but she did find a match for the man: Danny Sullivan, listed as co-owner with Paul McKinley of McSullivan property development. There was a photo of Danny on the website. It was definitely the same man.

Petra wasted no time in emailing Danny at the address listed on the website:

My name is Petra McCarlin and I am spending a week at a writing retreat on the Rothmore estate. Your sister was here, too, but she's disappeared. I don't want to alarm you, but I think she ran away. And I think it might be my fault. Please message me as soon as you see this. She might be in danger.

It was after ten o'clock. If he wasn't checking – or responding to – work email this time of night, she would have to wait until morning. There was nothing else she could do, it seemed, but wait, and hope she had struck the right note of urgent insistence and personal culpability in the email. There was no right way to send the kind of message she knew she'd needed to send, and she hadn't meant to sensationalise the situation. She was telling the truth about the danger. With every minute that passed, she was more and more convinced that something had happened – or was about to happen – to Clodagh.

Less than ten minutes after sending the message, she received a reply:

Hello Petra. I'm on the other side of the world at the moment, but I've asked someone back home to make contact with you. Thank you for reaching out to me about my sister.

Petra stared at the words. The email was matter-of-fact, and showed that he was taking it seriously, but there was something almost blasé about what he had written. Maybe Clodagh and her brother were not close. But, if that was the case, why did they look like they were in the photographs? Had they had a falling out since then? And why was Danny on the other side of the world, if he co-owned a property company in Edinburgh?

It was back to a waiting game, until the other person made contact with her.

A bit before two o'clock in the morning, Petra abandoned

all hope that the person would email her that night. She was too tired to stay awake a minute longer. She told herself she had to get a few hours of sleep, and then be ready if the person contacted her early in the day.

Her alarm went off at six. Disappointed, she saw that there were no new messages. She had a quick, hot shower, and was happy to see that the fog had lifted and the sun was coming up – red and hazy on the eastern horizon. She made a cup of coffee and ate a few shortbread fingers, staring alternately at her phone and the view out the window.

Petra was in no rush to see Gill, but she was going stir crazy in her room and needed a change of scenery. When she got to the guest lounge, she was relieved to see Samuel, drinking a cappuccino. She made one too, and joined him at the table. Petra was just about to ask if there was any news about Clodagh, when Jane appeared.

"Good morning. I was just checking to see if anyone was awake yet – I know the fog has lifted, but I thought it might be a good morning for porridge."

"That would hit the spot!" Samuel enthused, and Petra said that she would love some, too. Jane looked slightly less-than-pleased to see her there, but at least Gill wasn't there to cast more eye-daggers at her.

Jane came back a short time later with a bowl of the creamiest porridge Petra had ever eaten, some warm apple compote, and a little jug of salted caramel sauce.

"These are like little mouthfuls of heaven," Samuel said, scoffing the contents of his bowl. "Di-vine."

Petra nodded her agreement. Samuel gave her a sad smile and said, "Maybe there will be good news today."

Petra set her spoon down. "I really hope so."

Samuel excused himself, telling Petra that he was going to try to write, since mornings were when his head was at its clearest.

She checked her phone: still no message. Petra finished her coffee, cold by that point, and made a decision: the sun was out, and she was going to emulate Erik and have a quick swim in the sea. It was partly for the shock of the cold, she told herself, which might also kick her brain into gear and allow her to work, while they waited for news of Clodagh. But the icy cold water would also serve as self-inflicted punishment, and one that she deserved, for the stupid decision to do the reading in the old prison.

***

Walking back through the woods after her swim in the sea, Petra's head felt so cold it was like it belonged to someone else. Her thoughts were slow and juddery, almost painfully slow as she tried to make sense of what she was thinking.

Back in her room, clutching a hot cup of tea, she could feel her thoughts loosen up, like dipping a warm spoon into a jar of honey. When her mother had gone under the water in the burn, she wondered, had her head been that cold? It had been the middle of October when she died, and the water would have been icy. Strangely, the thought of it comforted Petra, that her mother's brain had been too groggy to register what was happening to her. She had never before thought that her mother had died peacefully, and without fear, but she wanted to carry this hope forward.

She checked her phone: still no message.

She sat at the desk, and wrote and wrote. It was difficult, reliving the images she had seen the day before of Lilias, Margaret and Lady Rothmore, but she had to, she knew. When she had finished, she realised how much she wanted to share this with Clodagh. Not just the story of the Midhallow witches, but also to be honest with her about how these stories came to her. *It's not just you*, she wanted to say to her, *I see things too. It doesn't mean we're crazy – just tuned-in.*

She lit a candle, closed her eyes, and chanted words of protection and of hope, asking that Clodagh be kept safe from harm. Whether it was hope or something more, Petra could feel that Clodagh was not very far away, almost as though a thick cord bound the two of them together.

She opened her eyes just in time to see a Police Scotland car arrive. Her heart fluttered: had they found Clodagh? Was she safe? She did not know what the protocol was in these situations, but did not think it was appropriate to run downstairs and ask. The police would speak with Jane and Fingal, she figured, and any news would come to her through them.

She checked her phone: still no message.

She left her room just before noon, hoping that Jane or Fingal – or both – would be waiting for them with news. As she approached the guest lounge she heard voices – one belonged to Gill, and although she was speaking quietly, Petra could hear her say, "I just know she did *something*! Why was her scarf with Clodagh's jumper if she wasn't with her? She's been lying to all of us!"

The low, deep rumble of Samuel's voice followed, the words indistinguishable. Petra was turning around to leave, when she came face-to-face with Erik.

"Decided you aren't hungry after all?"

"Something like that." Petra tried to smile, but couldn't manage it.

"Is everything okay?"

"I just – I know that some people blame me for what happened but I –."

"Hey – you haven't done anything wrong. It's okay, we'll get lunch later, when the coast is clear. This is going to sound really egotistical, but would you like to come and have another look at the exhibition with me?"

They walked in silence, until they got to the exhibition room. Erik switched on the lights, and asked Petra to follow him, over to a stand with a poem about one of the Finmen. "You see this poem? This is an important one, because I wrote it after months and months of not being able to write. I mean, not even a word."

Petra looked at him in surprise. "It was after Lena's accident. You could say that the poetry pipe – well the whole *word* pipe, actually – was blocked up. I couldn't think of anything to write. I felt like a fraud, accepting their offer to come here, when I was no longer writing."

He took a deep breath, staring at Fingal's sculpture. "But then I came here, and went to Midhallow with Fingal and had the idea for the poems. I wrote this one first, very slowly. And then I wrote the others, more quickly each time."

"The poetry pipe was unblocked."

"Exactly! Grief does this to us, and sadness." He looked at Petra, compassionately. "For you, and for Clodagh, you've been the guardians of the words that you wanted to write, but couldn't. The pipe has opened for you, but not yet for Clodagh. I think she is working through some things in her life that are unimaginably difficult."

Petra raised her eyebrows, encouraging him to say more. "What I mean is, if you had set out to harm Clodagh that would have been one thing. But you didn't. We don't know why Clodagh ran away. All we can do is hope that she will come back to us, safely."

Petra nodded. She was relieved, and grateful to Erik for making her feel better. She realised that he also believed that Clodagh ran away, not that she had been abducted or had come to harm. "Thank you, Erik. You know, I have a sense that Clodagh isn't very far away. I hope she's safe, and hasn't come to any harm."

She hesitated a moment, and then she told him about her message to Clodagh's brother, and his reply.

"But you haven't heard from this other person yet?"

"Not yet. I can't imagine why not – unless they haven't seen Danny's message yet."

"Are you going to tell Fingal and Jane?"

"I will – as soon as the other person makes contact and I know more."

"Let's hope you hear from them. Soon."

"Erik, I hope you won't mind but I'm going to take a rain check for lunch. There's something I need to do."

His look was full of concern as he told her to take care of herself, and watched her walk away.

CHAPTER 19

Although Petra was concerned that the car wouldn't start up again, it did so without much protest and she drove back along the gravel drive, and away from the Rothmore estate. Early on a Thursday afternoon the coast road was mercifully quiet, and she tootled along with frequent glances out over the sea as she drove through the small village high streets, until she reached North Berwick, where her father's care facility was.

She pulled the car into one of the tiny spaces, and walked into the building, bracing herself for the onslaught of smells that never changed from visit to visit, a co-mingling of odours that no one wanted to breathe in: gravy gone bad, unwashed bodies and hair, human waste. A new, annoyed-looking receptionist was at the desk, and she made Petra show identification before checking her father's record, and telling Petra he would most likely be in his room.

When Petra knocked on his door and stepped inside, her heart caught at the sight of her father sitting in his wheelchair, watching TV. His eyes shifted to Petra, and she saw something in them – happiness, she hoped.

She kissed his cheek, which someone had shaved recently, and said, "Hi Dad. It's good to see you."

His hand jerked, and he reached it out and placed it on Petra's. He grunted something that although Petra did not strictly understand, she could guess at.

"I've missed you, too. You'll never guess where I've been this week." He grunted, an inquisitive sound. "I've been at a writer's retreat." His left eye widened, slightly. "At the Rothmore estate." Another grunt. "Aunt Alice paid for it."

She wanted to tell him what she was writing about, but did not want to upset him. "It's good to be getting back to doing what I love. I've never told you this, but someone stole my under-graduate dissertation and published it as his own work." His fingers fluttered against hers, and his eyes narrowed. "It kind of sent me into a downward spiral. But Aunt Alice gave me a pep talk and I'm feeling better. I really want this."

His eyes were glassy and watery as he stared at her, and Petra tried to guess at all of the unspoken words between them. She longed to open up to him about what had happened with Clodagh, and Gill, and the police, but it wasn't fair to subject him to even more worry. She wondered if he could see it in her eyes, the disappointment in herself, the shame, the confusion. Petra had never asked her father if he thought she had some-thing to do with her mother's death. They had never had that conversation. *She* believed it, so she believed that he must, too. What thoughts ran through his head, in the many years since his stroke: was he angry, did he think it was history repeating itself and Petra'd had something to do with his accident, too?

Only on her darkest days did Petra wonder whether her father wished that he had died, too. When Erik had told her about his wife, she thought about her father. He did not scream at her when she came to visit, but he should have. He looked at her, tenderly, and she did not deserve it.

Petra felt a sudden, unexpected rush of tears. "I want to make you proud of me, Dad. You've been waiting a long time."

He squeezed her hand, and she lifted it to her lips, then pressed her forehead onto the leathery skin on the back of his hand.

***

When Petra left her father, she drove south, putting even greater distance between herself and Rothmore. She followed the coast road south, to the tiny former fishing village she'd spent the best weeks of her childhood summers in – Eastmouth. She parked the car in the small gravelled area adjacent to the steep wooden steps that led down to the white sandy beach, deserted like it had been nearly every time she'd visited in the past. Half way down the beach was a small hideaway where the rock face was interrupted. Petra squinted and could see her younger self there, inspecting her beach finds of the day along with her one true friend from those early years – Maggie.

Every summer, Petra's parents rented the small cottage that was attached to the one Maggie and her mother lived in all year round. Maggie's mother, Jean, rarely stepped outside of the cottage. She was a small, pale, pinched woman, who always made young Petra feel awkward. With hindsight, Petra knew that Jean had most likely been depressed, anxious, and afraid of social contact. Maggie was, in effect, her carer – she bought groceries, ran errands, and served as her mother's sole companion. She was home-schooled, and rarely came into contact with other children her age. During the one week of the year they were together, Maggie asked Petra endless questions about school and, as she stared intently with her pale, gaunt face and saucer eyes - thirsty for information about a world that was closed to her - Petra felt she had no choice but to embellish the truth. She couldn't bear to tell Maggie that school was a living hell.

Most of the time, though, Maggie was happy to do the talking. She devised elaborate games and explained them to Petra with great care and attention. She shared endless tales about her daily beach adventures, which often involved catching and killing fish and shellfish; she had a clinical approach to her accounts of procuring food for their meals which Petra both admired and was disgusted by. Even though she knew Maggie didn't have an easy life, Petra envied her life by the sea, and especially the school-free part. It was Maggie who first showed Petra the joys of beach combing, teaching her about the ethics of what was acceptable to take away, and what should be left there. She ate shellfish, but said no one should take their shells away purely for decoration, as stealing the creatures' homes resulted in their unnecessary deaths.

Maggie's domestic and caring responsibilities meant that she carried an inbuilt mental clock with her at all times, and she never left her mother alone for longer than an hour or two. Petra noticed that Maggie never talked about her mother; instead, she learned about Maggie's caring commitments from her own mother.

Those lazy, languid days on the beach with Maggie – often, they were the only people there – sustained Petra through the remaining weeks of the year. They were kindred spirits, two lonely girls whose imaginations broke them out of the confines of social isolation when they weren't together. When they were, their joy bubbled up and spilled over, and the air around them crackled with their energy.

When she was at the cottage, Petra wouldn't allow herself to think about the last day of the holiday. Damp, grey sadness descended over both cottages as Petra and her parents packed up and said their goodbyes to Maggie and her mother. Her parents were kind, but Petra had never understood why they never allowed her to visit Maggie outside of the holiday week. Eastmouth was only an hour away from their home, but they made the journey only once a year.

***

Petra walked the full length of the beach, to the impassable cliff face at its southern tip and back, her memories so clear and sharp it was as though she could see Maggie and her younger self wading into the water, scooping to collect treasures, their delighted cries ringing out. Once she'd climbed the steps, Petra lingered only for a moment outside of the cottages, wondering if Maggie and her mother still lived there. She imagined knocking on the door, Maggie opening it and recognising Petra instantly, welcoming her with tears of joy. Petra feared the truth was Maggie wouldn't recognise her, or wouldn't respond with any enthusiasm even if she did. They'd spent their last week together the summer before Petra started high school, when Petra still had hope that she'd find new friends there. As far as she knew, Maggie didn't know why Petra and her family had never returned to the cottage. A ripple of pain coursed through her as she imagined telling Maggie everything. As much as she wanted to see her old friend, Petra couldn't open up that particular old wound. With a final, mournful look at the cottages, she said goodbye to her cherished childhood friend, and walked back to the car.

She checked her phone, but there was still no message about Clodagh. Suddenly bone weary, Petra decided to take a quick nap, and then look for somewhere to buy some food and park the car for the night. She climbed into the back seat, curled up and draped her long cardigan over her body like a blanket.

She slept soundly for two hours, until a fierce storm blew in from the west, bringing with it gales that rocked the tiny car. The storm lasted for hours and, although she considered driving inland to a sheltered place, she was transfixed by the motion of the clouds as they raced across the ever-changing hues of the sky. When it grew calm again, Petra closed her eyes, but slept fitfully. She was worried about Clodagh, and frustrated by her inertness. She watched as the sky turn a deep blue, then a dappled soft grey, and when the sun poked up over the horizon, she took in the glorious view of the sunrise over Eastmouth, which still echoed with joyful moments from Petra's childhood.

***

At Rothmore, the others realised Petra was missing late Friday afternoon, when Fingal was trying to round everyone up for a house meeting. Petra didn't answer when he knocked at her door and when he asked if anyone had seen her, Erik reported that she had left, because she had to take care of something. She had not said what it was, and he had not asked, he said.

A quick check of the car parking area confirmed that Petra's car was not there.

"This is further proof, isn't it?" Gill asked indignantly. "You should let the police know that she's scarpered, Fingal."

Fingal cleared his throat, looked at Jane, who was wringing her hands, and said, "About that. We have something important to tell you. Um - this is a little delicate. The police were here this morning. Clodagh's parents haven't heard from her, and there's no evidence she's gone back to her flat in Edinburgh."

"Oh, dear God," Gill said, her voice catching.

"They also wanted to talk to us about the circumstances surrounding her disappearance, about certain – um – inconsistencies. There is no evidence that Clodagh was in the boat after she disappeared."

"But what about the fact that her jumper was found on the beach?" Gill asked.

Fingal looked at Jane, who was staring at the floor, looking close to tears. Fingal said, "You see, we need to apologise to you. When we found out that Clodagh went missing we had what can only be called a lapse of reason, and panicked. We untied the boat and let it drift to make it look like she'd taken it out. And we left her jumper on the beach to make it seem as though she'd just been there."

There was a sharp intake of breath, from Gill. "You mean you staged her disappearance? Why on earth would you do that? We thought the poor girl had drowned!"

"We can't tell you how sorry we are," Fingal said sadly. "We hope you'll be able to forgive us."

"You have to understand," Jane added, "that we have worked so hard to build this haven for writers. Something like this – well it can undo years of hard work." Although Fingal had sounded sincerely apologetic, Jane's tone leaned more towards self-pity.

"Someone we care about went missing," Samuel said quietly. "And you deceived us. And more to the point, you led the police to believe that certain things were true. The whole time, a young woman has been missing. And now a *second* one is gone. Did you make it look like she'd been there with Clodagh by putting her scarf on the beach, too?"

Jane said nothing. Fingal answered for her. "It was a foolish thing to do, and we apologise. But now that we know Clodagh wasn't out in the boat, or down on the beach, we can start to focus on where she might have gone. She might -."

All eyes were on Jane. Fingal realised what he had just admitted, which told the others that Jane had been solely responsible for planting the evidence, even though Fingal was now sharing the blame.

"Okay, so the police are going to redirect their search," Samuel said. "Is there anything we can do to help find Clodagh in the meantime?"

"Unless you have any new information to share, I don't think so," Fingal said.

Gill fizzed with angry energy. "So that's it? You put us in the centre of this huge charade, and all you can say for yourselves is sorry? I think this is disgraceful. You've been treating us all like fools."

"We're very sorry that you feel that way," Fingal said, his head bowed. "Of course, we can understand why you'd be angry, and disappointed in us."

"And very worried about Clodagh," Samuel said. "And Petra."

"Of course, we're all very worried about Clodagh. And now Petra."

"Huh!" Gill huffed, crossed her arms, and let out another angry sigh.

***

The ancient oaks on the Rothmore estate had witnessed centuries of the folly and selfishness of human nature. They were not surprised by it and merely observed, that night, the five people who remained inside Rothmore house reacting, in their unique ways, to the news that Jane had done her best to make it appear as though Clodagh had left of her own accord.

Jane stayed in the kitchen, from the time Fingal admitted what had happened to the others until the small hours of the morning. She baked an enormous collection of tarts – both savoury and sweet – which she put in the freezer once they had cooled. Rolling out the dough and lacing the threads of pastry together in a delicate act of lattice work was soothing, she had always felt. The smells filling the kitchen – rhubarb and apple in brown sugar, spinach, dill and cheese and caramelised onions – lifted her mood. Baking rubbed away some of her restlessness, and her self-righteousness. Up until the moment when the final tarts came out of the oven, she had been angry with everyone else but herself. She blamed Petra for driving Clodagh away with her ridiculous notion of reading her work in the prison, Clodagh for running off to god-knows-where and not telling anyone, and Fingal for telling the others what had happened.

Long after midnight, she slipped into bed next to Fingal's warm body, and was filled with worry about where Clodagh was, and what had happened to her. Images of what she had done to try to stage Clodagh's disappearance flitted through her mind, which she watched as though it was a film about someone else – some nasty, lamentable person.

She didn't sleep that night but she felt no self-pity because she didn't deserve sleep, after everything she'd done.

Fingal kept busy in his studio all evening, and had only gone to bed minutes before Jane. Wide awake, he heard her deep, quavering breaths, and knew that she was trying to hold back tears. He had forgiven her already, and felt pity for his wife. She had acted terribly, it was true, but it was a terrible thing, when a young person leaves and never returns, and Jane had never recovered from the loss of their only child. Jane had told the others that she had acted to protect their business, and Fingal knew that this was in part true; but Jane had once suffered a loss whose scars would never heal, and Clodagh's disappearance had sliced the wounds wide open again.

He knew that he should reach out to comfort his wife – he

could move his arm an inch, lay his hand on hers, and let her take whatever comfort she could from his touch. But he could not bring himself to touch her – not yet; instead, he hoped his silent forgiveness would somehow work its way through the space between them.

Gill was raging, still. Samuel had provided a calm, patient ear for a couple of hours, until he incurred some of her rage by saying, "I'm angry too, Gill. We're just going to have to let this go. It's bad, but it's happened. Being this angry won't help bring them back."

Gill was indignant. If she wanted to be angry, she would bloody well be angry – it was her right, she told him. And Samuel could stop telling her what to do, by the way.

She continued to pace, and rage, in the guest lounge. Samuel went to his room, where he tried to distract himself from worrying about the young women by working on his book. But it was in vain. How could they have lost her? And where had she gone?

Erik knew part of Clodagh's secret. She had told him, during one of their meetings, that she was meant to finish a manuscript she was under contract to write while she was at Rothmore, and then start the sea witch story. She had deadlines she didn't think she would be able to keep. But, she had said, there was a serious crisis in her family and she was so distracted by it that she could not concentrate on her work. He had told her that deadlines could be shifted, but crises could not. That had made her cry, and they had sat together, on the beach, as she cried for her family and he stared out to sea, hoping that this enchanted beach would work a little bit of its magic on him, and bring his wife back to her former self. It was what he hoped for, every day, and he was not ashamed for believing that it might come true.

CHAPTER 20

The next morning, Petra's car started with only minor protest and, when she stopped at a food truck in a layby heading back north along the coast, she left it running while they fried her an egg and stuck it in a bun, because she knew it was running on a wing and a prayer. She ate her breakfast in seven substantial bites and washed it down with hot tea, then was back on the road quickly, before her stomach could protest.

After her online search for information about Clodagh, she'd carried out a different search, one she'd forbidden herself from even thinking about for more than seven years: she looked up her high school tormentors. After the night that her revenge spells went wrong, she had not allowed herself to think about what might have happened to those girls, good or bad. Any time she pictured Bethany sneering at her on Princes Street, she pushed the image out of her mind. Bethany's co-ringleader was a tall, willowy girl named Kirstie McCulloch. Cruelty had not dimmed her beauty at the age of twelve, and when Petra found a photograph of present-day Kirstie online, she saw that she was still beautiful.

Her profile showed that she lived in a small village just a mile east of the Rothmore estate, in a distinctive-looking large white house with a wrought-iron balcony on the first floor. Petra knew the village, knew it was tiny, and figured she could find the house without much difficulty.

She drove into the village, and found the house in under two minutes. It was just off the main street, on a narrow road leading down to the beach. She knew it would be too conspicuous on such a quiet street to leave her car running, so parked it a few doors down from Kirstie's house, close enough to be able to see anyone coming or going.

It was a beautiful morning. The sun lit up the white-painted houses on the street with a warming rosy glow, and burned moisture off the grass in little wisps of steam. With the window rolled down, birdsong drifted into the car, and Petra breathed in the fresh, crisp smell of the sea. She was surprised by how calm she felt, this close to an encounter with the person who'd caused her so much pain all those years ago.

Just before nine o'clock, the front door to the house opened, and a woman and a young girl emerged. Kirstie was yoga-toned in her skinny jeans and red silk floaty top. The little girl looked so much like Kirstie that she had to be her daughter. She skipped down the front steps, and Petra could hear them talking as they walked along the front path, hand in hand.

"Mum, what's a wamhole?"

"I don't know – somewhere to put your wams?"

"No, it's not a joke Mum - I want *you* to tell *me* what it is. Jamie Ritchie told me yesterday to stick it up my wamhole."

"Well, I wouldn't repeat it to anyone else. I think it could be something Jamie Ritchie made up. It doesn't sound very nice anyway."

"Has anyone ever called you a wamhole, Mum?"

They climbed into a tank-like black Range Rover, and drove off towards the direction of the high street. Petra did a quick three-point turn, using Kirstie's driveway, and followed them.

The Range Rover ploughed its way along the coast road, heading east, towards North Berwick. Petra willed the old, tattered clunker of a car to keep going. The Range Rover pulled off the road into a car park near West Bay beach and Petra followed, parking on the opposite side, and watched as Kirstie and her daughter walked quickly towards a group of people – children and a few adults – on the beach. Kirstie's daughter went inside a striped beach tent, and came out a few minutes later in a wetsuit. The adults led the children into the water, and Petra watched them learn to paddleboard. Kirstie's daughter had good upper body strength and balance, and Petra watched her for several minutes, impressed. She was in awe of the children generally, as she watched them master the cold waves of the North Sea.

After a little while Petra got out of the car and, to avoid drawing attention to herself, walked along the beach, glancing at the children but trying not to stare. She heard their excited voices out on the water, shouting encouragement and praise to each other. After a few minutes, she watched Kirstie walk back towards a coffee truck on the shore road, engage in animated conversation with the kiosk owner, then carry a large tray of coffees back to the group. What kind of person was Kirstie now, Petra wondered – kind and generous, or governed by appearance and status? If she ever thought about her behaviour in the past, did she regret any of it, or was she proud of the power she'd held over others? When it was happening, all those years ago, Petra had wanted nothing more than to fade away, to blend into the background so that Kirstie and the other girls stopped seeing her, stopped making fun of her. But as the years passed and she assumed that they were untainted by any thought or concern about what they'd done to her, she had a strong urge to rise up from the swell like a huge sea creature and demand that they see her, see what had happened to her because of them.

After an hour passed, the children loudly splashed their way back to the sand, and took turns going into the beach tent to get changed out of their wetsuits. There was something so dignified about the way they stood in their tiny seal-like wetsuits, talking to each other in adrenaline-rushed, excited voices. For reasons she didn't quite understand, Petra found it deeply moving.

Kirstie and her daughter skip-walked back to the Range Rover, and Petra hurried back to her car, hoping to catch snippets of their conversation. But she was too far away, and their words were lost.

The Range Rover drove back along the coast road, in the direction of Kirstie's house, and pulled into a diagonal parking space in front of a bakery on the high street of the neighbouring village. Petra cruised past and parked further up the street, then watched until Kirstie and her daughter emerged, each carrying pastries wrapped in paper. They crossed the high street, Kirstie's daughter skipping as she walked towards the play park across the street, where a small group of children played animatedly.

Petra kept a safe distance, watching Kirstie from behind the trunk of a large oak tree. She asked herself what she really wanted from Kirstie in this present moment: recognition that she had been cruel and nasty; awareness that she had incited horrible behaviour from others; acknowledgement that her actions had changed Petra and her family irrevocably; an apology?

Petra had sought retribution once, after her run-in with Bethany, to horrible effect. She wasn't interested in trying it again. She felt an urge to confront Kirstie as she stood eating her pastry, unaware that she was being watched. Petra imagined different scenarios in her mind, and how each might play out. Every one of them involved the unavoidable fact that Kirstie's daughter would witness any confrontation, would hear the truth about what her mother had done to Petra all those years ago.

As clear as a bell she heard Isobel's voice, telling her that choosing the light was always the difficult choice, that it was easier to let the dark take hold of your emotions and behaviour. She knew that Isobel was right. And, she told herself, it was always possible that Kirstie regretted what she had done to Petra. She might be a completely different person now.

In the end, Petra chose to stay in the shadows, to continue being the voiceless shape from Kirstie's past; in other words, she chose the light.

**

She was grateful that her car started up again, and she nosed it out into the lazy traffic on the high street, and headed south, inland. She had never gone back to the house she had grown up in, not once after she had moved away to live with her aunt. Her father had wanted her to come and see him, before he had lost the house, but she could never bear the thought of seeing the place – the exact spot – where her mother had died. And then, after a few months living with her aunt, the phone conversations she had with her father confirmed what she had feared: he was drinking - a lot by the sounds of it - and she did not want to be in that house with him when he was drunk, especially. With his filters down, she had no idea what he might say, or what he might accuse her of.

Petra didn't know what had happened to the house, who had lived in it these past sixteen years. She drove past the neighbouring farm, which had belonged to the McManus family when she was a child, and was pleased to see their name plate still affixed to the front gate. But the black-faced sheep that had once roamed their land had been replaced by goats – and two llamas. Someone had cut the tall beech hedge that had once shrouded their house down, and as Petra drew near she had a full view of the house, and right down the garden to the burn.

She had not expected to see it from the road, and her body jolted as her brain registered what she was looking at. She'd seen it in her dreams for years, but she never thought she would see the real thing again. Like a shadow from the past she saw her mother, standing right by the water's edge, and heard her singing. So much of her mother's life was spent in that very spot, and it was where she'd died.

The apple trees still stood on the land across the burn, and the pears. Petra's eyes welled up when she saw them, because her mother had loved those fruit trees so much. The garden looked well-loved and well-tended. A small plastic orange swing-set stood on the grass near the house, and it made Petra happy to think of a child – or children - living there.

Did *they* see her mother, she wondered, the people who lived there now? Was she still there, on the land she had loved so well, watching over the current tenants, trying to keep them safe?

Petra drove slowly past the house, and pulled into a passing place on the road where it curved behind the house, so she could sit and watch. It was a minor road through the countryside, not very well-travelled, so it seemed safe enough to park and sit for a while. She pressed her forehead against the driver's side window, and drifted off to sleep.

Something woke her, jerked her body into consciousness. The heat from the sun blazed through the window onto her face, and the inside of her mouth was chalky. She looked over at the garden – *her* garden – but it was still empty.

She realised it was her phone, buzzing with a message:

It's Ruth – Danny gave me your number. Have been at a silent retreat – no phones! Ring me back when you can.

Petra saw then that she had just missed a call. With fumbling fingers, she dialled back.

"Hi – Petra?"

"Yes, thanks for getting back to me. Listen, I'll get right to the point. I'm worried about Clodagh. She ran away from the retreat."

There was a pause, and Ruth said, "I think I know where she is. She's not answering her phone, but I think she's okay."

"Really? Would – would it be okay to tell me where she is? I want to apologise to her. I'm the reason she ran away."

"I'm sorry but I can't tell you - I promised her. But I don't think you should worry that it's your fault. She likely just needed some time to herself."

"Something bad happened to her – she was scared, and she ran off. I should have known it might happen. And I'm feeling more and more convinced that she needs help."

The pitch of Ruth's voice changed as she asked, "Why do you say that?"

"It's just that – I've got a bad feeling about it."

Ruth sighed. "Okay, listen, where are you – at Rothmore House?"

"No, I've left, but I'm not very far away from there."

"Can we meet there in – say half an hour?"

Petra did not want to go back to Rothmore, but she knew of a place just off the main road nearby where she could ditch her car and wait for Ruth, and said she would send her directions. Before she drove away Petra looked, for a long moment, over at the garden that had been the centre of her world for so many years. She could almost see herself there, in that special place where she had been able to play and think and imagine and just *be*, the place where she found peace after another lonely, sometimes hostile, day at school. She could definitely see her mother there, and had a fleeting but comforting thought that her mother had possibly only ever felt she belonged in that place, too, and that her spirit – her life force, as she had called it – was suspended there, forever.

PART TWO

THE COTTAGE

CHAPTER 21

Clodagh ran.

Her own ghostly face loomed up at her through the fog, and she ran out of the witches' prison and back to the house. Terrified, and afraid she was losing her mind, she cursed Petra for making them all traipse out to the prison in the fog. Was Clodagh the only one who could smell sulphur in the air mixed with something older, like dried blood creeping up from the ground? The fog was so dense it had clung to everything – her hair, clothes, face. It reminded her of a child's hand, soaked and sticky, pressing up against her cheek. She had hoped, in vain, that the fog would shroud any hallucinations, but she hadn't been so lucky.

The first time it had happened, when she and Petra had arrived at the camp on Midhallow, cold swirls of air had reached right under her skin. As they stood there, Clodagh's head filled with the sound of hushed voices all speaking at the same time, the words inaudible. It had frightened her, even as she tried to tune in to what they were saying. She thought they were trying to tell her something, speaking across the centuries. As she strained to listen, she saw the apparition of a girl, lying on a rough blanket on the ground, slowly lifting her head ever so slightly up, and reaching out her hand. Quickly and violently, another hand swatted it back down onto the blanket. The apparition looked exactly like Clodagh had as a girl. She recognised the hand, too, by its wedding ring – her mother's gold band, engraved with her name and that of Clodagh's father.

Clodagh never should have agreed to go along to the

witches' prison. Every instinct screamed at her to stay away. But she had gone, and the apparition had appeared again, lying on the floor of one of the cells, and again lifting her head and hand towards Clodagh, straining in obvious pain. The girl turned to look at her, with a face just like her own, only even worse than the first time, because the girl was levitating - like something out of a horror film.

And this time, the hand wearing her mother's ring closed over the girl's face, smothering her.

When Petra had told Clodagh that it was not uncommon to see visions in places where terrible things once occurred, she hoped it might alleviate her concerns about her own sanity, after what had happened on Midhallow. But after the second vision, she was convinced that something was seriously wrong with her. Seeing and hearing things that were not actually there could not be the sign of a healthy mind, she feared.

Afterwards, when Erik knocked at the door and asked her gently if she was okay, Clodagh told him to go away. She couldn't bear the thought of more people coming to check on her, wanting to know what was wrong with her. More to the point, she couldn't even begin to think about telling everyone what she'd seen on Midhallow and in the prison. She'd told Petra, who'd seemed to understand – had even offered up a reason for her hallucination – but had then put her at risk in the witches' prison.

Raw, scared, too ashamed to admit to anyone else what had happened - that was when she decided to run away. She reckoned she could be at her brother's cottage in twenty minutes, as long as she didn't get lost in the fog. She couldn't carry all of her belongings on her back, so she chose some essentials, and packed them into her smaller rucksack. She changed into her running gear, put the head torch on, and opened the door slightly.

No sound, no sign of anyone.

She tiptoed down the stairs, grateful that the accommodation wing of the house was quiet. Clodagh opened up the front door carefully, and fog washed across her face like a wet flannel.

A quick look over her shoulder assured her that no one was there to witness her escape. She switched on the head torch, clumsily found her way to the coastal path to the east of the house, and started running in the direction of Danny's cottage. The distance was roughly four miles, which should have taken around half an hour to run, but in the thick fog it took her more than double that time.

Half-way there, visions of being pursued by professional fugitive-hunters flashed through her mind; she panicked and threw her phone over the cliff into the sea. It was gut-wrenching to lose it, but she was too paranoid about being tracked to keep it in her possession. Almost immediately, she regretted her action: without her phone or laptop, how would she keep in touch with Danny and Ruth, the only people in the world who knew where she was? Except they expected her to be at Rothmore until Sunday, so in actual fact *she* was the only one in the world who knew where she was.

Great start, she chided herself, *you're doing really well at this fugitive business so far.*

She passed two other old cottages as she got close to Danny's, but the curtains were drawn, no faces peered out into the night. Danny's cottage was on its own, part-way up a hill, not overlooked by any other houses.

It was the perfect place to disappear to.

***

An escape route, her counsellor Martina had called it. A place to think, a place to make the impossible decision. Clodagh knew that to say no was worse than cruelty, and the consequences would be deadly if she did. She had already tried to say no – or at least had tried to tell them it was an answer she was prepared to give – but they hadn't listened. She knew that they didn't really want to hear anything other than *Yes, of course I'll do this for you.* Although she had planned to go straight to Danny's cottage for a few days after the retreat ended, to be completely alone with her thoughts - and her fears - to work out what to do, she hadn't intended to run away mid-retreat and she knew, even as the adrenaline still coursed through her, that it was an extreme reaction.

It seemed now, in the dark silence of the old, abandoned cottage, that she was in self-imposed solitary confinement. She had planned her stay as best she could. She'd spent countless hours in outdoor shops, asking endless questions. She knew more about how to cook safely indoors with camping equipment than she ever imagined she would. Clodagh shone the torch at the supply of food stacked up on the kitchen counter: plenty of beans and pulses for protein, three different types of soup, a few steamed puddings for her sweet tooth. A tin of coffee, a tin of tea. Oats and long-life oat milk. Oatcakes. Peanut butter. She reckoned that she had enough food to last her a month, if she needed it. She really only planned to be at the cottage for a few days, but had thought it was better to be prepared, just in case. *Just in case I stay here and don't go back*, was what she really meant. Hiding out in the cottage and not going back home – back to face her parents - would be the coward's way, but she knew that her preparations had factored this possibility into the equation.

She'd bought two gas canisters, the warmest sleeping bag she could find, and a self-inflating air bed. Two thermal blankets to keep her warm when she was not in the sleeping bag. Some warm jumpers, fleece-lined trousers, woollen socks. Soap to wash in the sea (or rather, in the stream of water that ran down the hill, past the cottage and into the sea). Two fluffy bath towels that she kidded herself would warm her up after bathing outdoors. There was no electricity in the cottage, so she had a giant pack of tea lights to burn in little glass votive jars.

She kicked herself again for the hasty disposal of her phone, and thought mournfully of her laptop, sitting on the desk back at Rothmore. She would get that back, at least. Probably.

The fog had sneaked its icy fingers into the cottage, which was damp and freezing. There was a dusty, dirty smell that she imagined was from decades of mice coming and going as they pleased. Even though she had a spare gas canister, she planned to ration gas in case she did end up staying longer. She used the light from her head torch to locate the gas heater and start it up. Then she wrapped up in a thermal blanket and hunched over in front of the heat, trying to stop her teeth chattering and her body from convulsing with shivers. Clodagh tried not to think about what would be happening back at the retreat: had they noticed that she was missing yet?

This was the selfish dance of those who ran away, she thought: when circumstances make it the only option the brain will entertain, there were always consequences for other people.

***

When Clodagh's brother Danny and his partner Paul bought the run-down coastal cottage, her brain did not immediately identify its potential as an escape zone. They had already booked an extended holiday in New Zealand before they decided to buy the cottage, and Danny told Clodagh that although he was excited about starting the renovations, they would have to wait until he and Paul were back home. Danny said the photographs didn't do the place justice, so he drove Clodagh out to the cottage the day after he got the keys so that she could see its potential. As they drove along the coast road he pointed out the entrance to Rothmore House.

"When are you going on the retreat?"

"In just over two weeks."

"Paul and I will be in New Zealand then. How would you feel about coming out and checking on the cottage after the retreat is over? You wouldn't have to spend any time there. Just have a look and make sure no squatters have moved in, no windows are broken."

A little flicker of electricity lit up in Clodagh's brain then, as she recognised an escape route. She realised she could go and stay in Danny's cottage, just for a few days, which would give her time to think about what to do. And, if she decided to go through with the surgery, it would give her some time to mentally prepare for the experience, although she was not sure that was even possible.

Clodagh ran the idea past Danny. He sighed, and tears welled up in his eyes. He pulled her into a tight hug and said, "Of course you can stay. For as long as you want. But you know what I think about this."

Clodagh *did* know. Danny shared her view that to say yes was to put herself at serious risk. He also shared her feelings about their mother.

Their visit to the cottage became a scouting mission after that. *No electricity*. Cons: no light, no power for her laptop. Pro: no lights would be visible to any passers-by, supporting her endeavour to hide out from the world. *No running water.* Cons: The need to purchase and deliver bottled water, and having to figure out how much she would need for a few days, or possibly longer. The possibility of having to bathe in the sea - serious con. *The sky was visible through some bits of the roof.* Cons: Creature infestation, water everywhere. Pro: Danny said it would be repaired before they left for New Zealand.

"It wasn't this bad when we viewed the property before putting an offer in. We think parts of the roof must have blown off in that last winter storm."

Danny's car was parked just off the dirt road, where there was a small gap in the sea buckthorn hedge. A hedge bordering the cottage provided a good deal of privacy from passing folk. Clodagh asked Danny how busy the road was.

"Oh, not very. It narrows so much just there below the cottage that it's impassable for cars. It's mostly just people wanting to climb to the top of the hill for the view walking past. But it's nowhere near the coastal path, so there aren't too many people, I imagine. We'll have to see what it's like in summer, I suppose."

Someone had once shaped the sea buckthorn into an archway, now overgrown and scraggly, which they walked through to get to the cottage. An old fisherman's cottage, its white façade was covered in dirt and moss stains. It was L-shaped, with a red door at the far end, in the crook of the building.

The kitchen looked like someone had installed it in the 1950s: powder blue Formica cupboards, white Formica countertop with metallic speckles. The cooker had been ripped out. Still, Clodagh thought, she could use the space for storage and food preparation. She realised she would need to find out about a camping stove that could be used indoors. There was a small two-person table, the same colour as the counter-top, with two red vinyl chairs, both ripped. Clodagh pictured herself sitting there, eating meals, reading books, drawing, writing.

At the far end of the kitchen was a door to a room that housed only a toilet and a small sink. There was no bath tub or even shower. Another door off the kitchen led to a small sitting room, with an open fire. Clodagh could imagine how cosy it would be in the colder months. The window was boarded up, just as it was in the kitchen. Pro: No prying eyes could see her inside.

Oddly, the bedroom was right off the sitting room. Another open fire, another window boarded-up.

"Small but perfectly-formed," Clodagh said to Danny.

"What do you think, really?" he asked, looking concerned. "There's no electricity or running water."

Blind ignorance was bliss, she told him. "I'll think of it as a silent retreat, after the other retreat. A place to come for quiet contemplation."

"But you don't want it to be a place you come to starve."

She told him she would figure it out. "And don't worry – I won't do anything dangerous and set the place on fire."

"I wasn't even thinking about that. I was picturing coming home to find your skinny little skeleton sitting in that chair over there."

And here she was, sitting in the chair, feeling ashamed of herself, both for running away and for wanting to stand in front of her parents and firmly tell them *I can't do this*.

CHAPTER 22

Primum non nocere. Above all, do no harm.

Clodagh was not any kind of hero. She had always known this about herself, that she lacked courage. Her nocturnal escape from the Rothmore estate to Danny's cottage was the most recent evidence of this. She knew that she could have chosen a different way – could at least have let everyone know she was leaving. But she hadn't wanted to stay in that place for another minute. If it wasn't so over-the-top dramatic, it might be funny; *I mean, I'm the kind of person who represses my feelings, bottles them up, puts the cork on and pretends that everything's fine.*

Everything was not fine, though, and it had not been for quite some time. And Clodagh had stopped pretending – at least with some people. But seeing and hearing things that were not there – they just *couldn't* be – and running off into the night were new territory for her.

Sitting in the intense heat of the camping stove, by weak candlelight, she acknowledged that fleeing like a fugitive was not the right course of action. Even though her addled brain had been pushed to its limit of coping in a rational, reasoned way, and had responded by sending out a message to get the hell out of there, it didn't leave her with an easy way to resolve the situation. Go back to Rothmore and apologise? Or go back and say that she had done a runner because she was overwhelmed with emotion and feeling, and needed to be alone? She could put an end to their worry. But Clodagh had lacked courage to tell them the truth before she ran, and couldn't face being honest with virtual strangers about her anxieties.

Neither was she courageous when her mother's kidneys had stopped improving on dialysis; if she had been, she would have offered to help, before being asked for it. Clodagh's mother was on a transplant list, but the doctors had told the family that it was more unlikely than likely that she would get one. When the talk turned to live organ donation, Clodagh assumed that her father would be the hero. And he was – or at least he had tried to be, but their blood types did not match. All of Clodagh's brothers apart from Danny were working away - the nearest one was in London, but he said there was no way they would give him time off work for the operation, so there was no point in finding out if his blood type was a match. Danny had the wrong blood type, and Clodagh would not have wanted him to go through with it anyway, even if he was a match.

Clodagh was the only one left, and the test revealed that she had the same blood type as her mother. A further test revealed that their tissue types were also a match.

In those early stages of getting information from the doctors, who were careful to talk about the risks to Clodagh as well as her mother, she wouldn't have described herself as stoic. Instead, she was living each day in a haze of disbelief and denial. She could not really bring herself to think about what the experience of surgery and recovery would be like, despite the discussions with doctors and nurses and the leaflets they gave her. The bottom line was that she didn't want to be sliced open, and have one of her kidneys removed and placed in her mother's body.

It seemed so barbaric. Even though she knew that transplant surgery was not rare, that plenty of people survived it – and some people even donated organs to complete strangers, never mind their own mothers – she could not get past the horror of having her body carved up.

Clodagh was so overwhelmed by the thought of what would happen if she did – or did not – go through with the surgery, that she could hardly sleep at night. After a few weeks, she noticed that her centre of gravity was off, that she had trouble keeping her balance.

One Thursday afternoon she was alone in the flat, pretending to work but actually looking online at expensive face creams that she would never buy, and she heard a voice say:

If you go through with it, you'll die.

Heart racing, she closed the lid of her laptop and hurried away from it as though it was possessed. She had just switched the kettle on when she heard the voice again, saying exactly the same thing:

If you go through with it, you'll die.

She switched the kettle off, rushed into her bedroom, and pulled the duvet up over her head.

The voice was telling her what she was thinking deep down, that the risks were too great. Although she'd been telling herself that what she felt was natural worry and anxiety, because the risks *were* great, the voice – that seemed to come from some disembodied space - was like the foreteller of truth. She *would* die if she went through with the operation, Clodagh was sure of it.

And yet she also knew that her mother would die if she did not.

Clodagh tried to talk to her father, explaining that she wanted to help her mother and she knew she was the only one in the family who could, but that she had a terrible foreboding about dying during the surgery.

"Oh love, of course you're nervous about it. Anyone would be. You're young and you're strong, love. You'll be fine."

Later, she had tried to talk to *both* parents about it, and they had been dismissive. Neither parent was willing to give her an out-clause, it seemed. On another occasion, she tried to use the informational leaflets from the nurse about the physical and psychological risks associated with the surgery to start a conversation with her parents, but they had downplayed these, and her father told her they were minor compared to the risk of her mother dying.

No matter what Clodagh tried to say, her mother had the moral high ground. She also had a history of failing to adequately and assertively stand up to her mother, a poor track-record. The day that she made her clearest attempt to say she was afraid, that she could not go through with it, both parents dismissed her concerns and she responded by running out of the room. Clodagh's father ran after her. He caught up with her by the front door, grabbed her tightly by both wrists and said he was so proud of her for being so brave and so strong.

"I will never forget what you are doing," he had said, tears in his eyes. Clodagh had the strong feeling they were having a different conversation, one in which he was warning her against failing to go through with it.

Clodagh talked to only three people about the situation, and each one told her the same thing: she needed to be honest with her parents about her feelings, to keep communicating with them no matter how dismissive or unwilling to listen they might be, and to take some time to think through her decision.

But her mother did not have much time, she knew that: she had to make a decision, and quickly.

***

Clodagh believed that saying she had a difficult relationship with her mother was like saying that komodo dragons were a bit unsettling. For years, she had wondered how a mother could stop loving her daughter. That supposed, of course, that her mother had ever loved her. Clodagh wanted to think that she did. Maybe she *needed* to think that she did.

Clodagh was not sure when she first knew – really *knew* – that her mother did not. It was long before she banished Clodagh from the family home, although that particular incident was a very physical, very public marker of their estrangement from one another. Looking back at it, a decade on, Clodagh could see the disturbing signs of sexual competitiveness. Did all mothers feel this, she wondered, when their daughters became sexually active? Did the awareness of their ageing trigger a streak of envy and loathing? Or was it just the more insecure mothers, the ones whose identities were bound up in their sexual attractiveness?

Clodagh was not even sure that was true for her own mother, because she did not really know her. She certainly did not understand her. She only knew that her mother hated her that day, could see it in her eyes as she cursed her, and forced her to leave home.

Was it different for other daughters, when their mothers discovered they were in love, and making love, for the first time? Clodagh's mother's fury turned her first love – which had been sweet, and wonderful, and surprising - into something shameful.

Clodagh believed that a boy as socially-in-demand as Aidan never should have been interested in her – short and plain looking with a boyish figure. She felt like an outsider at school so she acted, and dressed, like one. When Aidan had invited her to his seventeenth birthday party he had seemed too sincere for Clodagh to suspect she was being made a fool of. She was surprised, and puzzled, but she went.

The mixed crowd of boys and girls were not friendly towards her, but they were not hostile, either, not until some of the girls clocked that Aidan was spending most of his time talking to Clodagh. After that, they made conspicuous attempts to distract him, to attract him away from Clodagh, but he stayed at her side, asking her questions and really listening to her answers.

Aidan invited Clodagh to see a film the following weekend and then they began to spend most of their time together. They were seventeen, full of raging lust and hormones, but somehow, they managed to wait four months to have sex for the first time. His parents both worked full time, so most days they went straight from school to Aidan's bedroom. He walked Clodagh home afterwards, every time, and although she tried to keep him from spending too much time with her mother, he always came to the door to say hello to her. He did not even seem to mind that she would haul the door open, and stand there with a glowering face, although her rudeness embarrassed Clodagh.

Clodagh's memories of the day of her banishment remained painful, nearly a decade later. She had felt so loved as Aidan walked her home that day, and so lucky. Her mother was not waiting at the door, which enhanced her good mood, but the crackling tension hit Clodagh as soon as she closed the door behind her. She naively assumed her mother must have been having a go at her father again, and felt a rush of pity for him. When she walked into her room to change out of her school uniform, there was her mother, sitting on Clodagh's bed, the contents of her jewellery box spread out on the duvet. Clodagh kept her birth control pills in there, under the mistaken assumption that her mother would never look inside.

The names she called Clodagh then were foul and degrading. They cut right through her, the shame of them, the shame of her mother finding out this private and special part of her life and attacking her for it. Her mother forbade Clodagh from seeing Aidan, of even speaking to him. If she saw him at school she was to turn around and walk the other way. But it was Clodagh she cut into with her words and accusations – this indecency was all Clodagh's fault. She said she was stupid, too, for risking getting pregnant and ruining her life when she should be concentrating on studying for her exams, and getting into a good university.

And then she kicked Clodagh out of the house.

Clodagh stayed at her friend Carol's for a few nights, grateful to her family for taking her in, but self-consciously worried that they knew why she had been kicked out, as though she wore her shame like a giant plumed hat. Danny asked their older brother John, who was making his fortune in the City of London, to send Clodagh some money, which enabled her to rent a room in a flat with three young women in their first year of university.

Their studiousness should have been conducive to her own studies, but instead she became increasingly depressed, and angry, and dropped out of school. Her mother's hostile rejection had cracked something in her, and carrying her shame and embarrassment around every day wore down her energy. She stopped talking to Aidan. For a couple of months afterwards he tried to reach out to her, but Clodagh ignored him, and eventually he gave up.

Clodagh had treated him badly, and she knew it. She mourned the end of the relationship as it had once been, before it had become tainted by shame. Clodagh convinced herself that Aidan deserved to be with someone from a normal, loving family – one like his.

That was the absolute low point in Clodagh's relationship with her mother, but she told herself she needed to try to remember the good times, too. Her mother was calmest when in the kitchen, baking, and they had baked together regularly, right up until the time she had left home.

And there were their back-to-school shopping days. Before the start of each new school year, Clodagh's mother took her shopping for provisions: new shoes, underwear, her first bra, ridiculous pens with feathers on the top that were all the rage one year, soft notebooks in her favourite colours. Once Clodagh had what she needed for school, her mother took her out for lunch in the local café. Clodagh had loved that unassuming, comforting place dearly, with its window panes always covered in condensation from the hot water urns and the tiny kitchen that churned out food all hours of the day and the breath of the chattering customers. It always felt like twilight inside for some reason: cosy and happy.

There was the time Clodagh was named Harvest Queen at her school's harvest festival, and got to wear the harvest hat – a wide-brimmed straw hat onto which plastic vegetables were glued. It was ridiculously heavy and the plastic carrots and turnips hanging down over the brim made it almost impossible to see anything, but Clodagh remembered standing on the stage while people cheered. Her mother was standing right at the front, smiling and looking proud.

There was the time her mother had submitted a poem Clodagh wrote in her last year of primary school to a poetry competition – without telling her – and Clodagh had won first prize.

Sitting in the cold, dark cottage, Clodagh clung to those happy moments in their relationship, probing her own strength and stamina, trying to decide if she could give the answer her mother needed to hear so desperately.

CHAPTER 23

Clodagh was starting to worry about the noxious, chemical odour coming from the heater: with no ventilation in the cottage, what if the fumes killed her? Danny's joke about finding her corpse when he got back from New Zealand suddenly seemed like it might be a real possibility. She was desperate for a cup of hot chocolate, but she didn't want to add to the chemical content of the cottage's interior by lighting the camping stove, so she ignored the craving. She considered setting up the air mattress and climbing into her sleeping bag, but the hideous image of mice running across her face in the dark bedroom stopped her. She decided to stay in the chair by the heater, and force her brain to focus: she had some serious thinking to do.

After she dropped out of secondary school, Clodagh got a job in the pub down the road from her rented room. She worked evenings and she drank to excess after work, because alcohol was readily available, and also because her colleagues did so. She drank heavily because she was ashamed about being kicked out of the family home, and about the reasons why it had happened, and she was ashamed whenever she compared her life trajectory with that of her flatmates. Sure, she was making money and living a more hedonistic lifestyle than they were – all three of them took their studies very seriously, already in first year – but in leaving secondary school without any qualifications she had squandered her dream of going to art college.

She hoped it might happen somehow, in the future, but she was not really sure how to make it happen, apart from finishing secondary school, one day.

And then one sleety, grey afternoon in January, Danny appeared at her door, crying, as she was getting ready for work. He had taken the bus to Clodagh's flat straight after school, telling her that he was never going back home. Their parents had learned of his relationship with Mr Taylor, his English teacher, and had given him an ultimatum: end it or get out. He had been planning on ending it, he told Clodagh, but he also wanted to get out. Their mother had said some vile things to him, although he would not tell her what they were. He said there was no way he could go back and live with their parents.

"Danny, what were you thinking though, love? Your English teacher?" He was sobbing into Clodagh's shoulder.

"I know, I know. That's the thing – to be forced to come out to them because the school called them in – it was just horrible. And then Mum was horrible – *really* horrible - about me."

"Well, she would be. She has horrible tendencies."

"But Dad was so kind. He asked me a few times why I hadn't come to him to talk about it. Like I could tell him I was having sex with my teacher every day after school."

"Every day! Oh, Danny."

He snorted into her shoulder. "It's terrible, I know it's terrible. I feel so ashamed."

"Danny, *he's* the adult in this situation. Your teacher - the authority figure. He never should have done it."

"He told the head teacher *I* was the predator. He made it sound like I was the one who'd forced him to do it."

"Well of course you weren't the predator. Did he force you to do anything?"

"No." He started crying again. "Not really. One day I went to see him after school about an essay and he told me that he'd fancied me since third year, and that was that. I started going to see him every day after that, for what we called extra help."

Danny looked at Clodagh, pain stamped on his sweet, sincere face. "I'm sorry for showing up like this. I'm a complete mess."

Clodagh felt like a complete mess, too, but taking charge of

Danny's welfare suddenly became her top priority. She asked her flatmates if Danny could move in with them, expecting them to refuse, but was delighted when they said yes. One flatmate, Diane, even offered to move out of her spacious double room and into Clodagh's box room so that Danny and Clodagh could share. Clodagh made a deal with their parents: she would pay for Danny's room and board, and would make sure that he kept up his schoolwork so that he, at least, would go to university. Their father had gone into the school to demand that Danny be moved to another English class, so that he did not have to see Mr Taylor.

Clodagh's part of the bargain was easy. Danny was so motivated that he required no supervision. He got himself up in the morning, made his own breakfast and went off to school. Every day, they had an early dinner together when Danny got home from school, before Clodagh went in for her shift at the pub. She was as quiet as possible when she got home in the early hours, trying her best not to wake him. Danny was conscientious, and he studied most evenings, or sometimes watched a bit of telly with her flatmates – who all loved him - and saw his friends at weekends.

The scandal with his teacher gave Clodagh a reason to give up drinking at the end of each shift, because she didn't want to come home drunk. She loved Danny more than anything, and didn't want him to see her in that state every night.

***

Danny and Clodagh had, for as long as she could remember, drawn cartoons for each other. They both loved doodling and sketching, and it kept them quiet, so their mother had never once complained about how much time they spent drawing. As a boy, Danny was obsessed with cars, and he drew everything with an exhaust pipe sticking out the back: animals, buildings, people, trees.

They'd often draw each other, with speech bubbles holding words and expressions more outlandish than anything they'd actually use in real life. They also drew their parents, mocking the more ridiculous things they said, and embellishing them. Those cartoons were for their eyes only, and they were careful not to be caught or let anyone else see them. Danny's one attempt to include every member of their family in his work had made their mother so angry that he had never again attempted it.

When he was six years old, Danny wrote and illustrated a book. Each member of their family had the body of a fish, but their own facial features and hair. In the book, their fish family mostly got into arguments. But one day, a new fish appeared - bald with large, round black glasses, and black sandals attached to his back fin. He introduced himself as the Gandhifish, whose mission was to bring peace to this squabbling family.

Clodagh didn't know how or where Danny had learned about Gandhi, and she adored the book. Their mother, though, told Danny the book was an insult to their family, and belonged in the bin, which is where she threw it.

After her mother kicked her out, mostly as a way to deal with the pain of it, Clodagh started to draw her. At first, Clodagh found it painful to write down the words her mother had actually used, and then to see them on paper in black and white. But Clodagh found that the more she read the words, the easier it was to remember them – or rather to live with them, she supposed.

And Clodagh could make her mother's facial expressions and gestures as exaggerated as she wanted to because there was no longer any chance of her mother stumbling upon her illustrations. Clodagh changed small details – her mother's hair, her height and weight, the type of clothes she wore – and as she became a version of her mother that Clodagh could control, an idea for a story was born.

Clodagh built her dystopian world, sketch by sketch, over a period of three months. She worked all day while Danny was at school, taking breaks only for cups of tea and snacks. The story began with the government instructing Scottish farmers to use a pesticide that they claimed was safe for organic crops. But soon the farmers, their families, people who lived near the farms, then the general population – anyone who had been eating the food from the farms, basically – started to get sick. It was not a typical disease, with physical symptoms, but rather started as small changes to a person's personality, things that were hardly noticeable to other people. Slowly, the changes became more obvious, until the loved ones of the infected people were sure they were living with a completely different person. Eventually, the afflicted got very violent.

In a scene that was particularly gruelling for Clodagh to create, the mother's increasing acts of violence towards her husband and children (barely-disguised versions of Danny and Clodagh) reached a crescendo.

Gradually, it seemed to the children that their mother was living somewhere else in her mind, tuning into a different world. She burst out laughing for no reason – a light, bubbly laugh that they had not heard before. She continued to cook and clean for them, and might even sit down and watch television with them from time to time, but with a vacant, dazed look on her face. Her teenage daughter became like a clingy child, asking to be tucked in at night, hugging her around the neck when she did come to say good night.

On one of those occasions, she caught her daughter's arms in a tight grip when she reached up for a hug. "Let's not do that anymore," she said in a gruff voice.

A couple of days later, she began to hit their father. Every night, after the children went to bed, they heard dull thuds followed by their father's muted cries for her to stop, then scuffling sounds as he tried to stop her, which were followed by their mother's shrieking – loud, pained, hideous and high-pitched – and, finally, her sobbing.

Two weeks on from the first attack on their father, the usual terrible sounds were followed by loud footsteps on the stairs and the voice of their father, pleading. There was a loud thud, and then the boy's voice, thick with sleep, called out.

Another thud and a scream followed, and the daughter was out of her bed and in her brother's room so fast her head was spinning. Their mother stood over the boy's limp body, which she had pulled out of bed by his feet. As the daughter rushed at her, their mother turned her rage on her, reaching out and grabbing a clump of her hair tightly in her fist. She gripped her daughter's neck, choking her.

All at once their mother's body went slack, and her hands relinquished their grip. The boy stood above her body, clutching his bedside lamp in his quivering hand.

It was a crude, but effective, way for Clodagh to gain a bit of a power stronghold over her mother, a way for her to exact some form of revenge. The character, who'd evolved from early sketches of her mother, became the first victim of the crop plague; however, Clodagh had to admit that the teenage daughter, who was the main character, bore little resemblance to her. The main character, Genoa, was brave, courageous, and strong, and she tackled the problem with an in-your-face gusto that Clodagh knew she did not share. When the world woke up to the fact that the main character was immune to the disease, and the scientific community made aggressive moves to get her into labs to perform tests on, she fled. She was a fugitive in the world, needing help from strangers to keep safe, but never entirely trusting anyone.

Clodagh loved the character of Genoa and, after she had finished the story, she made sure that Genoa stayed with her in her day-to-day life. If Clodagh was feeling afraid of doing something, she would ask herself what Genoa would do in that situation. If someone tried to intimidate her into doing something, she pulled out her Genoa moves and resisted. Clodagh found it an incredibly powerful way of imagining herself into being someone else, or behaving like someone else, even if Genoa was a fictional character. After she finished the book, she realised that she had missed writing Genoa's life every day, missed seeing how she would develop and survive in that terrible world, and she wanted to try to hang on to some of the power that Genoa had brought her.

It did not last long.

After Clodagh had finished about a third of the story, she'd shown it to Danny, who raved about it and said she needed to get her work out in the world, to share it. She told him she was worried about their mother seeing it. He told her she could use a pen-name. She told him she was too shy to show her work to anyone else, and Danny countered that they could set up social media accounts, using her pen-name.

Clodagh already closely followed the work of a few illustrators and writers online, and realised that Danny was right: she could be whoever she wanted to be. They set up a webcomic, using the pen-name Audrey deVere. Danny's gorgeous friend Daphne agreed to be photographed as the face of Audrey, and both she and Danny actively shared and promoted Clodagh's work through their social networks.

Once a week, Clodagh dropped new content online and, after just six weeks, she had a substantial following. In actual fact, Clodagh thought, it was Daphne-as-Audrey that had developed the following, but she loved reading the enthusiastic and mostly positive comments from her ever-growing group of fans.

By the time Clodagh had finished the story, the requests from fans for her to publish the online content as a graphic novel were multiplying, and she began to look into the possibility of self-publishing. Ultimately, she chose to publish with a fledgling company based in Edinburgh, started by two university graduates in English literature, who were full of enthusiasm and energy. They were fans of the webcomic, who said they wanted to use their impressive social media network and contacts to promote the graphic novel. Clodagh's book would be their first dystopian fiction publication.

The next hurdle was coming up with the funds, and the publishers suggested a crowd-funding campaign.

CHAPTER 24

Clodagh met Ruth when she was crowd-funding to self-publish *Genoa's Run.* Ruth owned an independent book shop in the south side of Edinburgh, where the entire lower floor was devoted to comic books and graphic novels. Clodagh aimed to set up events in as many book shops as she could, to generate interest in her story and encourage people to contribute to its publication, in exchange for a signed book, a signed print, or a private reading for a small group of people, depending on how much they paid.

Clodagh's first impression was that Ruth was effortlessly cool – tall and willowy. Speaking on the phone to set up the visit, Ruth described herself as a super-geek, who had been following *Genoa's Run* since the earliest blog posts and videos.

"I'd love to host an event," she said, enthusiastically. "And I can't wait to meet you."

Ruth led Clodagh downstairs, where the walls and book-shelves were painted navy-blue, giving the space an inviting feeling, like entering a cosy den. She led Clodagh to the back, closer to the smell of fresh coffee, and the sound of jazz. The space was long and narrow – a bit like an Aladdin's cave.

Ruth ordered a hazelnut macchiato and Clodagh had a black coffee with a caramel shot. A tempting range of cakes peeked out at Clodagh from the display case, and Ruth asked what she would like.

"I'm fine thanks - I just like looking."

"I'm afraid that's not acceptable. You're my guest and I'm going to have to insist."

Clodagh chose a chocolate brownie – so rich and luscious

it made her cheeks tingle. She was glad that Ruth took the lead in the conversation, so that Clodagh could focus on eating the brownie without having to talk.

"I'm such a fangirl," Ruth said, taking a delicate bite of brownie. "One of my regular customers showed me the first post of *Genoa's Run*, and I was hooked. A lot of us are fans – I don't think you'll have any trouble raising the money to publish it."

Clodagh washed the brownie down with a few swigs of coffee, and said she was glad to hear it. She told Ruth about the idea they'd had for the event – a staged reading, with costumes, and the accompanying illustration projected as a backdrop.

"I love it. We have a courtyard area out the back – if the weather is good we could set up there. It's not very big, but people can sit at the tables inside to watch. The wall would make a good screen. If it's raining, we'll figure something out in here – we'll just have to move a few things around. We'll make it work."

Clodagh thanked her profusely, but Ruth waved her hand, stopping her. "Please – it's such a pleasure. I mean that. Now tell me how you came up with the idea."

Clodagh stumbled her way through an answer, not really able to explain exactly where Genoa had come from. It was a strange and mysterious process, and she didn't want to talk about the story's origins as a way to deal with what had happened with her mother. She was also too shy to tell Ruth that Genoa was who she aspired to be.

Possibly sensing Clodagh's discomfort, Ruth made her laugh by describing her own attempts at creating comics, when she was a girl.

"My drawing skills are so poor, that I would literally have a space with an arrow coming out of it and an explanation of what should be there, like *two-headed alien with suction cups sticking out of its face* or *double-decker bus spaceship with armour and rocket-propelled engine*. Not that it stopped me from showing it to people. I'd show the other children in the playground, expecting them to be really impressed. They weren't."

Clodagh laughed. "There's probably a market for that kind

of book. A kind of draw-your-own comic. With prompts."

"I hadn't thought of that! I'll pitch it to the publishers – see what they think."

Nibbling on her brownie, Ruth gave Clodagh a curious look. "I have to be honest – you don't look very much like the photographs of Audrey deVere."

Mock-indignantly, Clodagh said, "How insulting!"

Ruth laughed. "It wasn't meant to be an insult. It's just that when you rang me, I pictured you as Audrey from the photos. If anything, it just goes to show how shallow I am."

"I didn't really want to be photographed. Well that's not the whole story, actually. I was reluctant to share my work until my brother suggested I use a pen-name. And he just happened to have this gorgeous friend who was willing to pose as Audrey. I have a feeling I wouldn't have quite so many followers if we'd used a photo of me."

Ruth looked at Clodagh with a wry smile and asked, "You don't mind that this other person is becoming the face of *Genoa's Run*, not you?"

"Not at all. She actually looks like Genoa, doesn't she?"

Ruth nodded, enthusiastically. "If they ever make a film of *Genoa's Run*, she'll have to take the lead role."

They talked for more than an hour, until Ruth said she really needed to get back to work. The next time they met was the day of the event, and they were both excited, if a bit fraught. It rained on and off all day, and Ruth decided it wasn't safe for the performers to use the courtyard. The shop shut at six, and the event started at seven, so they had only a short time set up the seating area and the stage.

To Clodagh's great relief, the event was a huge success. Danny and Daphne were outstanding – Danny as the narrator and Daphne as Genoa, the perfect embodiment of Clodagh's beloved main character. Danny and Daphne put their all into their performance, and Clodagh was so proud of both of them. The audience lapped it up, greedily, then demanded an encore, which they hadn't planned for, but which Danny and Daphne delivered flawlessly nonetheless.

At the end of the event – their first – they had raised more than half of their total target amount. It was so much more than Clodagh had hoped for. She invited Ruth and her staff to the wine bar across the street afterwards, to celebrate. Several bottles of prosecco in, Ruth raised a toast to Clodagh, calling her "a bright new talent" and "my new best friend".

Clodagh was too choked up to reply, so she raised her glass, and everyone cheered.

Clodagh gained a new best friend in Ruth, as well as an unofficial manager. With her contacts and connections in the book world, she set up two more fundraising events at other local book shops, with the result that Clodagh reached her target much more quickly than she'd expected to. During the whirlwind months of pre-publication, Ruth guided Clodagh through the process of self-promotion, helping her to whip up a small frenzy of excitement ahead of the launch of her book. They had fun, too. They shared a love of the cinema, and sitting in a darkened theatre with Ruth on Sunday afternoons before her shift became Clodagh's favourite part of each week.

When *Genoa's Run* was published, Ruth organised a series of events – similar to the fundraising event – to promote the book. Throughout the summer and into the autumn, Clodagh, Danny and Daphne – and Ruth when she could manage it – visited book shops, community centres, private gardens - anywhere large enough to act as venues for the performances, really, to present Genoa to the world. Well, to the people of Edinburgh, Glasgow, Dundee, Fife and the Scottish Borders.

Clodagh was surprised whenever they had a crowd, was surprised generally by the success of her book. Sales were modest, she knew that, but the numbers delighted her nonetheless. This was *her* book people clutched in their hands, wrote reviews about, posted wildly excited reactions to on the website. It was the best time in her life by far, and she didn't underestimate

Ruth's role in making it happen.

It couldn't last forever, she knew, and it didn't. The manager of the pub had limited patience for her requests for time off, and she was on the brink of being sacked. Danny had started working for a property renovation company and he loved it, but the work was demanding – as were his bosses – and Clodagh knew she couldn't keep asking him to request more time off for the events. Although Ruth seemed to have an infinite supply of patience and enthusiasm for Clodagh's work and burgeoning career, she had a business to run.

She also became the unwitting victim of an obsessive fan of Genoa, and by extension Clodagh, who came to see Ruth as the main obstacle between him and his obsession.

**

Sid came into their lives on a grey, wet afternoon in late September. It wasn't their usual type of event, since Danny and Daphne couldn't get any more time off work, so Ruth suggested an "in conversation with..." session, in which Clodagh would answer questions about the evolution of Genoa at a branch of a large chain of book shops in central Edinburgh. Anxious about being centre-stage for the first time, Ruth responded by rehearsing the format with Clodagh, and assuring her that she'd be with her every step of the way.

The conversation itself wasn't as bad as Clodagh feared, but afterwards people brought books to her for signing and, as she sat in a corner of the lower ground floor with a swelling crowd of people near her, she began to feel more than slightly claustrophobic. She wanted a break, and could smell coffee brewing at the concession upstairs, but it mingled with stale breath, and more than a few unwashed bodies, and a putrid tang that wafted up from the old, worn carpet.

During her first encounter with Sid, he marked himself out as odd in two key ways: he manoeuvred his body so that he was standing almost right beside Clodagh, rather than across the table from her; and he talked nervously – incessantly – about his favourite scene of the book. It was the mother's death scene, the scene Clodagh wanted least to discuss with a complete stranger. On the mother's deathbed, she had a brief return to her kind and loving self, the way Genoa remembered her mother when she was a young child. It was a redemption scene of sorts, before the mother's chest imploded. It was violent and bloody and there had been more than a little criticism posted online about the intensely graphic illustrations.

But Sid clearly loved it, as he was telling Clodagh enthusiastically, spittle flying dangerously close to her. Clodagh had signed his book and thanked him for coming, but still he remained. Ruth was sitting right beside Clodagh, and she stood up, gesturing for Sid to move on. Eventually he did, looking back over his shoulder at Clodagh as he walked away.

"Jesus," Ruth said quietly. "That did not seem like normal behaviour. I wonder if we should talk to the manager about that guy."

But before they could act on it, the next person in the queue was already talking to Clodagh, asking her to sign the book, "To my muse, Hayley".

Two hours later, exhausted, Clodagh accepted without any hint of protest Ruth's offer to come back to her flat and put her feet up while Ruth made them something to eat. Ruth was bubbling with excitement about the event and the number of people who'd turned up, but Clodagh was weary of body and mind. She'd have quite happily curled up for a nap. Neither of them thought of Sid as they left the book shop, had no sense of any danger as they walked east along George Street.

Sid stood on the opposite side of the street, watching as they came out of the book shop. He followed them as they walked, huddled together in the rain, cutting across St Andrew Square gardens and down to York Place. The sound of the rain drowned out any noise his footsteps made, as he followed them along London Road to a quiet, narrow street, where Ruth opened the door to a building at the far end. He watched as lights came on in the first floor flat, and waited patiently for hours for one or both women to emerge.

But he was disappointed.

Ruth didn't want to wake Clodagh before she left the next morning to open the shop, so instead she wrote her a note telling her to stay as long as she wanted, and help herself to anything. Most mornings, she walked to work, but it was raining heavily, and she opted for the bus. As she stood in the bus shelter, reflecting happily on the previous day's events, she had no idea that she was being watched.

She felt her legs give out and she stumbled forward, grasping at air before falling on her knees. She didn't see her attacker, who pinned her down, and slapped her face several times. He stopped when the owner of the newsagent beside the bus stop ran out of his shop and shouted at him, and he ran off. The police were called, but Ruth's attacker was long gone by the time they arrived. She hadn't seen her attacker's face, but she knew it was the man from the day before, because she recognised the peculiar rank smell coming off him – like mouse droppings mixed with ammonia. One of the police officers laughed at her description before catching himself and stopping abruptly.

"I know how ridiculous that sounds but that's exactly what came to mind as he stood there yesterday, hovering over my friend in the basement, and again today when he pinned me to the ground. I'd advise you to ask the shop for CCTV footage and then go on the hunt for him with your noses."

The same police officer who'd snickered was tempted to tell Ruth that they knew how to do their jobs, but he bit his tongue, and simply nodded.

Clodagh's phone buzzed, waking her up. It was a message from Ruth, instructing her to call as soon as she was awake. She did so, immediately, and listened as Ruth told her what had happened with Sid, the din of the other people on the bus competing with her voice. Clodagh realised the hand holding the phone was shaking as she listened to Ruth's account.

"God, Ruth, I'm so sorry. If you hadn't been there with me yesterday this wouldn't have happened."

"Clodagh, listen to me – this is *not* your fault."

"But he knows where you live!"

"Yes, he does, but hopefully the police will catch him today and we won't need to think about it again."

"Ruth, that's it. We're not doing any more of these events. It's too risky."

"Nonsense – we just need better security. This is likely a complete one-off. We're not stopping now, when we've built up this momentum."

Clodagh admired Ruth – everything about her. She admired her loyalty, her commitment to helping Clodagh become a successful writer, and above all her strength. Ruth had all of the traits she admired about Genoa, she realised as she sat shaking on her sofa that morning. But the characteristics she loved in both women – real and fictional – were those she knew were most lacking in herself. Clodagh wasn't the one that was attacked by Sid, but what he did to Ruth – and Clodagh's conviction that she was unequivocally to blame for it – caused a crack to form in that previously blissful time in her life. As the crack grew and spread, Clodagh became more and more anxious about life, more and more convinced that she couldn't sustain the early success of her work, and more alienated, and isolated.

The police identified Sid from the CCTV footage, but he'd done a runner, and the fact that no one knew where he was did nothing to assuage Clodagh's anxieties. She knew he was out there, somewhere, possibly preparing another attack on Ruth, or on herself.

CHAPTER 25

Clodagh slept fitfully in the chair that first night in the cottage, troubled by her dreams. In one dream, Sid tracked her to the cottage. He snuck in while she was sleeping, and set the cottage alight using the camping stove. He propped heavy objects against the door's exterior so that Clodagh was trapped inside. As she banged on the door, screaming at him to let her out, he yelled back that he was going after Ruth, and Danny.

Clodagh awoke with a start, her mental clock telling her it was close to dawn. The camping stove had only been off for a few hours, but it was freezing in the kitchen, and very dark. She shuffled over to the countertop, found a match and a tea light and, with numb fingers, lit the camping stove. She opened a tin of barley broth and warmed it on the stove for her breakfast. The soup made her insides tingle with warmth, and fortified her. She needed to get out of the chair and loosen her stiff and sore muscles and bones.

With no running water in the cottage, her first task was to sort out some kind of outdoor toilet. Danny had suggested she get a chemical toilet to use indoors but Clodagh refused, telling him that she would dig a hole outside.

"Okay, if you're sure. Don't build your poo-pit too close to the cottage, though. I don't want you attracting rats."

Rats. Until that moment, Clodagh hadn't even thought about rats. She imagined squatting over the pit, a snouty little rat-nose poking up at her nether regions. No, it wasn't going to happen, she told herself. *Get on with it.*

She put the head torch on, grabbed the brand-new shovel

she'd brought to do some garden work at the cottage and opened the front door to a rush of fresh, tangy air. She chose a spot far enough away from the cottage to avoid attracting unwanted visitors, but close enough should she need to use it in the night. An image of her beautiful room at Rothmore, with its elegant bathroom, popped into her mind, and she forced herself not to think of it. She'd made this choice, and she had to deal with it.

She was no survivalist, but she was reasonably pleased that she had managed to cook breakfast and dig the pit, all before the sun was fully up. Her first full day at the cottage stretched out ahead of her and Clodagh had some hard, physical slog planned.

She had things to do.

Clodagh knew that she should have started the day with a wash, and there was a stream running down from the hill into the sea that would be nice and close, if freezing. But she decided to save it until later, as she would get grimy doing the kind of work she had planned.

As she waited for the sky to lighten up enough for her to start work, she made a cup of tea and ate a second breakfast of a few oatcakes with peanut butter, keeping the door to the cottage open, and breathing in the smells and sounds of the morning. The birds filled the air with beautiful birdsong, some of which Clodagh could identify – blue tits, great tits, blackbirds, gulls squawking over each other. This close to the sea, the salt in the air was sharp, and she took a deep breath to fill her lungs. It was a perfect day to start work in Danny's garden.

Danny had originally wanted to have a vegetable patch, an idea that Paul vetoed since they would not be at the cottage often enough to take care of it. Danny agreed, but then had looked so disappointed that Clodagh suggested they could try a cottage garden. This idea had cheered Danny up, and when she had offered to help him, his smile had grown even wider.

On their last visit to the cottage, Danny and Clodagh

had brought some newly-purchased gardening tools along. After only ten minutes of digging, she discovered that the ground at the front of the cottage didn't want to be dug. It was claggy, clay soil, only recently released from the long grip of winter frost, and most likely also waterlogged with years of run-off from the hill. Centuries maybe. She persevered, and dug out common fiddleneck, plenty of thistle, couch grass, ground elder, and cleavers, which she set aside to dry out for tea. After an hour, she stopped working, drank every drop of water in her bottle, and ate a banana in three bites. She knew that it would be hard work, but wasn't prepared for the physical fatigue so early on. She had hours of digging ahead – days, most likely – until the ground would be ready for planting.

Clodagh was in good shape from all of the walking she did, but digging used dormant muscles, which now ached. She had started her marathon walks shortly after moving into Danny's flat, which was off Broughton Street at the east end of the city centre. She'd walk along Regent Road, through and around Queen's Park and up Arthur's Seat, enjoying the burn in her lungs as she climbed the steep hills. One of her favourite walks was out to Portobello beach, east along the sand as far as Joppa, then stopping for an unhurried coffee before walking back to Danny's. On these long walks, she discovered corners of Edinburgh she never knew existed.

After a few months she sought wilder spaces, taking the bus to the outskirts of the city – to Cramond in the west, and the Pentland Hills in the south, walking through their bleak splendour with only sheep for company, or the occasional dog and its owner. One of Clodagh's favourite places was Old Swanston, a cluster of thatched-roof cottages in which Robert Louis Stevenson had spent his summer holidays. She sat on the bench at the foot of the hills staring out across the city, feeling wonderfully distant from the worries that awaited her back in Danny's flat.

Clodagh's main source of anxiety stemmed from her inability to start working on the follow-up to *Genoa's Run*. She was plagued by insecurity and self-doubt. She had several ideas about what might happen next in Genoa's world, but couldn't decide which would be best. *Just start drawing*, she told herself, *and you'll find out if it works.* But, whenever she sat down to try out one of her ideas, she froze. Her pencil hovered over the page, almost like it was afraid to make a mark.

And then, to break the deadlock, she'd grab her rucksack, put on her shoes and go out walking. She hoped to walk off her insecurities, to keep moving, and be able to write again.

She discovered that she worked best in the evening, so she quit her job in the pub – they seemed relieved when she handed in her notice – and got one she loved, working as an assistant in the Central Fiction Library. The job was part-time, and the modest sales of *Genoa's Run* weren't flooding her with royalty payments, so money was tight. Danny, who'd worked hard learning the property development business as a paid employee, took the big step of setting up his own business with Paul. Paul's parents gave them money towards the purchase of their first project – a small one bedroom flat – which they renovated and sold within three months.

In just a little over two and half years after leaving home, Danny was co-owner of his own property company, and Clodagh couldn't have been happier. And then they'd invited her to live in their spare room, rent-free until she got back on her feet financially.

"Of course, we're expecting you to dedicate your next book to us," Paul said, not realising that he was rubbing salt in her wound.

One evening Danny came home with food from his favourite Vietnamese restaurant, and while they ate he talked about the latest property they were developing, which Paul was showing to potential buyers that evening. Clodagh thought their strategy was clever: buy and renovate small, one-bedroom flats that needed cosmetic work they could do themselves and then, after they'd built up some capital, work their way up to larger properties needing complete renovation. Clodagh was so proud of Danny, and of the success he had achieved. As he reached across the table for more noodles and she saw the sinewy muscles of his forearm she was, fleetingly, surprised, wondering why a grown man's arm was attached to her younger brother's body. She still thought of him as a little boy although, in so many ways, she knew he was much more grown-up than she was.

The flat in the West End that Danny and Paul had recently finished renovating had only just gone on the market, and there had been an open viewing the night before. Danny told Clodagh, "The flat was jammed with people, and I was trying to give people tours *and* answer questions and I could see one couple practically running towards the door."

He took another mouthful of noodles, and swallowed them quickly. "My first thought was that they must have stolen something, but then I saw it – black, greasy footprints all the way along the new cream carpet. It turns out the guy had come to the viewing straight after work and hadn't changed his work boots. He'd only gone and tracked engine oil all the way down the hall and into the sitting room, before his wife spotted them, which is when they tried to scarper."

"So, what happens now?"

"He agreed to pay for an industrial carpet cleaning. I'm not convinced it will get rid of all the grease, but hey-ho, it's worth a try."

"Did the greasy footprints put everybody else off?"

"Possibly. I don't think they helped, anyway." They ate in silence for a few minutes, and then Danny asked how Ruth was.

"She's so strong she acts like it hasn't affected her, but I don't know if that's possible. She's keen to organise more events, but I've been putting her off. They still haven't found the guy, and I'm worried he'll show up again."

"What a terrible thing to happen to her." Danny took another bite of food, chewed it while looking at Clodagh. "And to you, too. It's been traumatic. I've been wondering whether you might want to talk to someone. I've done a bit of searching, and I think I found a really good person."

Clodagh didn't know what he was getting at. "Talk to

someone about what?"

"About what you've been going through. It might help to talk to a counsellor."

Clodagh stared at him. "I'm not sure what you're getting at, Danny."

Danny looked at her gently, and reached over and took her hand in his. "I'm worried about you. You're restless, and anxious, and I think you might be depressed. I think going out walking is a great way of dealing with it, I really do. But I also think talking to someone might help. I'd like to pay for it."

Clodagh glared at him. The topic was a sore spot, because of their mother.

"Look, Danny, just because I'm having some issues right now doesn't mean I'm depressed. I'm not crazy. I'm not *hysterical*. Jesus. That is so offensive!"

He kept looking at her kindly, and holding her hand. "The last thing I wanted to do was hurt you. I'm sorry. I've just been so worried about you."

As quickly as Clodagh's anger had spurted up, it faded away. She could not be angry with Danny. She knew he just wanted to help her. But the thought of talking to a stranger scared her.

"Thank you, but I'm fine. I feel terrible about what happened to Ruth and now I'm scared that I'll never be able to start the second book, never mind finish it. Walking around Edinburgh is like a giant procrastination technique."

He gave a sad smile and said, "Okay, I can see that. Do you think talking to someone might help you work through the fear of the blank page?"

"Well it might – but I can't help but think that this is your sneaky way of getting me to talk to someone about my so-called depression."

Squeezing Clodagh's hand, he shook his head. "I'm not trying to be sneaky. At all. I think walking is good – a *little* bit of walking. Disappearing all day, every day might be a bit over the top." His eyes crinkled and Clodagh had to laugh.

"Who is this miracle worker you've found, anyway?"

"Her name is Martina, and she has appointments in her flat in Stockbridge. So right there you have half an hour's walk to get there, and another half hour back. Counting the hour that you'll spend with her, factor in a coffee and maybe a look around some of the shops there, that's nearly a whole day gone. Perfect opportunity for procrastination!"

Clodagh squeezed his hand as hard as she could, but it did not seem to cause him the discomfort she was hoping for. "Fine, give me her details and I'll think about ringing her."

Later that night, Clodagh tried to imagine what it would be like, sitting opposite a stranger, talking about herself. She did not want anyone to drill down into her emotions, making her talk about the past. Danny had lived the past with her, so they never had to talk about it. He just knew why she was the way she was. And Clodagh preferred it that way.

CHAPTER 26

At the start of their first session, Martina asked Clodagh to identify what was troubling her most about her life. Clodagh told
her, briefly, about Sid's attack on Ruth, and that she broke out in
a cold sweat whenever she thought about sitting down to write
the second book. Clodagh told Martina that, despite adopting a
pseudonym, her mother had found out about the book and read
it, which had unleashed a new strain of nastiness. As Clodagh
had feared, that led Martina to ask a number of questions about
their relationship over the years. And, although Clodagh had not
wanted to talk to a stranger about her mother, she realised that it
was not as bad as she'd feared. Martina was kind, and calm, and
the dimly-lit sitting room they were sitting in smelled like van-
illa, which Clodagh found relaxing.

Martina asked why Clodagh, her father and her brothers
kept allowing her mother to get away with such bad behaviour.

"If you keep accepting it, she'll keep doing it. You need to
tell her, and then show her, that it's not acceptable to treat any of
you that way. Until she changes."

Clodagh had never thought about it as *her* responsibility
for her mother's bad behaviour. She had come to think it was
something that had to be borne, not something that she could
change. But she could see that Martina was right: by not challen-
ging her mother, Clodagh was allowing her to keep acting that
way.

Months later, when Clodagh did finally find the courage
to confront her mother, she dealt with the confrontation the
same way she had treated Clodagh since her adolescence – by

showing complete disinterest, almost as though she wasn't listening. Clodagh told her mother that she had felt either ignored or rejected for much of her life. But her mother did not even acknowledge that she had heard Clodagh.

Clodagh had tried a few more times to tell her mother how she felt, urged by Martina not to give up. Martina said that it would no doubt take time, but that Clodagh needed to be consistent with the message that she would not allow her mother to continue to treat her that way.

And then Clodagh's mother had become very ill, and all of the problems in their relationship and communication came to a head when she had assumed that Clodagh would donate one of her kidneys to her, rather than ask her directly. Clodagh was silenced, her concerns ignored. Her mother made it clear, through Clodagh's father, that having the surgery was not just expected, it was her duty.

Clodagh tried to say "Listen to me, I'm saying no, I can't do this, I'm sorry." But neither parent was listening.

**

On Clodagh's second visit to Martina, she was asked to name the three people she loved most in the world. *Danny.* She didn't have two others. Martina asked for the most important relationships, the people that mattered most to Clodagh, as well as Danny, past and present. Clodagh pictured Aidan, and she saw him so clearly, so full of earnest love, but she still couldn't bring herself to talk about him. *Ruth.* Martina asked about Ruth, and Clodagh explained how Ruth had helped with the fundraising and promotion of her book, and had become a close friend. Ruth was loyal, patient, kind, and fun to be with. Clodagh said that she was worried their friendship would never be the same because of Sid's attack, and she wished she could have prevented it.

"Is it possible you love Ruth?" Martina asked.

"You mean in a romantic way?" Clodagh was getting a panicked feeling, like Martina had misunderstood her completely. She had the sudden urge to run away from their conversation.

"I mean in the widest sense of a loving relationship. It seems like Ruth plays a central role in your wellbeing."

"Well, I love our friendship." Clodagh realised that she loved Ruth almost as much as Danny. "I love her like a sister."

Martina then asked, "Is there anyone else important to you? Past or present."

"Not really. Look, I just don't feel like sitting and talking about myself today. I'm not up to this right now." Even as Clodagh said it, she knew she was setting up a huge flag emblazoned with *"evasion"* written across it, but she just wanted out of there, away from the conversation.

"I'm sorry if I've made you feel anxious, Clodagh. I didn't mean to. Tell me why Danny is so important to you."

Martina chose the right approach to defuse Clodagh's panic, and she settled back into the chair. It was easy to talk about Danny. She talked about him like other people talk about their children. Clodagh told Martina how she had known, even as a young girl, how much she loved him, how special he was to her. He had always been so sweet, such a good person, and from a very young age he proved himself to be unique.

Martina was a kind person, and Clodagh knew that she had not meant to make her feel inferior about her lack of personal relationships. That was her own doing, she knew. And Clodagh's resistance to what she was trying to help her understand disappeared when Martina said that it was wonderful that she had such a close relationship with Danny, that not all siblings had this, and that it had given her a good grounding in life. She also said that Clodagh's unconditional love for Danny must have been good for him, with the chaos and instability in their parents' relationship.

Clodagh had never seen it that way, had always credited Danny with saving her, but it was good to think that her love had been good for him, too.

Martina then said she had not meant to imply that there

was an ideal number of close loving relationships that any one person should have. She asked whether Clodagh considered herself a shy person, and Clodagh said that if she could avoid social situations like parties, or places where people gathered to look at her – like book readings - her mind came up with plenty of excuses to try to avoid them. Martina explained that some people were simply more comfortable in their own company, alone or with one or two others whom they loved. For those people, situations that required enforced socialising could result in a sensory overload that took time to recover from, so great was the impact on the person.

Clodagh was grateful to her for this framing of her life. She had always thought that the abrupt end to her relationship with Aidan, and her mother's extreme reaction, had left her too damaged to want to get involved again. Seeing it, instead, as a preference for solitude made her feel that this was her natural state.

One of the problems with the way Clodagh dealt with enforced socialisation, as Martina described it, was to overcompensate by acting like a friendly, confident person. Clodagh had done it at parties, where an evening of being with people was enough to tire her out for days afterwards. She had never been with the same group of people for days on end, as she had been at the retreat. She had not wanted them to know what a recluse she was, so she had projected confidence where there was none. Clodagh had been over-performing, and the stress that had caused her had contributed to her heightened emotions and anxieties, she knew, which had come to a head the night she ran away.

Clodagh was trying to use this new knowledge of herself, that Martina had helped her develop, to understand how she could have done something so drastic, so extreme. She knew that she could choose to feel guilty or not, but in this case she knew she *deserved* to feel guilty. The decent thing would be to go back to Rothmore and explain herself, or at the very least to make contact and let everyone know she was safe, but the easiest action was to stay hidden, and to bury the guilt deep inside. She told herself that she needed to focus on making a decision about her future, rather than dwell on the past, but she also knew that could be seen as a way to avoid facing up to her actions.

Clodagh could see her imperfections clearly, and she knew that Danny and Ruth could see them too. That they cared so much about her and were loyal to her despite her significant failings was a gift and a treasure that Clodagh clung to, as she went through the lonely process of deciding whether to have the surgery or not.

***

During her marathon walks around the city, Clodagh tried to work out what would happen to Genoa in the second book. If it was too happy it would not be realistic, she knew – but as she imagined all of the horrible fates Genoa could suffer, Clodagh also knew that she didn't have the heart to put Genoa through any of them. Genoa was smart, and she was strong, and she was courageous – and there had to be a way she could figure out how to stay alive in that terrible new world.

And then another effect of Clodagh's anxiety took hold: she stopped being able to eat most things. Weak cups of tea were fine, and she could still eat bananas. On a good day, she could also eat a bowlful of frozen peas, cooked until just warm. Everything else gave her the dry heaves, either before she put the food in her mouth, or as soon as she tried to take a bite of something. It made it incredibly difficult to manage her anxiety with long walks, because she had so little energy. A banana could keep her going for an hour, or sometimes two, but then she would feel weak and shaky, and had no energy to continue. And, most days, she could only eat two bananas in an entire day.

She felt light-headed and weak most of the time, and struggled to concentrate enough to answer questions, or carry out conversations. Her speech was slurred because her blood sugar was low. She was sure that people thought she was drunk or high, when really the problem was that her body just would not accept any nourishment.

When Clodagh saw Martina for the first time since the eating crisis, she had been unable to eat anything all day, and her speech and balance was off-kilter. She knew that she looked terrible, like a hollowed-out addict. As Clodagh tried to tell Martina what had been happening, it was as though the connection between her brain and her tongue was severed. She stuttered a bit, working hard to find the words to explain, but it all tangled up and came out as one long choking sob. And then she started to cry, a stream of hot tears running down her cheeks and into the open neck of her jumper.

Martina passed her a box of tissues, and came to sit beside her on the sofa. "Clodagh, I can see that you have been going through a terrible time since we last met. You don't have to say anything right now."

And she sat next to Clodagh, rubbing her back with her arm, until the sobs died down into sniffles. Clodagh felt physically worn out, as though a burning hole had opened up in her chest, but she also felt comforted by her kindness.

After a time, she was able to speak, and she told Martina what had been happening with food. Martina continued to sit beside her, and Clodagh felt the warmth of her body through her clothes. It was a nice, soporific feeling, and she realised that instead of talking she just wanted to lay down and sleep.

"Would I be able to have a nap?" Clodagh asked her. "I'd pay you for an extra session if I could just lay here and sleep."

Martina did not reply, but she stood up and left the room, and came back with a blanket, covered Clodagh up, then left the room and shut the door. Clodagh could hear her voice in the next room, speaking quietly, but she could not make out anything she was saying. And then Clodagh was away, carried into sleep again, the place of safety she had been retreating to for most of the day, every day.

When she awoke, she did not know where she was right away. There was no sound, there was not very much light and she did not recognise the back of the sofa she was staring at. And then she remembered: her emotions had crashed in a big way, and she had asked Martina if she could pay her to sleep in her flat. She looked down at her phone, and saw that she had been asleep for almost three hours. Clodagh wondered how much she had inconvenienced Martina, how many appointments she'd had to cancel. Clodagh sat up, and pulled the blanket up around her shoulders, feeling the chill of the newly-awoken. And then she saw a glass on the table, full of a whitish liquid. Not sure if Martina might be busy with another person, Clodagh decided to send her a text:

I'm awake. Sorry.

Within a minute there was a gentle knock at the door, and Martina poked her head through, and asked if she was okay.

"I'm so sorry, Martina, if I've messed up your day."

"You haven't."

"Is someone else here? I can just leave."

"It's just the two of us here. There's no rush to leave. I made you a drink, if you want it."

"I won't be able to drink it."

"It's what I drink when I'm not able to eat. It's kind of a meal in a glass. You could just take a sip and see what you think."

Clodagh just stared at the glass, not able to stop the mental images of taking a sip and then projectile vomiting all over Martina's room.

Martina said softly, "I've had problems with food for as long as I can remember. I stopped eating when I was eleven, and my parents tried to force-feed me. Then, whenever I would try to eat something, it would trigger vomiting. I was hospitalised a few times throughout my teens."

She paused, and Clodagh said, "I'm so sorry to hear that. Before this, I'd never had a problem with food. This has all come out of the blue. It's like I have no control over my body anymore." She took a breath, and more tears ran down her face. "So, you drink these instead of eating?"

"Not all the time, but when I need to. Sometimes I'm just not able to eat, and I have these instead."

"Anything I've tried to eat apart from bananas has made me puke."

"I'll go and get a bucket, if that makes you feel better." She was smiling, and it made Clodagh feel better to know that she did not think she was completely screwed up, that she understood what was happening to her.

Martina did get up, then, and came back a minute later with a bucket and a straw. "I find that texture can be a problem for me, sometimes. A straw helps."

Clodagh took a sip, and did not have the instant gag-reflex reaction she was expecting to have, and took another tentative sip, and that was okay too, and within a couple of minutes she had finished the drink. Martina explained that there was protein in it, and iron and glucose, and it should leave Clodagh with more energy than the only-banana diet.

The addition of the drink to her diet meant Clodagh could get back to her marathon-walking routine, enabling her to avoid writing on the days when she felt she just could not muster up enough brain power, and to burn off some of the anxiety that was plaguing her. She could feel the urge to work on the sequel returning, slowly, and she savoured the thrill of returning to the world she had created again. At last, she wanted to be there. She needed to finish Genoa's story.

CHAPTER 27

Clodagh had been seeing Martina for more than a year when it happened: *the big ask*. Her mother had been on dialysis for a couple of years at that point, and she was frailer and angrier every time Clodagh saw her. When Clodagh visited one Thursday afternoon, with a raspberry cheesecake her mother liked from the Italian bakery, her mother didn't get up from the kitchen table once. It was not uncommon for her father to fuss around, making pots of tea and organising snacks, but the temptation to show him how it should be done was always too strong, and her mother would push the chair back, huffing, and do just that.

But that day she just sat there, letting him make the tea, even letting him slice the cheesecake. When Clodagh asked how she had been doing, her mother did not answer, just looked at her with glazed-over eyes. After a moment her father said, "We wanted to talk to you about that, love. You know how you and mum have the same blood type? Well, if your tissue types also match, that means you can be a donor. You give her one of your kidneys and you'll be left with a perfectly healthy one."

At that stage, Clodagh hadn't taken the time to read much about kidney disease and treatment, and had no idea that this was even a possibility. She'd believed that her mother would keep getting dialysis and would either get better or not, and possibly would either get a dead person's kidney and get better, or not. She was not at all prepared for this discussion, or for this to be asked of her.

"You want one of my kidneys?" she asked.

"Mum will die without it, love," Dad said.

When Clodagh told Martina about this exchange, she listened and gave Clodagh her usual kind look, waiting until she took a pause.

"What are you thinking about doing?" she asked.

"The doctor and nurses I've spoken to have told me about the risks, and they've not been pushy about it in any way. But my parents don't seem to think there is any answer other than *Of course I'll do it*."

Martina nodded. "If you agree to it, what do you think is the worst thing that could happen?"

"I could die. During the operation or afterwards."

"And what do you think is the worst thing that could happen if you refuse to have the surgery?"

"My mother will almost definitely die."

Martina nodded again. "She might die anyway, even if you do give her one of your kidneys. You would be risking your own life to give her a chance to extend her life."

"If I say no, I'm effectively a murderer."

"If you say no, you are saying that you will not be a kidney donor for your mother. That isn't the same as murdering her."

"My parents don't see it that way. I'm not sure if I would ever be able to see it as anything other than knowingly killing her by saying no."

Martina shook her head. "This is life or death, Clodagh. That consideration exists for both of you."

Clodagh repeated what the medics had told her about the surgery, and how she couldn't get past the images of what would happen to her body. She told Martina that she had been doing some reading to find out more, and knew there were people who donated kidneys to complete strangers.

"This feels like something I should be automatically agreeing to. She's my own mother. There's the fear of the surgery, which at this point is huge. I know that I have a difficult relationship with my mother, so I'm also afraid that I'm being petty if I refuse. No, worse than petty - vengeful."

"Are you also a little bit worried about what other people will think of you, if you say no?"

"My dad made it fairly clear that he wouldn't even listen to no. I don't think he believes that I would refuse. I know I have the right to say no, but what does that really say about me – that I'm okay knowing that decision will kill my mother?"

"It's your body. It's your decision to make. The way other people react to that is their responsibility, really."

That was essentially what Danny had said to Clodagh, that she could only think of herself, and what *she* felt was the right thing to do. Clodagh asked Danny whether he knew what decision he would make, if he were in her position.

"Absolutely – I'd say no. I would not risk my life for hers. I know she's our mother, and she gave us life. But then, for reasons I will never understand, she systematically set out to tear apart any sense of self-worth we had. And Dad just stood by and let it happen, while he looked in the other direction."

He hugged Clodagh close to him. "I don't want anything to happen to you. Not ever – and certainly not because of this." His voice broke when he said the last word.

Danny knew his sister's self-esteem was fragile. Clodagh told him that she did not want to be responsible for their mother's death. Even on the days when her memories of their mother's emotional neglect were most powerful, Clodagh only wished her dead in her work – not in real life. She did not really want her to die, and she told Danny this.

"But Clodagh, sweetheart, she's quite happy to run the risk of you dying. She isn't even talking about the risks to you. It's still all about her."

"It must be terrible for her, though, Danny. Dialysis is bad enough, but to know she's dying…"

"It must be terrible. You're right. But we're all going to die. I just don't want you throwing yourself into its path, willingly."

***

Clodagh downed tools and leaned against the cottage, inspecting her work. She had made two piles of weeds, which looked like tall towers wilting in the sun. She grabbed a bottle of water and ate a protein bar, and then another.

It was early May, and yet the sun at midday felt like it was the height of summer. It was like this, on the east coast of Scotland, cold fog one day, hot sunshine the next. Clodagh liked Scottish weather, because it was never boring. Her back was complaining as she stood looking at the work she still had left to do, before the garden became a space Danny would love. Hot and sweaty, her skin stinging from the heat and the accumulated dirt, she decided it was time for a stream-bath.

She grabbed a towel and a bar of soap – inhaling the fresh lemon scent – and put on her bathing suit. She had not seen any sign of another person all day, but she didn't want to risk bathing in the nude just in case. Back outside, the sun warmed her as she walked to the stream. She slipped off her shoes, dipped a toe in, and pulled it out again quickly. It felt like she imagined water running off an iceberg would feel, in the coldest place on earth. The water was only up to mid-thigh level, so she stepped in with both feet, quickly, and started splashing water up the length of her body. She rubbed the bar of soap as quickly as she could, over all of the bits that needed it, including the roots of her hair, then knelt in the water and splashed water all over her body to rinse off the soap. Kneeling in the icy water made her gasp, and her body started to shiver, in an attempt to raise her core temperature.

She had hoped it would be invigorating, but painful was a more accurate description she thought, and she jumped out of the stream as soon as she had finished rinsing off. The experience had certainly cooled her down, and she was undoubtedly cleaner than she had been.

Back at the cottage, she grabbed her notebook and pencils and took them outside, hoping that the combination of the cold bath and the sunshine would spark even a tiny creative burst, and she could get some work done on the sequel. It was like stage fright, she thought, being so afraid of people looking at what she produced next that she could not find her way forward with Genoa. A few weeks before the retreat Clodagh had done a few preliminary sketches, which she thought had some potential. Genoa escaped from Scotland and flew to Canada with an RAF pilot who was also immune, probably due to a genetic condition and a presupposition to feeling invincible. His extreme arrogance caused Genoa to ditch the pilot when they landed in Canada, and begin her coast-to-coast search for other survivors, and for a cure.

Clodagh drew Genoa's face, which stared out from the page at her with a look of defiant resignation. Clodagh wanted to shout at Genoa to rage – to refuse to accept whatever terrible fate Clodagh might have in store for her. She drew her again, and this time Genoa's face was full of forlorn regret, as though she was saying goodbye to her world, and to the person who had created it. Clodagh tried to draw Genoa as a Valkyrie – to give her the chance to throw off the shackles Clodagh had placed on her – but it did not work, the illustration was unconvincing.

It was as Clodagh feared: she just was not in the right frame of mind to work on the sequel. Genoa's fate was inextricably linked to Clodagh's, and she could not see how her own crisis was going to turn out.

The publishers wanted the sequel to *Genoa's Run* next – of course they did – but Clodagh decided she would work on the sea witch book, instead. She had spent the past few days thinking about the story, and being right by the sea inspired her. The first sketch of her sea witch looked very much like Petra, with her long red hair and electric green eyes; Clodagh gave her skin an iridescent shimmer.

She drew her again, emerging from the sea, and this time the sea witch was statuesque like Ruth, with her elegant facial features, and undisguised mischief and mirth in her eyes.

She drew the lighthouse, standing tall and imposing, and its mirror image at a ninety-degree angle to the edge of the promontory, facing downwards into the sea. The upside-down lighthouse would be the sea witch's underwater lair.

The next drawings came quickly, a sequence of events as imagined by King James I of Scotland in 1590, when he was convinced that witches had caused a terrible storm at sea that threatened his life and that of his new bride, Anne of Denmark, as they crossed the North Sea. One of the women accused of witchcraft confessed that two hundred women – from Scotland and Denmark – had sailed in sieves to North Berwick, where the devil urged them to kill the king and his bride. Clodagh drew the ravings of the king's paranoid mind, including the women plotting and planning at Tantallon Castle, overlooking the mighty Bass Rock.

Clodagh's sea witch, Madrigal, calmed the storm that raged when the king and his bride crossed, ensuring that they were able to dock safely at Leith, in north Edinburgh. She had saved their lives, but she could not save the lives of the women who were accused of plotting to kill them.

Pleasantly tired from her flurry of activity, Clodagh set the pencil down and looked at her last drawing, of Madrigal standing at the top of the lighthouse, staring out over the sea in the direction of Edinburgh, where so many women accused of involvement in the North Berwick plot were executed. Her face was etched with sadness, compassion, and pain for the women she could not help. It was uncanny, Clodagh thought, that Madrigal's face staring through the window looked just like her mother's.

Clodagh took the notebook back into the cottage and, as the water boiled on the camping stove, she had a conversation in her mind with Danny. She told him about the drawings, and he told her he was happy that she had made a start. He did not make any comment when she told him the sea witch had their mother's face in the last frame. She told him she was going to have a cup of tea and then walk back to Rothmore, to explain her actions and to apologise. He seemed happy with this decision, too. She told him that she had made a decision about the surgery and he was silent. At long last, when she was almost finished drinking her tea, he said *You know I will support you whatever you decide.*

CHAPTER 28

As Clodagh crested the dunes, the choppy, white-capped waves reared up and then crashed down on the shore. A storm was whipping up, which she had been oblivious to in the sheltered cove of the garden at the cottage. She walked west, straight into the sun, in the direction of Rothmore. With every step, she fought against the coward's walk, back in the direction of the cottage; instead, she told herself that she had to go back, to apologise to Jane, Fingal and her fellow guests for running off.

Clodagh watched as the storm rolled in from the west, turning the sky from dark grey to almost black. After twenty minutes of walking, the coastline receded enough that she could see Midhallow Island, sitting in the sea like a great beast turned to rock. A great beast that had swallowed twenty-eight people whole and kept them in its belly. She shuddered to think about what she had seen, the whispered voices she heard that night on Midhallow and how - instead of trying to listen – she had done her best to silence them. She had poured alcohol on them, and disbelief. Nor did she want to remember what she had seen – the ghostly vision begging her for help. And then, when it had happened again in that terrible place where women accused of witchcraft were imprisoned, she had fled.

She realised that she was not just symbolically walking back towards Rothmore – she *needed* to go back. It was wrong to let the others think that she had just disappeared into thin air, and she was ashamed of herself. She kept walking into the storm, bracing herself for their anger, for whatever else they threw at her.

She picked up her walking pace, determined to get to Rothmore as quickly as possible. After a few minutes, a sharp scream pierced the air, and Clodagh looked back over her shoulder to see a woman running towards her.

"Help!" she shouted and although Clodagh could see that her mouth was still moving, the rest of her words were lost to the wind. She was pointing wildly at the sea, stabbing her arms towards the rough waves. Clodagh looked into the water, but could see nothing, and so she began to hurry towards the lashing waves. The woman shouted again and then Clodagh saw it: a long red strip of fabric that might have been a scarf, a ribbon or - a dog's lead.

Clodagh ran towards the sea and as she got closer it became clear just how far out the lead was. The water was murky grey, making it impossible to see anything below its surface. She could not see any dog attached to the lead. She tried to run into the sea but the water was so rough she could only wade in, every step happening in super-slow motion. At one point a strong wave caught her and dragged her under, as though it was a sea creature, and then she was spinning and rolling in the water. After what seemed like hours, she broke the surface, sputtering, salt water stinging her eyes. At last, when she was close enough to reach the lead, she pulled on it, hoping there would be a dog attached.

And there was. Clodagh pulled his little soaking body out of the water, and carried him back to shore where his owner was waiting, crying hysterically. Clodagh passed his lifeless body to the woman, who begged her to do something. Her medical knowledge was limited, acquired through medical dramas on TV and in films, and all she could think to do was compress his tiny chest five times, then wait, then do it five times more.

With a splutter and a hoarse bark, the little dog's eyes opened, and with that his owner started crying even harder. She buried her head in his fur, no longer aware of Clodagh's presence. Clodagh tried to say that she hoped the dog was okay but she was shivering so much her mouth would not work properly.

Trying to get the blood pumping through her veins by moving as quickly as she could, Clodagh started walking back in the direction of the cottage. But her legs felt like they were buried in sand, she was dizzy and light-headed. Her centre of gravity was off, and she struggled to keep her balance.

At last, she made it back to the cottage, shivering so violently that she could barely pull off her wet clothes, as if they were welded to her skin with sea water. She dried herself as best she could with a towel, then pulled on every single item of warm clothing she had. She wrapped both of the thermal blankets around her body, then switched on the heater and sat as close as she dared to it, hoping the blankets would not catch fire.

Clodagh could not stop shivering and, although she knew that meant her body was warming up, it was a terrible feeling, as though she had no control over herself. Her teeth were chattering so much her jaw ached. She knew she needed to drink something hot but was shaking so much she did not trust herself to use the stove. She tried to think herself into warm, tropical places, hoping her imagination would help warm her, but she found it difficult to stop feeling the cold, grey sea bubbling up all around her, pulling her under.

Clodagh lost all sense of time sitting there, staring into the heater, shivering, overcome with latent fear about the dangers of wading into the angry sea. She hoped the wee dog had recovered. When she realised that her hands were shaking less, she thought it might be safe enough to work the camp stove, but before she could give it a try she was overcome with a sudden rush of pure exhaustion. She switched off the heater, moved clumsily through the dark cottage to the bedroom and climbed into her sleeping bag. Her limbs felt like lead weights, and she was asleep instantly.

***

She dreamed about the sea witch, who was in the sea with her, pulling on the red lead. In her dream the sea witch held the dog under water and Clodagh dove into the roiling grey waves, grabbed the witch and the little dog, and pulled all three of them to the surface. The sea witch and the dog ran off down the beach while Clodagh stood in the waves like they were quicksand, unable to get onto solid ground. As she watched their bodies retreat, she felt a sudden sharp stabbing pain in her head, as though the claws of a giant sea creature were pulling her back under the surface of the water.

***

Clodagh awoke, a sharp pain piercing through her ear and straight through her head. Her jaw throbbed dully, pain which became sharper when she swallowed or tried to move her head. She cupped her hand over her ear in an attempt to dull the pain, thinking that she needed to get up from the mattress and search for some ibuprofen.

A wave of nausea and exhaustion rippled through her, and she fell back to sleep.

***

Clodagh was back on the beach in the middle of a terrible storm, trying to keep her balance against the wind. Her father was there, cupping his hands against her ears, yelling to be heard against the wailing wind.

"Clodagh, you don't have to think about it anymore. Your kidneys were washed out to sea. We've found a new pair for your mother. But right now, we need to get out of the storm."

And then her father led her to a boat, a small white boat that looked insubstantial for the scale of the storm. Its name, *Kidney*, was painted in blood-red on the side of the boat.

"I'm not getting in that boat with you," Clodagh told him. "We'll drown."

"It's going to take us back to Edinburgh, and you're going to sleep in your own bed tonight. Come on, sweetheart, get in. I promise I'll keep you safe."

Clodagh climbed into the boat, sitting at the front with her elbows jutting out either side. As her father rowed she yelled, "Heave! Heave!"

Her father's voice dropped several octaves as he chanted, "Great gods of the sea, carry us back to our home without peril. Keep us safe from harm."

But her father's chant-prayers were in vain, because at that moment a giant wave in the shape of a monster's hand reared up out of the sea and swept him out of the boat. Clodagh could see the lights of Edinburgh in the distance as she gripped the oars and rowed the boat steadily towards them through the storm. When her arms became too sore and too weak to carry on rowing, the boat kept moving forward towards the lights, as though some unseen hand guided her home.

***

Clodagh awoke to what sounded like the roof being ripped off the cottage. The storm had worsened, and gales were battering the old building. She tried to lift her head up, but it felt like someone was cutting into the right side of her head with a sharp knife. She wanted a painkiller, and a glass of water. But when she tried to sit up, the pain was so intense it triggered the heave reflex. Nauseous and weak, she let her head sink back down, and slipped into unconsciousness once again.

***

When Clodagh opened her eyes again the sea witch was there, standing over her, holding a glass of water. Clodagh reached for it greedily, and the sea witch leaned down so that she could pour some of it into Clodagh's mouth. Although the witch's mouth did not open, Clodagh could hear her say clearly, "The sea has made you ill. Drink, and it will heal you."

Clodagh spat the salty water out onto the floor beside the

air mattress. "I can't drink polluted sea water! Are you trying to kill me?"

The witch reached down and put a cool hand on Clodagh's forehead, gently pushing her head back down.

***

The wind rattled the windows, the brass knocker on the front door tapped the wood relentlessly. Clodagh knew she should get up, find some ibuprofen, and drink some water. Every movement was painful as she worked her body out of the sleeping bag, and as she sat up the pain was excruciating. She tried to stand up, but her legs were like wet noodles, unable to take her full weight. But she needed a painkiller – badly – so she tried to move towards the kitchen by shuffling on her knees, cupping her hand against her right ear, hoping the pain would abate.

But it did not. Clodagh feared her head was about to explode. She needed to get back to the mattress, and lay her head down. She knew, though, that she was not going to make it, that she would most likely pass out from the pain. She needed to get back inside the sleeping bag, and keep warm.

Just then Clodagh felt arms around her, lifting her up, helping her walk. And then Ruth was saying, "Come on, Kidneys, let's get you back to bed."

"Ruth, it's me – Clodagh. Don't you recognise me?"

"Of course I do. That's why I'm here. I've come to rescue you."

"Ruth, could you get me some water, and some ibuprofen?'

"I've got them right here. Just lie back down and you can have them."

"Ruth, where have you been? Why didn't you come sooner?"

Ruth said that she had been at the cemetery, to mark the anniversary.

"Of what?"

"My sister Emily died ten years ago. Don't you remember

me telling you about her?"

Clodagh could not remember, but she did not tell Ruth that. She did not want to appear any more self-absorbed than Ruth must already think she was. An image of Ruth's double, only younger, flashed through her brain. Had she seen a photograph of Emily, perhaps?

"She'd been unwell for such a long time, but the thing was, I actually thought she was getting better. She'd started eating again, we were spending more time together, and then – one night she disappeared on a night out. The next day her body washed up on the shore in South Queensferry. She'd jumped off the Forth Road Bridge."

Clodagh reached her arms up towards Ruth, trying to hug her. "Oh Ruth, I'm so sorry. You've been carrying this sadness around all this time. And now *I've* disappeared."

"I knew where you were, though. Unlike some people, I have to say. People who are worried sick about you."

"I know I shouldn't have run away, but I saw a ghost, Ruth. *My* ghost."

"The people you were with at the retreat, they're really worried about you."

"I feel terrible about that."

"You should. I understand why you did it, but you *should* feel terrible. I'll tell them you're safe, tell them where you are."

"Oh, please don't do that. I just want to be alone."

"Clodagh, you're really ill. You need our help."

She tried pleading with Ruth not to tell anyone where she was, but no more words would come out. Sleep washed over her again.

CHAPTER 29

Petra switched off the car engine and thought, for the ump-teenth time, that might be the last time the old car ever ran. It had served her well, had unexpectedly and without any problem enabled her jaunt after she fled Rothmore, and she was grateful. She leaned against the back of the car, stretched out her stiff muscles, and watched as the cars drove past. About ten minutes later, a black sedan stopped, and a bald man leaned out the win-dow and asked if she needed any help. She said she was waiting for a friend, and thanked him. As he drove away, a child sitting in the back seat stuck two fingers up at Petra, while shoving the index finger of the other hand up her nose.

Fifteen minutes later, a red car pulled off the road, and nudged up beside Petra. Petra recognised Ruth from one of the photos she had found of Clodagh: she had a friendly face, green eyes that exuded warmth, and an anxious smile.

"Petra?"

"Hi Ruth. Thanks for meeting me."

"Hop in and we'll see if we can't find our girl."

Our girl. Petra heard affection, and warmth and maybe some exasperation and worry in Ruth's voice.

Ruth fiddled with her phone, and explained that she had GPS co-ordinates for the location, but had never been there be-fore. "Danny told me how to get there, so hopefully we'll be okay."

She looked over at Petra, "Buckled up? Okay, let's go. You'll have to forgive me if I bunny-hop the car a bit while we get going – it's a hire car and I'm not great with it yet. I needed it to get to *my* retreat last week."

Petra wanted to ask more about that but, before she could, Ruth asked her to explain why she was so worried about Clodagh. Petra described what Clodagh told her she had seen on Midhallow, how upset she had been at Beltane, and about the reading in the witches' prison.

"I mean, I never should have suggested it. I honestly didn't even think about the chance it would cause her to have another hallucination. It's my fault completely that she's run off."

Petra gave Ruth the details about how they had realised that Clodagh was missing, their search, the lifeboat, and the police.

Ruth took a deep breath. "Petra, I can't break Clodagh's confidence, but I can tell you that she has been going through a very difficult time recently. Family issues. She had planned some time by herself after the retreat, at her brother's cottage, and I think that's where she is. I *hope* that's where she is, anyway. Although why she would have gone there in the fog is anyone's guess." She looked over at Petra. "She really said she saw an apparition on Midhallow?"

"Yes, that looked just like her."

"Jeez-o. She's likely worried that she's losing her mind, on top of everything else."

They drove in silence, mulling over their worries and thoughts as Ruth drove along the coast road. The coastal landscape changed from mudflats at Aberlady to grand dunes and tall sea grasses at Gullane, where they could see the Bass Rock looming white in the sea, looking like an iceberg, or something that would not be out of place in the northern Atlantic. Ruth turned off onto a single-track road, where they bumped along slowly through a continuous stream of pot-holes.

After about ten minutes the road jogged sharply east and then came to a complete stop in the face of a row of white birch trees. "We'll have to walk from here," Ruth said. "It should be just ahead."

They got out and walked past the trees, then were faced

with tall, sandy dunes that separated the road from the beach. The air was sharp with the tang of the sea, and they heard sea birds calling noisily to each other. They walked along a narrow sandy path up a steep slope, and then came to a tall hedge of sea buckthorn. There was a large hole shaped in the hedge, through which they saw a white cottage with a red door. The ground had recently been dug, and two tall piles of weeds threatened to collapse under their own weight.

"That's it," Ruth said, rushing to the door and trying the handle. It was locked. She knocked on the door, calling out to Clodagh, but there was no answer.

"Now I've got a bad feeling about this, too," she said, looking worried. "I think she's in there, and can't get to the door."

Ruth searched in her bag and when she pulled out something metallic she looked at Petra and said, "Don't judge me."

Petra was not judging - she was impressed when Ruth slipped the tool in the keyhole and jiggled it a bit. There was a soft clicking noise, and the door opened.

They were just inside the door when they saw a thick pile of clothes stretched out across the kitchen floor, giving off a rank smell of must and brine. Ruth called out to Clodagh again, moving her way through the small cottage. It was cold and damp and dark, lit only by the light coming in through the door. They could both sense that something was wrong, and Petra stood there, taking in the camping equipment and the tins of food and the terrible state of the place.

Petra heard Ruth's strangled cry of "Clodagh!" from the other end of the cottage, and Petra rushed through. In the dark, small space of the bedroom, a figure was lying inert on a mattress. Ruth put her arms under the small body and pulled her towards her.

She said, in a trembling voice, "Clodagh, sweetheart, can you hear me? It's Ruth, and Petra."

Ruth touched Clodagh's cheek, gently, and felt for a pulse. Even in the darkness of the room, or perhaps because of it, Petra could see how ill Clodagh looked. Petra feared the worst, as Ruth reached out again and pinched Clodagh's cheek, and then the skin on the top of her hand.

"Clodagh, wake up love. I'm going to get you some water." Ruth reached into her bag and pulled out a bottle of water, then put her thumb on Clodagh's chin, which opened her mouth up slightly, and poured a trickle of water in. There was a quiet sputter, and Clodagh's eyes opened.

"Ruth," she said in a hoarse voice. She started to say more, but Ruth put her hand on Clodagh's arm and told her not to talk.

"Oh Clodagh, what happened to you?" Ruth asked, her voice choked with tears.

Clodagh's eyes had closed again. 'She's burning up, and I'm guessing she's seriously dehydrated. I'll call an ambulance." Ruth took out her phone, but could not get a signal.

"I'll go outside and try," Petra said. But outside, she was dismayed to find that she had no signal either. She rushed back inside, and found Ruth trickling more water into Clodagh's mouth. She told Ruth she thought they should take Clodagh to the hospital, since there didn't seem to be any way to get an ambulance to come to the cottage.

With one deft motion Ruth scooped up Clodagh's limp body, and they ran to the car. Petra offered to drive, and Ruth tossed her the keys, then got in the back of the car with Clodagh, cradling her head in her lap and speaking softly to her, giving her small sips of water. Clodagh mumbled for most of the journey, incoherent words that Ruth responded to as though she knew what she was saying.

Petra drove like a bandit, determined to get Clodagh to the hospital as quickly as possible. Fever, dehydration, delirium – they both knew that Clodagh needed urgent medical attention. Fortunately, they did not encounter any police cars on the way, and twenty minutes later Petra pulled the car up to the front of the A&E department at the Royal Infirmary in Edinburgh.

***

While the medics did whatever they were doing to help Clodagh, Ruth and Petra waited, impatiently, in the waiting area. Ruth paced, and Petra tried to calm herself by doing silent spells for healing and recovery. Ruth phoned Danny and explained what was happening. Petra heard her promise to ring him again as soon as there was any news. She then phoned Clodagh's parents, who knew that she had gone missing from Rothmore and had been beside themselves with worry. Ruth phoned Jane and Fingal, and told them that Clodagh had been found. She asked them to let the police know.

Petra left, just for a few minutes, to buy some snacks. She knew that neither of them really wanted to eat, but she was motivated by the desire to do *something* useful.

When, at last, a nurse came to speak with them, she explained that Clodagh was in intensive care. She had a fever, and severe dehydration, likely caused by hypothermia. They were not allowed to see her until her condition had improved. Ruth phoned Danny, and then Clodagh's parents. She paced for hours, until she exhausted herself, finally. She slumped down in one of the hard, uncomfortable plastic hospital seats beside Petra and closed her eyes.

"Why don't you try to get some sleep?" Petra asked her. "I'll wake you up if anything happens."

"Thank you, but I don't think I'd be able to sleep. I can't stop thinking about what might have happened to her. It's like a horror film, playing over and over in my mind."

"She's strong. Do you want a coffee or anything?"

Ruth reached down and took Petra's hand in hers. "No, thank you. And I want to thank you for contacting us – Danny, I mean. Imagine what might have happened if we hadn't found her today."

"But we did."

Ruth squeezed Petra's hand, and then she told her what had been happening in Clodagh's life, about the decision she faced. Petra remembered Clodagh's tears the night of Beltane, how she had told them she was working through some things. She could only guess at how difficult it must have been for Clodagh, faced with such a decision and not having anyone to talk to. Her brother was in New Zealand, Ruth was away and could not be reached by phone, and her fellow guests were completely oblivious.

Petra wished she could go back to the start of the retreat, and do it all differently. She would have taken better care of Clodagh, looked out for her, and not placed her in the situation that had tipped her over the edge.

CHAPTER 30

Neither of them slept, but around midnight Ruth and Petra stopped talking, and sat silently together in a state of exhaustion, waiting for news. Just after four in the morning, one of the nurses came to see them and said, "Clodagh opened her eyes and called for Ruth, then fell back to sleep."

Ruth was up out of her seat in a flash, saying that she wanted to go and see Clodagh. The nurse nodded, but when Petra asked to see her as well, the nurse said, kindly, that it would be best not to overwhelm Clodagh with too many visitors.

At a few minutes after six o'clock, Ruth came back through to the waiting area. Her face spoke of physical and mental exhaustion, but she looked exhilarated, too. "Clodagh's awake," she said, beaming, "and she wants to see you."

Clodagh was sitting up in bed, still worryingly pale but with a spark in her huge brown eyes. She said, "Ruth tells me you saved my life."

"It was Ruth, really. She drove us to the cottage. I would never have figured out where you were."

"That was kind of the point," Clodagh said, smiling. "I was meant to be in splendid isolation. Well, she says I owe *you* my life. And I think I owe you an explanation."

She told Petra about what had happened since she had run away from Rothmore in a reverse chronology, starting with the dog in the sea, and her brief period of isolation. She told Petra what she had seen in the witches' prison, and apologised for running away.

"I know you didn't think I was going to have another vision there. I was feeling so fragile anyway, and when I saw it again – I just had to get away." Her eyes filled with tears and she said, "I hope you can forgive me. And I should have told you before I left. It was cruel not to."

Petra told her there was nothing to forgive, that it was *her* fault. She told Clodagh to focus on her recovery, instead of what had happened.

"I'm not out for pity. I don't want you to feel sorry for me, I just wanted to explain. The thing is, I had decided to go back to Rothmore to apologise for running away, when the dog went into the sea."

Petra wondered if she should give Clodagh a hug, or if that would be inappropriate or possibly even uncomfortable for her. Instead, she relied on the old standbys. "I'm so glad you're okay, Clodagh. Now, can I get you a cup of tea and some chocolate biscuits?" Clodagh laughed, and said that would be perfect.

Petra asked at the nursing station if she was allowed to take Clodagh some food, and the nurse said, "Not really, but I would never stand in the way of a cup of tea and some chocolate biscuits."

Petra told Ruth that she was going to get some snacks, and she came back with tea for all of them, a pack of chocolate biscuits for Clodagh and one that she left at the nurses' station.

When Petra walked back into Clodagh's room Ruth was there, and Clodagh was telling her what she could remember about her delirium. As she recounted some of the conversations she'd had with people who had appeared in the cottage, which she had believed were real, Ruth looked more and more uncomfortable. Sensing this, Clodagh asked what was wrong.

"When you woke up the first time you said that I'd told you about my sister, but I've never talked to you about it, not once."

Clodagh hesitated and then asked, "About the Forth Road Bridge?"

Tears bubbled up in Ruth's eyes and she nodded. "I've kept

that buried, because I can't bear to talk about it."

"Are you sure you didn't tell me before – maybe one night after we'd been drinking?"

"Do you remember me telling you before?"

Clodagh shook her head. "Just when you came to me in the cottage." Looking a bit spooked, she turned to Petra and asked, "You've read so much, Petra - is there any explanation for this?"

Petra had, in fact, read about dream telepathy, when patients in comas or other states of unconsciousness communicated with other people. It was said that they had gained knowledge of events and experiences they could not otherwise have known about. As she told Clodagh and Ruth what she had read about the subject they looked at each other, sharing some unspoken communication that Petra could only guess at.

***

After Ruth had phoned Clodagh's parents to say that she was awake, they arrived at the hospital within the hour, looking like they had not slept for days. Her mother had great difficulty walking, and her father looked like he was on the verge of tears. Ruth was in Clodagh's room, so Petra introduced herself and told them what she knew about Clodagh's condition and, also, about what had happened to her since leaving Rothmore.

Clodagh's father said, "We both thought she was dead. We thought someone had taken her, and we'd never see her again." Clodagh's mother did not say anything, but she looked like she was reliving days of stress and worst-case thinking.

After a pause, she asked, "Did she say why she ran away?"

Petra debated not telling her what she knew, as it did not seem her place to intervene in such a significant family event. The knowledge she had about Clodagh's relationship with her mother was derived from the little that Ruth had told her, and from instinct. As diplomatically as she could, Petra said, "I think she needed some time to come to terms with the surgery."

Both parents were crying then, and Clodagh's father

pulled his wife to him, tightly. "It's my fault," he said. "I just didn't listen to her. She told us she was scared."

There was a question Petra knew she could ask, one question that could have the power to take away Clodagh's fear and sadness, and to help this broken couple. And when Petra asked it, she received the answer she was both hoping for and dreading.

***

By nine o'clock there was practically a full-house of visitors, taking over the waiting area as they waited to see Clodagh. Samuel, Gill and Erik had arrived soon after Ruth had phoned Rothmore to let them know Clodagh was awake. They brought a huge balloon bouquet that they said was from all of them – Jane and Fingal included – even though it seemed to Petra like the last thing Jane would have approved of. Petra had stopped counting how many times they had been shushed by the nurses since they had all arrived.

Erik pulled Petra to him in a tight bear-hug, telling her that she was amazing for finding Clodagh.

"I didn't, really – it was Ruth."

"You both did, I know, but you made it happen. Now stop protesting and let me tell you that I'm proud of you."

The nurses told them all several times that they were concerned about Clodagh having too many visitors, and were insistent that they would have to ask everyone to leave, and that only a few people should come back during the afternoon visiting hours. Although everyone nodded compliantly, as soon as the nurses were out of earshot a plan was hatched to retreat to a nearby café, where they could get breakfast and regroup for the afternoon visitation.

As they were getting reading to go, Ruth appeared and told Petra that Clodagh wanted to speak to her.

When Petra walked into Clodagh's room, she had to laugh at the sight of her, propped up against the pillows, book-ended by two brand new stuffed animals and the ridiculous balloon-bouquet beside her, looking tired but happy. On the bedside table was an assortment of bags of sweets, some grapes, and several bottles of the copper-coloured soft drink so beloved in Scotland.

She saw Petra looking at them and said, "From my dad. He swears this is the cure for all that ails you."

"Scotland's other national drink," Petra laughed. "Maybe they could pump some of that straight into your veins."

Clodagh laughed, then looked at Petra sombrely. "My parents told me that you had a chat with them about the surgery."

"I hope you don't mind. I know it wasn't my place to tell, but I thought it might save you a difficult conversation with them."

"I don't mind at all. But I mean that you said you have the same blood type as my mum, and offered to be a donor if your tissue types match."

Petra nodded, and they stared at each other in silence, as Clodagh's eyes filled up with tears. "Petra, this is a serious operation, and there are significant risks."

Petra nodded again. "I'm aware of that."

"You hardly know me, and yet you've stepped up to do this so I don't have to." Two fat tears popped out of her eyes, and slowly rolled down her cheeks.

"Petra, just because I ran away – I mean, you don't owe me anything. I know you never meant for me to be scared. I just – well, I over-reacted and -."

Petra smiled at her. "That isn't why I volunteered to do this."

Clodagh gave Petra a look that was so sad, and so grateful, that she felt a twinge in her heart. "I'd decided I was going to do it, you know," she said. "Honestly – before I went in the sea after the dog I decided I would go and apologise to Jane and Fingal, and the rest of you, then go home and tell my parents I'd do it."

"Your body has taken a hammering in the last couple of days. You need to give it a proper rest."

"Petra, I don't know what to say. I want to say thank you, but that's not enough. You, and Ruth, you literally saved my life yesterday, and now – doing this – I just -." She was crying softly, unable to say any more.

"Hey, enough," Petra said, putting her arms around Clodagh gently. "You're making me out to be some kind of hero or something, and I'm definitely not that. Just think of how many karma points I'll get for doing this!"

***

There was a celebratory atmosphere in the waiting area when Petra re-joined the group, out of relief that Clodagh had been found and was out of danger. Her parents seemed a bit bewildered by the whole crowd and, although they were hanging back on the fringe of the group somewhat, Samuel and Erik were doing their best to include them in the conversation and make sure they knew they were welcome.

Erik put his fingers on Petra's elbow, gently, and asked, "How is Clodagh?"

"Tired. I think what she really needs is for all of us to leave now and take our noise with us. She needs rest."

"And you? Are you okay?"

"I'm tired, too. I can't pull all-nighters any more. Not at my age."

He laughed and said, "None of that! Fifty isn't that old."

Petra looked at him in shock, and saw that he was joking. "Erik, I'm half that age."

"Oh well, a spring chicken then." He was quiet for a minute and then he said, "I wanted to tell you that I read the writing you sent me. It's *very* good, Petra. Whatever happens, please make me a promise that you won't stop writing."

"I promise."

"And feel free to send me more. In fact, *please* send me more – I want to read it."

Pride bubbled up inside Petra's chest, as though all of the time that she had been so angry and resentful that she was unable to write – washed away, and she was left with a strong, pure sense that she had started something important and she would finish it this time, too. She would keep her promise to Erik, the same one she had made to the women who had told her their stories, and to her mother.

She thanked him, her voice breaking as she did so, and Erik pulled her to him in another mighty bear-hug. She thought it was just the kind of hug her father would have given her, if he could.

CHAPTER 31

They kept Clodagh in hospital for three days. The first day was a blur – quite literally at first, because she spent much of it unconscious, or so they told her. And then it was a blur of pure, raw emotions that she could not seem to hold back. In truth, she did not even try to hold them back. Rivers of emotion flowed through her, and right out of her: she cried, for happiness and relief and from sadness that had been stored up inside her for so long. Clodagh thought it might have been a bit like having an out-of-body experience, watching this happen to someone else.

Ruth.

The truth had been right there in front of Clodagh for years, and she had kept it at arm's length. The length of a whole *parade* of arms. But now that Clodagh realised how she truly felt about Ruth, it was like she was able to leave the old Clodagh somewhere else, perhaps in a remote part of the landscape that she had once traversed, when she had tried to walk off her insecurities, and her anxieties. Clodagh pictured that abandoned version of herself, the Clodagh of the past, who had been hurting, and trying to find her way through the pain.

When she had opened her eyes for the first time and saw Ruth sitting on the side of her bed, holding her hand, she asked with a croaky voice, "Ruth? Is it really you?"

"Yes, I'm here," Ruth said, breaking into a wide smile.

"I was trying to say it before, back at the cottage, when you were telling me about your sister. I love you Ruth."

"I know you do. And I love you."

Clodagh's parents.

Clodagh thought they looked like two little old people when they had first poked their heads into her hospital room. She was full of guilt because it was her actions – the fact that she had run away - that had caused them to look that way. *If only*, she thought, *I had just told them that I was going to Danny's cottage to get my head straight. If only I'd yelled and screamed at them before I went on the retreat, I'd have cleared that vein of anger, resentment and bitterness that has been flowing through me since I was a little girl.*

Clodagh had been so angry with her mother for so long, and then when she saw her in the hospital room, looking like *she* was the one who should be lying in a hospital bed, Clodagh had the clear understanding that she would have done anything to help her. No matter what had happened between them, inside her mother was the core of a good person, coated in layers of bitterness and frustration and resentment. Clodagh recognised that. That was who she was at risk of becoming. *Was.*

When Clodagh had a moment alone with the nurse, before her parents had arrived, she had asked what effect the hypothermia and dehydration would have on her ability to go through with the organ donation. The nurse told Clodagh that she would be in too delicate a state for the foreseeable future, that she would not be able to have the surgery. Clodagh had cried - hot, wet, angry, shameful tears. *If only,* she thought again – *if only I hadn't gone to stay at the cottage. If only I'd not been on the beach and gone into the sea.* She cried for the little dog she had saved, only to destroy her chance to help save her mother.

Petra.

A complete stranger until a week ago. Clodagh was trying to channel her energies into being grateful to Petra, rather than feeling guilty that she had offered to be a donor for Clodagh's mother after only just meeting her, when Clodagh herself had not been quick to make the decision about what to do. And, as nonchalant as Petra had been about it, Clodagh was sure that she had seen fear in her eyes. Not surprising, really – that kind of surgery was not a walk in the park. It was completely selfless and kind. Clodagh felt that she owed Petra a debt too huge to put into words, too great to ever repay.

But she would try. She would definitely try.

What was the story with these new psychic powers she had acquired? She had been unconscious for one day and suddenly she was able to communicate with people without actually speaking to them. Well, not *any* people: Ruth. Clodagh wasn't sure why that had not put Ruth off her completely, but it had not seemed to.

Clodagh'd had three video calls with Danny since she woke up, and he was relentless in his teasing, remorseless as he made Clodagh laugh so much that parts of her she could not identify hurt. His theory was that this so-called dream telepathy was completely fake. He accused Clodagh of reading Ruth's diary, which was the only way she could have known about what had happened to her sister. When Clodagh told him that she knew Ruth had never kept a diary because she did not trust them as either accurate personal accounts or as records that people could never resist reading – "Everyone wants to know your deepest secrets" she had said – Danny then accused her of stalking Ruth.

"Hold it – that's a bit close to the bone," Clodagh told him. "You know what happened to Ruth and I. With Sid, I mean."

"I know, but having it happen to you doesn't necessarily mean you would never do it yourself. I think you've been googling Ruth something rotten. You wanted to know everything about her. Including all about her family."

"Her parents fought to keep the story out of the news. Danny, come on, you know this about them. Very rich and very private. Especially about family business."

He was running out of steam, Clodagh could tell, but he tried out a few more possible explanations: Ruth must have told Clodagh about her sister, one drunken night, or it was a lucky guess, but Clodagh could tell he almost believed that this was some kind of new ability she had.

"Careful – if you tell anyone else about this, they'll take you back to Rothmore and throw you in with the ghosts of all the other women they burned."

"Danny! Not cool. In any way. Totally inappropriate." Clodagh was glad she was alone in the hospital room, that no one could overhear their conversation.

He changed his tune, then, and said he was so happy for Clodagh, and for Ruth.

"Tell me – did you ever guess that I was in love with her?"

He shook his head. "I really didn't. I knew you depended on her like you do on your right arm, but I had no idea how you felt. I suppose you've had such a tough time these past few years, you being in love never really crossed my mind." Clodagh saw his eyes mist up, huge as they were on her laptop screen.

He cleared his throat and asked, "So did you finish writing the sequel?"

"Not quite."

"Will Genoa have a happy ending?"

"I'm working on it," she told him, honestly.

That was why Clodagh had asked the nurse for her sketchpad, and pencils. The closer she had come to writing the ending, the less likely it had seemed that it would be a happy one for Genoa, most likely due to the mirroring effect and the state of her own life at the time. But, she realised, that was her life B.C. – before the cottage. Even before she had spoken with Danny, Clodagh had regretted the likelihood of an unhappy ending. It seemed wrong, after everything Genoa had been through and how much she had survived, to have her die at the hands of a crazed citizen who had eaten too much infected corn.

It was awkward, sitting propped up in bed, balancing the sketch pad on the rickety plastic tray table, but Clodagh was determined to give Genoa an ending she deserved.

***

New Genoa – the ending

Jake, the Canadian farmer who had engineered the construction of the biodome for the new civilization, called Genoa Gloriana. He was a staunch royalist – in that unexpected way that Canadians who had never been to the United Kingdom or had much of any real sense of what it was like to live there could be. It was blind loyalty to a kingdom they had only vague, romantic notions of. Jake saw Genoa as the visionary queen to beat all visionary queens, able to make decisions about what should be done and how they would reclaim this land for survival. He was astonished at her vast knowledge of pesticides - crop plagues as they had all come to call them - and he trusted her with everything he possessed to make the right decisions for them.

There were seventy people in their new civilization – New Genoa as he insisted on calling it. And he believed that Genoa was like Gloriana – or Queen Elizabeth I – because she sent out explorers to find other survivors, when signals were received from others with immunity from all over the world. But unlike sending sailors out to discover (or rather, to claim as their own) new worlds, Genoa sent out the brave, willing people – her comrades in immunity – to rescue their fellow comrades and bring them back to New Genoa.

The rescuers faced increasingly ferocious attacks and acts of violence from those who had been infected by the crop plague. It had mutated several times over, infecting people with a speed that meant only seconds passed between being a healthy human being, and being a crazed, rabid animal. The infected came at the healthy with everything they had, all brute force and unstoppable energy.

Well, *almost* unstoppable. Bullets worked, and the citizens of New Genoa had looted gun shops far and wide, to create an impressive arsenal.

While the explorers went out on rescue missions, Genoa and the non-explorers stayed behind, building the biodome on a vast expanse of Canadian prairie. They had chosen the land because it had not been hospitable to other vegetation, and their concerns about spray drift were therefore minimal. This was a good reason to choose soil that had not come into contact with the plague virus, but it was a bad reason to choose soil that they wished to grow the food that would help them survive. Not just survive, but thrive.

Some of the others had questioned Genoa's logic: if they were immune to the plagues that had sprung up first in Scotland and then all over the world, why would they need to protect themselves from air-borne viruses by building the biodome? Genoa explained that she strongly suspected that those who had waged biological warfare on them in the first place might well be plotting something new, something that they would not be immune to. But what if it was not warfare, some of the others asked, but a poorly-tested pesticide that had spread too far, too quickly without the proper safety measures being in place?

You've just answered your own question, Genoa told them. *You know the answer to that. These things don't just happen. The plan was to wipe us out – all of us apart from a select elite. There's something in each of us that they didn't plan on, because they couldn't predict it. That's why they are so desperate to get their hands on us. Not to create a vaccine, but to kill us.*

Genoa knew how to calculate the dimensions of the bio-dome to provide the kind of space within which to grow food on a scale that they needed for their survival. She did not know how to actually go about translating her designs into a real, three-dimensional structure that would provide safety and security. This was where Jake came in. He had studied to be an engineer before taking over the family farm, and he was able to build the structure from scratch, with salvaged and looted tools and equipment and supplies.

He also built dwelling houses within their protected space, designed to be cool in the summer when the heat on the prairies could fry the brains inside your head (his words) and to be warm enough in the winter when the cold was enough to crack the clothes right off your back (also his words).

And their other immuno-comrades were forces of strength and stamina, working from early in the morning until late in the evening, building, building, building. Genoa had some knowledge of the things her comrades had been through, the things they had survived. She had seen things that were now forever etched on the inside of her eyelids, forcing her to look at them whenever she closed her eyes.

So instead she chose, as much as possible, to stay awake, to keep planning, keep working, keep building. Keep moving her comrades forward into a safe, clean future.

None of the immuno-comrades had family members who were also immune. They were all orphans, brought together into one big family unbound by blood. But they were bound by *something* in their blood – something that had kept them all healthy when others had become so sick they became murderers.

If Jake was her right arm, Sanna was connected to her heart. Sanna was in charge of the rescue missions to find their immuno-comrades who had sent out calls for help, distress signals, to let them know they needed to be saved. Sanna had the cool level-headed intelligence necessary to plan and lead the missions. She was brutal, and she was efficient, and she was the most awe-inspiring person Genoa had ever met.

They knew how they felt about each other, but had never spoken the words aloud. Theirs was an intuitive love, one that lived on a plane of knowing and being that defied words.

One day, Genoa thought, when we are safe and our community is thriving and the threat has been eliminated, we will speak of it. Until then, I will be content with what I can see, and what I know. To know this kind of love, after everything that has happened, is not what I expected.

But it is what I deserve.

**

Clodagh closed the sketch pad, and sat back against the bedrest. It was done. There was no utopian ending for Genoa, but there couldn't be, not really. She had, though, deserved hope, and love, and the promise of a better life. She deserved not to be killed off in a violent attack. Clodagh owed her that.

She smiled, thinking of Ruth. Her newly-formed powers must have been working, because a moment later she appeared at the door of Clodagh's room, looking in tentatively. Clodagh smiled, beckoned Ruth in and in the next instant she was there, right by her side.

Epilogue

Petra reached for Clodagh's hand, which was trembling. "Are you sure you want to do this?"

"Yes." Clodagh's voice was a whisper.

"Just reach out and grab my arm if you want to stop at any point." She squeezed Ruth's hand, too. "Same goes for you, Ruth."

Ruth returned the squeeze, firmly. "I'm ready for this," she said.

A cool wind blew through the witches' prison, despite the warmth of the sunshine on this last day of October; it was Samhain Eve, the dawning of winter as marked by the Celtic people. Petra thought the chill air was either a breeze blowing off the sea, right through them, or the strength of the energy of the women she had been summoning all week. The prison thrummed with their combined force, as they surged forward in anticipation of telling their stories.

It was the final day of Petra and Clodagh's second-chance retreat, as Jane called it; she and Fingal had invited them back, to make up for their halted retreat in May, by way of apology for their actions in attempting to deceive the police, and in an attempt at recompense. They were the only two guests and, without the excursions and planned events they'd experienced during their first stay, they'd both knuckled down and worked hard all week. Petra had been physically and mentally exhausted for weeks after the operation and her short stay in hospital, so that she'd been unable to do more than edit what she'd written during the few days of the first retreat. And, truthfully, she hadn't wanted to summon any of the women anywhere other than in the prison, where she'd spent so much time during the past week that she had ample material for her book. The women's stories were gruelling and terrible, but Petra gave thanks that she was able to communicate with them about their lives.

When Clodagh wasn't spending time with the convalescing patients – Petra and her mother – or working in the library, she was working on the sequel to *Genoa's Run*. She'd delivered the manuscript to her publisher two weeks before coming on the second-chance retreat, and had spent the week at Rothmore working on the first draft of the sea witch story. Jane, who'd been walking on eggshells around her guests, provided delicious meals and snacks, but otherwise left them to use the spaces in and around the house as they chose. Clodagh planted herself either in the lounge or on the bench in the courtyard garden, so that she knew when Petra came back from her work in the witches' prison, and they would eat together, or take long walks on the cove beach.

She loved spending time with Petra, and she also felt it was her duty to take care of her as she recovered. She was attentive to Petra's fatigue levels, and recognised when she needed a cup of hot, sweet tea and some carbohydrates. The operation had left Petra with a slight weakness on her left side as the wound healed, and Clodagh knew by the way Petra held herself when she was in pain and needed a rest.

But she'd resisted joining Petra in the prison, until their final day. Ruth had hired a car to collect them and drive them home and, as they'd made the travel arrangements, Clodagh mentioned that although she knew she should face her fears and join Petra for a summoning, she just couldn't seem to bring herself to do it.

Ruth's voice was gentle as she said, "You were in a completely different place emotionally and psychologically when you saw the vision the last time. You've come out the other side. I don't think you have anything to worry about."

"Maybe not, but I'm still terrified about it happening again."

"Nothing says you have to do it. No one's going to think any less of you."

Clodagh thought of Petra, and everything she had done for her and her family, all of the sacrifices she'd made. "But I think Petra is going to carry around guilt about it unless I do it."

"Well then you should do it. Wait until I'm there and I'll

come with you."

The three women were sitting in a closed circle, hands interlinked. Petra had lit the candles, and the incense, and squeezed her friends' hands again.

"I'll do the incantation now. You might feel a rush of air, and hear some voices. I'll ask that only one woman speaks to us. You might not experience it the same way I do, but I hear each woman introduce herself, and then my mind fills with images, like I'm watching a film of her life. We're inside the protective circle, so no harm will come to us. I promise."

Clodagh and Ruth squeezed her hands tightly, but neither said a word. Petra began the incantation, low and steady, imploring the women to come forward if they wanted to share their story. Almost instantly there was a gust of air so powerful it startled her, and Clodagh gripped her hand even more tightly. Petra kept her voice steady as she asked that only one woman step forward to talk to them.

***

Summoning drained Petra so much that she wanted little more than to sleep right afterwards. Clodagh and Ruth, however, had a completely different reaction. Both had tears in their eyes, of sadness at the traumatic events they had seen. But they were exhilarated in a way that surprised and delighted Petra, as they spoke of their wonder at being able to see into the past, to spend time with one of the women who'd been brought to this place. They hugged Petra tightly, praising her skill and talent, in awe of the power she had to open this world up to them. The three women sat together, talking about what they'd seen, until the candles burned right down to the grass, damp with evening dew.

No one wanted to leave the prison. Petra performed an incantation of gratitude, and peace, and healing as they held fast to each other's hands, walking slowly in a circular motion at first, before the energy bursting through their bodies made them kick their heels up, and dance.

***

The ancient oaks of Rothmore looked down on the three women as they danced in the moonlight on Samhain Eve, like three fire-flies against the backdrop of the dark night, circling the earth that had borne witness to many terrible acts of cruelty. As the women danced in their tight circle, the oaks watched as faint concentric rings formed around them; these circles of women who came to dance with them from the past might have shone less brightly, but their energy burned on through the centuries nevertheless, silvered flecks of joy against the navy-black sky.

ABOUT THE AUTHOR

Maria Melo

British author Maria Melo divides her time between making miniature books and tinctures, balms and potions in her house in the forest by the sea in western Portugal. Previously, she lived in Scotland, whose dark, brooding coastal aesthetic is the inspiration for her writing.

Printed in Great Britain
by Amazon